# Critical Acclaim for *The Venetian Files*

"The Venetian Files is a delightful book which taps into a historical reservoir of criticism and suspicion of banks and their practices."

— *Alan Kirman, economist, Aix-Marseille Université and OECD*

"The Venetian Files is a fascinating read, that blends intrigue, math, love, and finance to tell a gripping story. It takes the reader from Renaissance Italy to the credit crisis of 2008, by way of murder, economic theory, and secret societies. I can't wait for the next instalment."

— *Tom Salisbury. Former president, Canadian Mathematical Society*

"The lines between reality and fiction are blurred in this spellbinding mystery novel taking us on a journey across centuries and continents, mixing history, politics, and finance with passion and verve and a surprising conclusion awaiting at the end."

— *Edward Frenkel, Professor at University of California,*
*Berkeley, and author of "Love and Math"*

**Library and Archives Canada Cataloguing in Publication**

Title:     The Venetian Files: The Secret of Financial Crises /
           Izaías Almada, Matheus Grasselli.

Names:   Almada, Izaías, author.
            Grasselli, Matheus, author.

Identifiers: Canadiana (print) 20190225793
               Canadiana (ebook) 20190225807

ISBN 9781771614849 (softcover) ISBN 9781771614863 (PDF)
ISBN 9781771614856 (HTML) ISBN 9781771614870 (Kindle)

Classification: LCC PR9306.9.A46 V46 2019
                  DDC 813/.6–dc23

Published by Mosaic Press, Oakville, Ontario, Canada, 2019.

MOSAIC PRESS, Publishers
Copyright © Mosaic Press 2020

Cover Design by Brianna Wodabek

**ONTARIO ARTS COUNCIL**
**CONSEIL DES ARTS DE L'ONTARIO**
an Ontario government agency
un organisme du gouvernement de l'Ontario

We acknowledge the Ontario Arts Council
for their support of our publishing program

Funded by the Government of Canada
Financé par le gouvernement du Canada

MOSAIC PRESS
1252 Speers Road, Units 1 & 2
Oakville, Ontario L6L 5N9
phone: (905) 825-2130

info@mosaic-press.com

# THE VENETIAN FILES

# THE VENETIAN FILES

## The Secret of Financial Crises

Izaías Almada

Matheus Grasselli

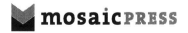
mosaicPRESS

*To Leonardo, son and grandson*

*"In one of the most dramatic days in Wall Street's history, Merrill Lynch agreed to sell itself on Sunday to Bank of America for roughly $50 billion to avert a deepening financial crisis, while another prominent securities firm, Lehman Brothers, filed for bankruptcy protection and hurtled toward liquidation after it failed to find a buyer.*

*But even as the fates of Lehman and Merrill hung in the balance, another crisis loomed as the insurance giant American International Group appeared to teeter. Staggered by losses stemming from the credit crisis, A.I.G. sought a $40 billion lifeline from the Federal Reserve, without which the company may have only days to survive".*

*The stunning series of events culminated a weekend of frantic around-the-clock negotiations, as Wall Street bankers huddled in meetings at the behest of Bush administration officials to try to avoid a downward spiral in the markets stemming from a crisis of confidence."*

New York Times – September 15, 2008

*"World events do not occur by accident. They are made to happen, whether it is to do with national issues or commerce; and most of them are staged and managed by those who hold the purse strings."*

*Denis Healey, British Secretary of State for Defense (1964 to 1970) and Chancellor of the Exchequer (1974 to 1979), founding member of the Bilderberg Club.*

*"Imagine a private club where presidents, prime ministers, international bankers and generals rub shoulders, where gracious royal chaperones ensure everyone gets along, and where the people running the wars, markets, and Europe (and America) say what they never dare say in public."*

*Daniel Estulin, journalist and author of "The True Story of the Bilderberg Group".*

# FOREWORD

D ear Reader: the book in front of you - "The Venetian Files" - starts with a prologue titled "Lehman Weekend: September 12-14, 2008, New York City - USA". When I read it, a wave of long forgotten memories rushed through my head as for me personally, it was also Merrill Lynch Weekend.

On Friday, September 12th, 2008, I left my desk located on the trading floor of the well-designed and ecologically friendly Merrill Lynch Financial Centre in London, UK, at 8:00 PM, taking with me all family pictures, "The Prince" by Machiavelli, bookmarked at Chapter 25, with the following sentence highlighted: "Nevertheless, since our free will must not be denied, I estimate that even if fortune is the arbiter of half our actions, she still allows us to control the other half, or thereabouts", and my own book, "Mathematical Methods for Foreign Exchange" bookmarked at Section 7.6, describing jump-diffusion models, which, I thought were becoming more important by the hour, given the severity of the market conditions. I was certain that the bank will fail and there would be no need to return to work on Monday. September 2008 was quite cold, in fact, the coldest in 10 years. With the temperature hovering around 10oC, I walked briskly along the Holborn, Fleet Street, past Goldman Sachs headquarters, then Strand, Pall Mall with its dark, silent, and imposing Buckingham Palace, the official residence of the Queen, on my left, and finally reaching Knightsbridge an hour later. As I turned the corner past Harrods, the ultimate luxury shop in London, I opened the door to my flat, where my family awaited my arrival. Our supper was marked by its brevity and gloom, rather than the usual lei-surely pace and gaiety. I retired to bed and slept for 16 hours straight, partly due to exhaustion from many a sleepless night in the office, and partly from the sheer enormity of the events unfolding in front of my own eyes. I was overwhelmed by the feeling that history was being written before my eyes.

The inability to comprehend what was going on and why, and who was pulling the strings and how, had begun to take its toll.

Over the weekend I tried to think of my future in the event of Merrill's collapse. Fortunately, my contingency plans needed not come to fruition as my premonitions proved to be overly pessimistic. While Lehman Brothers tried and failed to sell itself to the venerable British bank Barclays, mostly due to the justifiable reluctance of the Brits to allow such a risky transaction, Merrill Lynch & Co. had arranged to be acquired by Bank of America on Sunday. The transaction was completed in January 2009 and Merrill Lynch was formally merged into Bank of America in October 2013. I spend the next 8 years with Bank of America, co-running its Quantitative Research Group for most of my time there. I finally left the firm in 2016 to pursue my many academic and business interests, aiming to change the global financial system for the better.

Little did I know that the events affecting my life's trajectory were mostly due to a meeting of the world's most prominent bankers working around the clock over my sleepy but worrisome weekend to avert a global financial crisis. The world's heaviest financial hitters, including Treasury Secretary Hank Paulson, President of NY Fed Timothy Geithner, Chancellor of the Exchequer Alistair Darling, President of the European Central Bank Jean-Claude Trichet, President of the Deutsche Bundesbank Axel Weber, and numerous known and unknown other players were busy at work trying to find a buyer for the ailing Lehman Brothers. While Lehman failed and was relegated to the history books, Merrill was saved. Over the next few years Central Banks including the Fed, the Bank of England, the European Central Bank and the Band of Japan conducted a massive effort to stabilize and shore the global financial system by injecting enormous amounts of cash through the Quantitative Easing and other means.

Yet, despite the local success in restoring calm and avoiding a complete collapse of the world economy, the Global Financial Crisis failed to reorganize the world financial ecosystem. Too-big-to-fail banks became bigger rather than smaller by massively increasing their share of the banking business. Seemingly better capitalized, banking institutions have become so complex that their stability and creditworthiness can no longer be established with certainty. Their balance sheets are opaque and have risks that are too convoluted to be deciphered by their own management, let alone regulators, depositors, and investors. Together, these ever-increasing layers of complexity are rapidly creating banks that are too-big-to-manage.

In addition, due to the Quantitative Easing and other nontraditional measures undertaken by Central Banks and Treasuries, interest rates have become negative in many developed economies, bringing back centuries-old memories of economic stagnation and despair.

Frustration of the general public with the status quo manifests itself in numerous ways — in political turmoil, in deteriorating general discourse, and, most directly, in the stratospheric rise of Bitcoin and other cryptocurrencies.

How was such finely tuned coordination of the efforts by powers that be maintained? Was macroeconomics a guiding light behind this effort? Did the system self-regulate? Or was there a more sinister force acting behind the scenes?

One can certainly exclude any chance of macroeconomics saving the day. Mainstream macroeconomic theories cannot help in understanding the true nature of the financial system because they fail to capture and account for its complexities and hence are useless in practice. These theories are not only useless, they are dangerous and adversely affect both academic discourse and the practical actions of regulators and politicians. The latter fact is crucial because of its enormous implications for society at large: In the words of Austrian born physicist and Nobel prize winner Wolfgang Pauli, famous for his dry wit and sharp tongue, these theories are "not even wrong."

This leaves us with two possibilities - internal resilience of the system in the spirit of the invisible hand described by Adam Smith, or a conspiracy theory. I feel that the former possibility is more likely, while the authors of the book argue in favor of the latter. While it is hard to believe that a secret organization can perpetuate itself and thrive for hundreds of years, conspiracy theories sound plausible enough given the strangeness of the known facts. Regardless of whether a conspiracy existed, the authors have created a compelling thriller grounded in this possibility. And what can go wrong with it - a centuries old secret society currently run from the Ardennes Forest in Belgium by an elderly recluse Monsieur Henry; one of the first Venetian banks based on principles of the famous Florentine mathematician Fibonacci and launched with a pile of gold inherited from a fugitive Templar; a promising, if nerdy, Columbia postdoctoral student Willbe of the mixed American/Italian background and a Fibonacci descendant; his librarian girlfriend Sarah working for the NY Fed Chairman Geithner; and numerous other characters, some real, some fictional, and some real but with fictional names.

The Venetian Files is a fascinating detective story, written by a unique duo comprising of a prominent and experienced Brazilian novelist, playwright, and screenwriter Izaías Almada, with several novels and a wide variety of other output to his credit, and a very accomplished and clever mathematician Matheus Grasselli, for whom this novel is the first. Following the lines pioneered by Dan Brown, and characterized by seamless movements in space and time, the book effortlessly blends real people and fictional characters in the fine tradition of Leo Tolstoy's "War and Peace." For me personally, it was a pleasure to recognize some of my old friends.

This book excitingly lays foundation for a long book series, in which they explore the individual and entangled stories of Willbe, Sarah and Monsieur Henry. I look forward to the authors' rendition and explanation of financial mysteries old and new, and especially their take on my personal field of study, how and why Bitcoin and other cryptocurrencies were developed, and, of course, the true identity of Satoshi Nakamoto.

**Alexander Lipton**
*Chicago IL USA, October 2019*

# DISCLAIMER

This is a work of fiction. The story told here, although coloured by reality, is solely the product of the authors' imagination. The background for the narrative is the Global Financial Crisis of 2007-2009, its distant origins, and likely, perhaps even more acute, future crises.

The events of September 2008 were the *turning point* for the crisis, and for this reason we use the real names of some characters and institutions that played key roles in them. This is not meant, however, to constitute any judgment of their actions; rather, it is to assist in the understanding of a phenomenon that still baffles many people, and to help identify the elusive causes and unpredictable consequences of economic crises.

# ACKNOWLEDGMENTS

With the possible exception of the authors themselves, nobody spent more time thinking about the Venetian Files than Luke Taylor. Not only did he listen to one of us talk about the project for uncountably many hours, he also read every sentence of the many working versions and helped bring the book into shape. It is a much better book because of him.

Catriona Byrne was a constant source of encouragement and advice in navigating the intricacies of the publishing world, as well as valuable style tips.

Jiro Takahashi and Edward Frenkel gave generous support and advice.

Rafaela Figueiredo introduced us to Renan Paini, who gracefully provided the Italian translations scattered throughout the book.

Howard Asher, Brianna Wodabek and the team at Mosaic Press made the book a reality.

IZAÍAS ALMADA & MATHEUS GRASSELLI, October 2019.

# PROLOGUE

## Lehman Weekend: September 12-14, 2008
## New York City – USA

Hank Paulson managed to get Alistair Darling on the phone at 11:30 on Sunday morning. The Treasury Secretary was speaking to his British counterpart from the 13th floor of the Federal Reserve Bank of New York, in a makeshift office that Tim Geithner, the President of the New York Fed, had arranged for him. Paulson and Geithner, along with dozens of other Fed and Treasury officials, had been bunkered down at the Renaissance Revival fortress on Liberty Street since Friday night, when Geithner had summoned the CEOs of the most important banks in the country for an emergency meeting to avoid an impending financial Armageddon.

"We all know why we're here", were Paulson's opening remarks to the CEOs. "Without an intervention, Lehman Brothers will not be able to reopen on Monday."

"This will have to be a private bailout. Neither the Fed nor the Treasury has the legal authority to rescue Lehman", Geithner made clear before they broke for the night on Friday. "Come back in the morning and be prepared to do something."

Many of the men in the room (and they were all men) were aware of how closely their meeting resembled a gathering that had taken place ten years before, also at the Federal Reserve Bank of New York. There, representatives from the world's largest banks, including those same banks whose executives now sat in front of Paulson and Geithner on this Friday, had met to decide the fate of a sinking hedge fund. Notably absent from the current meeting, though, were representatives from the only two banks that had refused to assist in the 1998 bailout: Bear Stearns and Lehman Brothers.

The more historically minded in the room also thought further back, to the early years of the twentieth century. They had in mind the fabled meeting convened by John Pierpont Morgan Sr. in 1907. According to legend,

Morgan locked himself and his peers inside his private library on Madison Avenue and pocketed the key until they would agree to commit sufficient funds to stop the panic that then threatened to destroy the American banking system. The trauma caused by that episode, particularly the fear that someone like J.P. Morgan might not be around for the next crisis, convinced a reluctant Congress to create the Federal Reserve System some six years later.

On Saturday morning, Paulson greeted the re-assembled group of bankers with news that Barclays, the British bank, had emerged as a potential purchaser of Lehman. There were two sticking points, though. Barclays needed the approval of the British Government to complete the deal in such a short timeframe. "And Barclays won't take on all of Lehman's toxic assets," Paulson declared. "You need to help finance a competitor or deal with the reality of a Lehman failure."

It was not to be.

"There is no way I'm going to allow Barclays to buy Lehman", declared the Chancellor of the Exchequer, Alistair Darling, when Paulson reached him on Sunday morning. "You're asking the British Government to take on too big a risk", was Darling's only explanation to Paulson for refusing to allow the purchase to go ahead.

With no other buyers in sight and the U.S. Government refusing to step in, Lehman's time was up. By that afternoon, the once mighty financial group was the subject of bankruptcy proceedings, heralding the start of a new, much more severe chapter of the Global Financial Crisis.

"The British screwed us", was how Paulson summarized the news when he addressed the CEOs shortly before 1:00pm.

The news reverberated like shockwaves through the teams of accountants, lawyers, and investment bankers gathered in different floors of the building, who knew they had little time to switch to full damage control mode, whether they worked for one of the banks or for the government.

For most people gathered at the Federal Reserve Bank of New York, Darling's refusal to allow the sale was incomprehensible. A select few, however, sensed the almost invisible handiwork of a centuries-old, shadowy organization with roots in medieval Italy.

# PART 1

*Reality is often the best illusion*

# 1

*September 10, 2008*
*Ardennes Forest – BELGIUM*

The elusive man held in his hands a copy of the Belgian newspaper *Le Soir*. He sat with his back towards the door of his enormous library, in which were almost thirty thousand meticulously catalogued books, many of which filled him with pride owing to their extreme rarity. The section on medieval history, for example, included hundreds of works on art, religion, natural sciences, philosophy, and economics, some in first editions that were two or three hundred years old, impeccably maintained in an environment with controlled temperature and humidity designed to prevent unwanted fungus, moths, and mold – the resolute enemies of human knowledge and history.

His desk was located to the left of the entrance to this soundproof office, where he met the select visitors that occasionally arrived there, always with his explicit authorization. The large room, strategically situated in the middle of a labyrinth of other smaller rooms, shielded him from unwelcome intruders. More importantly, the space allowed him to hide who he really was: an eccentric gentleman, known only to a small circle that referred to him simply as "Monsieur Henry".

The library occupied most of the second floor of the neo-gothic castle in the Belgian Ardennes and was protected from curious eyes by a three-metre high wall and the thick tops of the surrounding beech and oak trees. According to some of the residents of the other estates in the hilly region, all of which were separated by considerable distances to guarantee privacy, the castle had its share of visits from luxury cars and the occasional helicopter.

M. Henry took his eyes off the newspaper and adjusted his glasses to look at the analog clock on the wall in front of his desk, following the last turn of the second hand with feline attention, waiting for it to strike midnight.

There was a lot at stake in the next couple of days and much of it depended on his leadership. It was time for his organization to take the reins of the current financial crisis, as it had done so many times in the past. This episode, like many other crises before, was about to become a lot worse before it could improve. It was part of the protocol. The details differed in each crisis, but the final outcome was certain: preservation of the wealth and power of the members of his organization. The only necessary condition for a successful outcome was obedience, both from the select members of the brotherhood and from the wider web of politicians and central bankers they controlled.

Both groups now required his attention. One of the brothers had gone rogue, there was undeniable evidence of it. Punishment had to be administered, traditions invoked, rituals observed. As the deadline he had given to the other brothers approached, he clicked an icon on the screen of his computer, which led him to a protected mailbox associated with an address known to only twelve other people. He clicked on "received messages" and found eleven of them, all in response to his previous email with subject "VF". He read them one by one, safely moving them to a removable disk that he then placed in a safe with an electronic lock, itself with a combination that was regularly changed. The messages contained the consent of the other members to his plan for how to deal with their treacherous brother.

He then proceeded to the next order of business and typed new messages containing instructions to be studied and executed in the following days, starting in the morning of the day that had just begun: September 11, 2008. The outgoing messages were also securely encrypted; they contained directions related to billions of dollars, and were addressed to high-ranking officials in all major world economies.

As the thirteenth and most important link in that chain, he could now retire for the night. Unbeknown to most, the world economy would not be the same from that point onwards.

*************

## Iguaçu Falls – BRAZIL

Three private G650-Gulfstream jets arrived at the Cataratas International Airport in the small town of Foz do Iguaçu, Brazil, at the end of the afternoon. Their origins were La Guardia, Charles De Gaulle and Kingsford Smith International airports, and each was carrying a top financial executive on his way to an emergency business meeting. Two other men, a South African and a Brazilian, had checked in the night before the meeting to ensure all the necessary preparations were in place to welcome their brothers.

Each of them had been trained in a system of rules and hierarchies built and solidified over more than 650 years. The five held the trust of the other members of the organization and their leader, and they had the authority to evaluate and discuss the instructions that would be received from Europe that evening. They also knew that any disobedience or carelessness on their part would lead to exemplary punishment.

An entire wing of the Belmond Hotel das Cataratas, on the border region between Brazil, Paraguay, and Argentina, had been blocked off for the meeting and only those authorized by the hotel management had access to it. During the three days of the businessmen's visit, the regular hotel staff was to be replaced with a private staff vetted by the organization's security personnel.

*************

The five men met in an elegant room overlooking the falls. They were served champagne and offered hors d'oeuvres by discreet waiters. The opportunity for these fraternizing dinners was a perk of such meetings, where the gastronomical offerings were meant to match the purposefully mysterious tone of the conversation. Power demands sacrifice, but compensates with luxury.

More than a meeting of the different continents they represented, these men carried with them the weight and responsibility of a tradition almost seven centuries old. In their positions, certain rules and pledges were for life. But who would not do the same? They received the highest salaries and perks ever paid to anyone in any country in the modern world, in addition to the dividends and capital gains from the shares of the corporations they led. As chief executive officers and major shareholders of large private and mixed public enterprises, they knew their place within the organization; it was a hierarchy that could only be broken by the death of another member. The pledges that new members of this brotherhood had to take, above all that of absolute loyalty, conferred on each of them the autonomy to create a network of informants who did not know for what or whom they ultimately worked.

They spoke in German, believing it safer from prying ears than the other languages available to them. In the briefest of exchanges, they confirmed that everything had been arranged to carry into effect their leader's orders for the following day. Two events would take place in different parts of the world and would appear in different sections of the news: one would make global front pages as a tragic accident; the other would not travel further than local news. A Malaysian Airlines flight from Kuala Lumpur to Tokyo would disappear somewhere in the South China Sea. Among the 200 passengers listed in the flight's manifest would appear a Mr. Hideo Akashiro, one of Japan's richest businessmen, whose private jet had been grounded after a routine inspection had indicated mechanical problems. Coming amid the developing financial crisis, news of the flight disappearance would lead to large stock market losses in Tokyo and other Asian exchanges. The real Hideo Akashiro would, however, meet his fate thousands of kilometers away.

At the end of the sophisticated dinner, the man who had arrived from France used the small silver bell to ask the waiter for a magnum of Dom Perignon Charles and Diana and five flute glasses. They needed one of the best champagnes ever made to toast the next phase of their good business and to welcome the new member of the select group, the first Brazilian to receive this distinction, restoring the numbers in their brotherhood to the traditional thirteen.

# 2

*August 18, 2008*
*New York City – USA*

William Benjamin F. Hubbard, born in Stamford, Connecticut, almost thirty years ago, of an American father and Italian mother, Princeton graduate, affectionately nicknamed *Willbe* by his mother when still in his early years - a play of words for good augury, as she used to say - took a seat at his favourite table by one of the mirrored columns of Café Tallulah on Columbus Avenue, not far from where he lived. It being the middle of summer, Willbe dressed casually in a light blue shirt, khaki pants, and moccasins. He enjoyed dressing well, and had a reason to do so today.

New York was still new to him, having arrived back in the country only eight weeks earlier, after four years studying for his doctorate in the vastly different environment of Pisa. In a few more weeks he would begin teaching at Columbia University as a postdoctoral fellow. His research in Pisa had focused on arcane matters of abstract risk measures. Recently, though, his interests had taken a turn towards those curious periods in economic history known as financial bubbles - what happens when the price of an asset, be it a stock, a house, or even a tulip bulb, rises exponentially because of speculation. The subjects were not as disparate as they might initially appear, with an increasing number of financial mathematicians like him paying attention to the nascent field of systemic risk. The truth, however, was that his interest in financial history was more than simply academic - it had been spiked by some unusual family connections that he had uncovered while in Italy.

He had adopted the Tallulah as a second office, where he read the news, especially on economics and politics, and devoured tomes on the history of financial crises while enjoying one of the best espressos on the Upper West Side. He would often stay at the café for an hour or more, well acquainted with all of the staff and even two or three regulars for that time of the day.

This evening he had chosen the Tallulah for his date with Sarah - someone still fairly new in his life, but who had the ability to surprise his mind, warm his heart, and ignite his desire.

The shopkeeper's bell above the front door rang and Willbe waited as Sarah made her way across the café towards him. Just under five feet, seven inches tall, with lively eyes and a few freckles on her face, she wore a light grey suit over a white blouse and only a little makeup, just enough to sharpen her youth; her red hair was styled with metal clips, and her feet were clad in braided leather sandals.

Willbe stood up and gently kissed her on the cheeks, pulling a chair for her to sit. He suggested an espresso with Italian almond cookies, *cantuccini*, accompanied by sweet kaffir lime liqueur, a novelty at Tallulah. Or a vodka and lime cocktail, a Serge Gainsbourg, famous and traditional at the bar.

"Sorry for the delay, Willbe," said Sarah catching her breath, "but the boss was obviously nervous today. He asked me to spend a few extra minutes searching for a document he needs to take to Washington tomorrow. They're all worried sick about this banking crisis."

The "boss" was Timothy Geithner, President of the Federal Reserve Bank of New York. Sarah had been working in his office for over a year.

"That's alright," replied Willbe, checking the time on his cell phone. "Seven minutes late in New York isn't really a delay, especially at the end of the afternoon..."

"And yet, you seem to have counted the minutes," quipped Sarah.

"Perhaps," said Willbe with a smile, "but I forgive you because your boss is a workaholic with not even half my charm..."

They both laughed.

"Any news?" asked Willbe.

"Perhaps," answered Sarah, removing the clips from her hair and letting it fall around her face.

"What do you mean, perhaps?"

"Let me see, how can I say this in a solemn tone?" Sarah smiled mischievously.

"Oh go on, let it out. Are you going to get a raise?"

"I wish."

Sarah took Willbe's hands and gently pressed them against her own. She looked him in his greenish hazel eyes:

"I started the research you asked me to do. I went to the rare books section of the Public Library and looked for books from the period you mentioned. I found a few - some of the oldest books they have."

"And?" Willbe asked drawing out the syllable hopefully.

"Before I tell you what I found, Willbe, explain to me again why you want to know about sects and occultism in the Middle Ages when your subject is financial mathematics. I still don't see the connection."

"It certainly sounds a bit obscure," said Willbe, smiling. "There's a lot to it, but for starters, I'm trying to confirm where exactly in Europe the first bank was founded."

Sarah refrained from laughing.

"In rare books on occultism? What do you expect to find?"

"I'm not entirely sure, but I have a hunch that it is all tied up with the Church and its prohibition on usury. The Holy Office saw the earliest banks as doing the devil's work because they lent money for profit. Jews and Christians who were involved were targeted during the Inquisition and labeled heretics. So I think there might be some as yet unknown details about these early banks in books of this sort. These bankers had to conduct most of their business in secrecy to protect themselves, but they might have left records in a disguised way."

Sarah listened with a raised eyebrow and a slight smile. Before she could respond, the waiter appeared at their table with the coffee, cookies, and liqueur that Willbe had ordered. Sarah asked for a vodka and lime cocktail.

"Go on, tell me more. I must confess I never thought about banks in this... conspiratorial way. I'm enjoying it."

"Some say that banks started in England, others say Holland, and also Italy. Most likely Italy."

"Ok, but why is it really so important to know for sure where the first bank was created?"

"Oh you cannot imagine how important! It's not just an academic question. It's..."

His enthusiasm stalled and he stopped midsentence. Perhaps it wasn't the right moment yet. He went on:

"Have you ever stopped to think, Sarah, how our entire lives depend more and more on banks, all the financial activity they manage and command? The businesses they control? The power they wield? Their role in economic crises, like this one?"

"I understand that, but not why you need to know about the *first* bank. Is there something you're not telling me, Willbe?"

"I'm not hiding anything, Sarah."

They each took a sip of their drinks. Willbe broke the silence:

"So tell me then, Sarah, did you find anything interesting in the books?"

Sarah stared back at Willbe, as if she were weighing up whether to proceed. Eventually, she spoke:

"I don't know if this is what you are looking for, but given what you just said, it might be something." Sarah paused and added at last: "Have you ever heard of something called the Venetian Files?"

Before Willbe could answer, Sarah noticed a change in expression and a slight loss of colour in her friend's face.

# 3

## *Circa 1350-60 AD*
## *Vicenza, Veneto Region - ITALY*

The delicate snowflakes of what was going to be an unforgettable winter for the village of Vicenza already covered the smaller shrubs, some late blooming flowers of the surrounding area, and the vineyards of much of the region - not far from the Dolomites in the Italian Tyrol, a land good for grapes and grappa.

The languorous sun, its summer vigor a distant memory, now lacked the strength for long days and failed to warm the damp and narrow alleyways of the village. As if to compensate, it spilled a gentle orange light of impressive beauty over the village, turning to gold the thin layer of snow that sat on the branches of walnut and peach trees up in the mountains. Birds had, by and large, already left for more hospitable climes.

Like the neighbouring village of Bassano Del Grappa, founded by a Roman soldier named Bassanius between the years 100 and 200 of the Christian era, Vicenza is said to have been established when the Roman army of Charlemagne established a camp there in the early ninth century. More than five hundred years later, the still few inhabitants of the small village, most of them peasants, were readying themselves for the difficult winter months to come. Everything was gathered and carefully stored beside the firewood that had been patiently chopped and left to dry - the fuel that would warm with its blaze the dwellings of each one of the village's nearly fifteen hundred people.

The shadow of the Black Death lingered on in these parts, not only in the scarcity of food, but also in the undercurrent of fear that continued to weigh upon the survivors. Rumors circulated that the plague spread not through the air, as was generally thought, but rather by fleas that fed on the blood of rats; many of the young men in the village devoted themselves to hunting down the rodents day and night, with hands and feet covered in thick rags. The few outsiders who ventured on to these lands, many simply looking for food or fleeing battles between neighbouring towns, were forced to undress and prove that their bodies were free of the telltale dark spots that spelled contamination.

Disease was not the only source of the villagers' fears. Three centuries before, Pope Urban II had organized the First Crusades against the Muslim Turks, and the memory of this violent campaign lived on, even in villages as remote as Vicenza. As the Church was once again campaigning against heretics and infidels, its inhabitants feared that once the winter passed, they would receive news of the death of Luigi Minardi, Vicenza's adopted but nevertheless illustrious son.

He was a strange character who sought notoriety and wealth within monastic walls, despite preaching the virtues of a simple and secluded life. He was responsible for the accounts of his small monastery, which discreetly produced wine, liqueurs, breads, sweets, and assorted cakes for Vicenza and its neighbouring villages. Word had it that Friar Luigi was a rich man thanks to his bookkeeping skills - a fact likely to raise suspicion among the higher powers in the Church.

Born Filippo Luigi Scoppi Minardi in the neighbouring village of Bassano Del Grappa, he had been adopted as an infant by the monks in Vicenza after his poverty-stricken parents left the boy to be cared for by the monastery. In his youth, he had been one of the first Italian followers of the Cistercians, a religious order that would become famous throughout Europe in the seventeenth century as the Trappist Monks, thanks to reforms introduced in La Trappe Abbey in France. Originating in the Bourgogne region, in the village of Citeaux, Cistercium in Latin, near Dijon, the Cistercians arrived in Northern Italy at the end of the twelfth century from the South East of France and preached, among other virtues, moderation. They led simple lives and slept on wooden planks. By tradition, they spoke little, even among themselves, and only in cases of extreme need. Luigi Minardi di Vicenza, as he eventually became known, acted in the same simple and cordial manner with his Italian compatriots.

When the time came for him to take his vows, Luigi had come to see simplicity as one of the central teachings of Christ and was ordained as a Franciscan, becoming a friar and fierce defender of the Church against apostates and the wicked. He observed his religious and secular duties with devotion, establishing himself as a faithful intermediary, whenever necessary, between landowners and the Italian peasants of the Veneto.

By the time Luigi joined the Franciscans, the Inquisition, officially formalized during the Synod of Verona in 1184, was a powerful institution of the Church, respected and feared by Christians and non-Christians alike. Men and women were accused of a multitude of heresies; their fate, if repentance was not given or believed, could result in burning at the stake. While some in Vicenza worried that Friar Luigi would face the Inquisition's forces because of his business dealings, others in the village secretly questioned whether he might himself be an agent of the Holy Office. The more superstitious in the village spoke of Luigi as an augur, a diviner of signs, capable of seeing the presence of the devil in banal, day-to-day events, especially where it concerned society's outcasts – the women who sold themselves for money, Jews, lepers, and worshippers of ancient pagan gods. Some even identified him as a descendant of one of the Knights Templar.

More than any of these things, though, Friar Luigi was a shrewd negotiator and analyst of earthly activities, particularly those concerning trade and finance. It was a profitable time for such talents. Using its powers of religious terror, the Church had steadily been acquiring parcels of land throughout Europe, establishing itself as a producer of wine, olive oil, cheese, seeds, sweets, scarves, and handkerchiefs, many of which were traded with the East for spices, silk and precious stones, mostly through the ports of Genoa and, above all, Venice.

Friar Luigi's monastery was a shining example of this blend of faith and commerce, with all of the money managed by Luigi himself. Beyond financial administration, his monastic life included the occasional work with two or three copyist monks, a task that he executed with special pleasure, courtesy of his proficiency in Latin.

Although Kings and Popes remained all-powerful, wealthy merchants of the fourteenth century were beginning to act in defiance of royal edicts and papal proclamations. In this environment, conservative but at the same time visionary, rational but paradoxically chaotic, Friar Luigi de Vicenza balanced impeccably on the edge of the wedge between divine teachings and secular businesses.

*************

## Pisa, Tuscany Region - ITALY

The final years of the 1350s were troubled times. War, pestilence, famine, roaming bands of destitute men and mercenaries, religious and royal fights; ingredients mixed in a cauldron of new economic and financial recipes. New ideas addressing new needs, as soon as they were being created were already the subject of fierce disputes by noble families, the clergy, and the newly enriched merchants.

In the midst of these turbulent times, the small city of Pisa was about to unveil its leaning tower, built with the pure white marble found in the fields and mountains surrounding the town. The inclination of the tower, evident right from the start of construction, could have resulted in tragedy, but the ingenuity of the builders ensured its survival.

Finally completed, the festivities to inaugurate the tower drew visitors from far and wide, including Vitorio Giuseppe Fibonacci – a man known, feared, and respected from the beaches of the Tyrrhenian Sea all the way to the piazzas of Venice. Not just because he was almost six feet, six inches tall, but above all for carrying the name of one of the richest and most honoured families in Tuscany – a valuable and necessary attribute in the times and places in which he lived and conducted his business.

Like his famous granduncle, the great mathematician Leonardo Fibonacci, Vitorio Giuseppe was born in Pisa and lived there until his adolescence. By divine influence, as he liked to say with some irony, and through the businesses started by his great-granduncle Guglielmo Bonacci, father of Leonardo, he became a competent and well-known merchant in the Tuscan and Veneto regions, where he had moved in his youth with the help of his father, settling in Venice. He was married to Marinella Luigia Lombardi Fibonacci, of whom he liked to say to all with pride that she had given him *tre figli maschi*.

At age forty-nine he had already acquired an immense fortune, to the point that he had pledged to help finance the establishment of the University of Pisa and had personally bankrolled a large part of the cost of the leaning tower. He was thus a doubly honoured guest at the celebrations attending its completion. Satisfied after a private tour of the tower's interior, he had spent the past few days visiting with family in the town and was now on his way back to Venice by way of Vicenza, where he owned land.

The trip from Pisa to Vicenza was long and tiring. For four days and three nights through the Apennine paths and shortcuts, Giuseppe travelled on horseback together with two servants and two extra horses. He had an ambitious objective in mind as he rode to see his old friend Friar Luigi Minardi di Vicenza. They had known each other since they were young. As the years had progressed, Friar Luigi had somewhat ironically become Giuseppe's most trusted advisor in matters of earthly business. He was also a partner, for much of what Luigi raised in his trading activities through the monastery he passed on to Giuseppe to invest.

On this visit though, he wanted to discuss something altogether new with the Friar - an idea, still embryonic, which had originated in conversations he had shared with Giovanni Acunto, an English mercenary turned Florentine, ambitious and equally cunning in business. It was an idea too advanced to be understood by most people in feudal Europe, but one that was already being discussed and embraced by some Florentine merchants; it pointed to Venice, with its port opened to the known world, as a diamond in the rough.

# 4

## September 11, 2008
## Venice – ITALY

The red rays of evening light reflected off the wavelets of the Grand Canal and disappeared behind the architectural silhouettes of hundreds of byzantine, gothic and neoclassical homes and palaces in that most stunning of cities at sunset, Venice. It being late summer, the city's streets and squares were flooded with people, its hotels, churches, and museums overflowing with awestruck tourists.

This splendid setting could not hide the strange sight that confronted a few of the tourists who, their attention roused by a dull thud, momentarily directed their gazes towards an arched passageway along the Grand Canal: a man, elegantly dressed in tailcoat and black bowtie, jumping from a small bridge into a smaller canal. Soaked by the sudden immersion, the man still managed, without apparent effort, to lift himself onto a gondola, silently disappearing through a narrow corridor of green water.

As the gondola rounded a corner and slipped from view, a woman's scream rang close to where the man in tailcoat had jumped, prompting a group of passersby in the alleyway to hurry to where she stood, shaking.

On the ground, another man, also elegantly dressed, twitched as he clutched the hilt of a Japanese katana lodged in his bowels. There was little chance the unknown man would survive.

*************

## São Paulo – BRAZIL

After delivering a parcel with precise receiver's information to the doorman at the headquarters of the Ministry of the Economy in São Paulo, the *motoboy* - one of the thousands of young men who deliver small parcels and mail in the big cities of Brazil – unzipped his yellow nylon jacket and consulted his pocket book for the next scheduled delivery. A drizzle fell over the city that afternoon, foretelling the start of spring.

The youngster was being closely observed through the tinted windows of a black SUV with blue license plates, the type used in Brazil to identify official vehicles of consulates and embassies of foreign countries.

Five minutes after the delivery, in pursuit of the *motoboy* in one of the busy motorways that encircle the city, the SUV accelerated and, in a fast and precise maneuver, threw the unsuspecting youth against a concrete wall, instantly killing him.

The boy's death was not even mentioned in the tabloid shows airing that evening on local TV stations or in the printed newspapers the next day, for the simple reason that at least two *motoboys* die every day in the savage asphalts of São Paulo.

And that day, a normal Thursday in the second week of September of 2008, was no different. The young man could not imagine that his last delivery was perhaps the most important of his short life: an envelope to be opened only by the Minister himself, who was in town that afternoon for an important meeting with business leaders and financiers. Fate, however, does not usually send word.

*************

## Washington DC – USA

The official mission of the United States Treasury is to protect the integrity of the country's financial system. Judging by his circumspect expression, this was certainly what was worrying Hank Paulson, who was speaking into the phone with some agitation, a scowl on his face. He was so focused on the conversation that he barely noticed when his personal assistant, quiet and discreet as usual, laid on his desk a white rectangular envelope with red letters stamped across the seal flap: TOP SECRET. His concentration momentarily interrupted, the Secretary glanced at the initials of the sender in a mechanical fashion that betrayed familiarity with such routine occurrences. He slid the envelope inside a leather folio positioned alongside his computer, taking care to leave visible just the portion with the red-letter stamp.

After finishing his call, still absorbed in what had been discussed and leaving for the time being the correspondence that had just arrived,

Paulson rose and moved closer to his office windows. Observing the end of summer scenery, he had a feeling that the worst was yet to come. He knew, though, that he had to convey a message of optimism to the nation, with the conviction and sense of duty required by the moment. President Bush had just asked him to do so. For about a year prior to this call, the international and American financial systems had showed signs of mounting volatility, with unusual nervousness on the part of banks, insurance companies, stock markets, and other agents in financial centres in Asia, Europe, and the United States. The number of American households defaulting on their mortgage payments had increased considerably in recent months. In international financial circles this was being watched with apprehension and incipient panic.

*Who is going to pay for the losses on these so-called toxic assets? For the folly of unscrupulous investors?*

The sale in March 2008 of the insolvent bank Bear Stearns to J.P. Morgan, which had been orchestrated by the Federal Reserve Board to avoid the unpredictable consequences of the bankruptcy of a large financial institution, had been the warning shot. But Paulson had to remain optimistic, as he had just told the President in their nearly twenty-minute conversation. In truth, the situation with Lehman Brothers, a much larger bank than Bear Stearns, was even more worrying.

*Why do I have to face an economic crisis of this magnitude in the last year of my term? The presidential elections are approaching. The financial system ought to find stricter rules to save itself from adventurers.*

He was sincerely torn between believing those who feared the worst – an out-of-control reprise of the Great Depression – and those, perhaps more realistically, who thought that financial crises plodded along more or less predictable paths. If the latter were right, everything should end well.

Dark clouds gathered over Washington. Paulson took his eyes off the city in front of him, turning his attention to the envelope he had just received. Returning to his desk, he opened the leather folio and stared at the seal for a number of minutes. Then, with a swift movement, he opened the envelope with a small silver paper knife that he kept in the top drawer of his desk. He pulled out a light blue sheet folded in half. Unfolding the sheet, he read with almost imperceptible relief the message typed above the sender's initials: *VF.*

His autonomy on the matter was over. The coded signature let him know that the mechanism for overcoming the crisis had been initiated. Other such envelopes, identical in every respect, would be delivered to finance ministers and central bank presidents of major economic powers around the world that same day. He would schedule a meeting with Ben Bernanke, Chairman of the Federal Reserve Board, for the next morning. Timothy Geithner, President of the Federal Reserve Bank of New York, would also be called.

The identity of the sender was of no relevance. When he took over this position he had been informed that some decisions, whenever necessary, would be above his powers.

He knew what he had to do. Before calling Bernanke, though, he used the prerogatives at his disposal in this kind of emergency and called the private line at number 11 Downing Street, London. He wanted to know, however informally, what the British thought about the Lehman situation.

*************

## London – ENGLAND

Ms. Brown Smith, given names Marian Louise, career civil servant in Her Majesty's Exchequer, wrote down with focused attention the message received by phone just after 6:35pm in her office at 11 Downing Street.

It was a call from Treasury Secretary Paulson, who was waiting for an update from the British government on the economic crisis that had been building up for more than a year, and which seemed about to erupt with the imminent bankruptcy of investment bank Lehman Brothers. The central banks of some other countries had already acted; others remained undecided. Paulson would wait for the Chancellor of the Exchequer to return his call. Any time, day or night, he emphasized.

Alistair Darling, the Chancellor, would return from Scotland before the end of the day and receive a complete report from his team, who were all working late that Thursday evening. His decision to authorize the use of twenty billion pounds just a few months before to prevent the bankruptcy of the Northern Rock bank had caused a stir in the press. And, above all, as one expects, among the opposition Tories. His position, however, was clear: nothing would be hidden from the taxpayers. In an interview with a left leaning British newspaper he stated that the UK was facing the worst economic conditions of the past sixty years, a recession that was likely to be deeper and longer than most people expected.

Darling, like most of those in power at the time, lacked previous experience in big economic crises like the one that now confronted him. But he was determined to do all he could to minimize the fallout.

Ms Brown Smith headed towards the Chancellor's office to find out from his personal assistant when the "number one" was supposed to arrive. She carried a folder with the annotated report he was supposed to read.

"I'm going to leave these documents on the Chancellor's desk."

"You can leave them with me."

"Keep on working, Alice, I can take them in."

Alice Malley, one of the longest serving employees in the Exchequer and approaching retirement, was known for her competence and loyalty, and also for her terrible moods when she felt underappreciated or opposed. The exception was her darling Alistair, for whom she would sacrifice anything.

As she left the folder on Darling's desk, Ms Brown Smith could not avoid noticing an envelope with the red TOP SECRET stamp. She glanced towards the door and overheard Alice speaking animatedly on the phone. Unable to control her curiosity, she took the envelope and moved it against the light coming from the window to see whether she could read anything.

*Idiot*, she thought. *And reckless. As if anyone who would send a confidential letter would not have taken the necessary care against prying eyes. Her Majesty must forgive me for such indiscretion.*

She did notice, however, and without understanding its significance, a small watermark in one of the corners of the envelope, only revealed against the light: a winged lion with his left paw over a book. A familiar image, although one she could not identify at that instant.

She replaced the envelope in its exact original position, hoping that Alice would not notice anything amiss.

*And much less Alistair,* she thought.

# 5

*August 18, 2008*
*USA – New York City*

Willbe wore an expression of amazement. With a rapid heartbeat, he held Sarah's hands in his:

"Venetian files? Did I hear you correctly? So they exist!" Willbe let the words out with a barely contained expression of surprise and incredulity. Sarah sat perplexed in front of him, unsure of the reason for his reaction.

"Where did you hear this, Sarah?"

Without noticing, Willbe grasped her hands more firmly.

"I didn't hear anything... I read something about it."

"Read!"

Willbe's surprise seemed to increase. Somewhat embarrassed by his own reaction, he let go of his Sarah's hands.

"What is it, Willbe? You're all agitated."

"I'm sorry. I'll explain, but first tell me, please, where did you read about these files?"

"Well, at the Public Library, where else?"

"Of course, but where, which book? Does it say anything about the contents of the files? Who wrote them? When?"

"Calm down, Willbe. I don't know whether or not they exist, I've never heard of them before. I was browsing and looking for words, expressions that could point me towards banks, like you asked. But I won't tell you anything more until you explain why you're so excited by these Venetian files. The only reason I even looked for them is that they were cited as a reference for one of those supposedly secret societies that were formed in the Middle Ages."

"A secret society?"

"Yes, in Venice."

"Incredible," Willbe murmured.

"What's incredible, Willbe? Tell me why this is so important!"

Before he could answer, her cell phone rang and she picked it up.

"Hello... hello?"

Willbe tried to relax while Sarah looked at her phone with a puzzled expression.

"Who was it?"

"I don't know, no caller ID, must have had the wrong number..." answered Sarah.

The Tallulah waiter, responding to Willbe's call, brought him a beer, while Sarah replaced the vodka cocktail with an espresso, giving Willbe enough time to take a deep breath and ready himself to explain his excited state.

"I'm sorry, Sarah, I'm probably being a little ridiculous. I heard about these files a while ago, but I never really thought that they existed. But now, if there are references to them, well, perhaps they do exist."

*************

They had met at the beginning of the summer at the Rare Book and Manuscript Library at Columbia University. Sarah, who had recently completed her graduate studies in Library and Information Sciences, laughed whenever she recalled the bewildered expression on Willbe's face when he was told that he needed a Special Collections Research Account to access any of the materials hosted there. That seemed to be one bureaucratic step too many for the new hire in the Mathematics Department. She overheard his plea for special consideration at the front desk – he just wanted to consult this one book, why did he have to create a whole new account for that? – and thought he was charming enough, in the clueless way often displayed by math geeks, to offer her assistance.

"You can use my account if you want, if all that you need is to consult one book," she had offered. "But you need to tell me why you need it, you know, due diligence and all that."

Willbe, struck by Sarah's beauty as much as her kindness in making this offer, quickly accepted.

"Alright, do you have time for a coffee?"

Thus, began their collaboration. Willbe was certain that, bureaucracy or not, he could manage to search through a bunch of old books by himself, but being helped by someone who already knew her way around archives and libraries couldn't hurt. In time he discovered that a recommendation letter from her boss could also open certain doors that would probably take months for him alone.

But, above all, their conversations about rare books, the Middle Ages, politics, and mathematics were the perfect excuse for the two strangers to get to know each other for the next several weeks, as it was apparent from the beginning that research was not the only thing they had in mind when they were together.

\*\*\*\*\*\*\*\*\*\*\*\*\*

"So what if these files exist, Willbe? Why are they so important?"

"If they really are the files I have in mind, they might have something to do with my ancestors. It's something that's been mentioned in conversation with my Italian family, but I've never known for sure whether or not they exist."

"Something do to with your ancestors?"

"That's right. My family, or more precisely my mother's family, comes from the Tuscan region in Italy, from the city of Pisa to be exact."

Willbe grabbed his wallet, pulled out a photocopy of the identification page on his passport, and showed it to Sarah.

"Look at my full name in the document."

"Ok... And?"

"Normally I don't use the letter *F* in my middle, or maternal, surname, even though for some Italians it's more important than the paternal surname."

"I'm still not following..."

"This *F* here stands for Fibonacci, the name of the first great Italian, or even European, mathematician. A distant relative, so to speak, from almost a thousand years ago, but a blood relation that fills this part of the family with pride, as you might imagine. You know, the Fibonacci sequence... Surely you've heard of Fibonacci numbers."

"You're turning into a little box of surprises today, Willbe. Hiding a famous surname? Why? In New York of all places!"

"I find it easier to just avoid the inevitable jokes and comparisons. But there's another reason, one that's actually a lot more serious."

"Well, well. Looks like today is the day for revelations."

Willbe lowered his voice even further:

"But not here, Sarah. Not in a public place like this, ok? Walls have ears, you know. Can we continue this at my place?"

"Of course," Sarah replied, a questioning look in her eye.

\*\*\*\*\*\*\*\*\*\*

As they entered his small but comfortable apartment on the Upper West Side, on 91st Street between Broadway and Amsterdam Avenue, Willbe motioned towards an armchair for Sarah to sit and turned on the stereo, letting the voice of Andrea Bocelli echo through the room. A little cliché, he knew, but the music reminded him of his time in Italy.

*Un amore così grande, un amore così…*

Bocelli gave the surroundings a romantic touch. Sarah did not understand much Italian, but she knew enough to be carried by the song.

*… Tanto caldo dentro e fuori, intorno a noi un silenzio breve.*

Their initial flirting in the library at Columbia had been the spark that led to many walks around campus and a few late nights in New York bars. Whenever they were free, their cell phones would light up with messages suggesting times and places where they could meet and talk. They shared an interest in many subjects, particularly history and the medieval era.

*… e poi la bocca tua si accende, si accende un'altra volta per me.*

"Did you know that Andrea Bocelli was born in Tuscany, Sarah?"

"No, I didn't."

"In a small village about 40 kilometers from Pisa. He and I have a lot in common."

"Are you also a singer, Willbe? This might be too much new information for me to take in a single day."

Willbe smiled.

"I'm afraid I'm no singer, but both of us attended the University of Pisa, how about that? He studied law and I did a PhD in mathematics, at different times, granted. Galileo and Enrico Fermi also studied there. *Tutti buona gente*, as they say in Italian."

"I'd be proud too."

"The university had among its early benefactors one of my ancestors, also a Fibonacci, called Giuseppe. To be honest, that played a small role in my decision to study there. It also made my mother and the rest of my family very happy, as you can imagine."

Sarah looked at Willbe with admiration, pleased that he was opening up to her in this way. "I'd love to travel to Italy, Willbe. I've been to many parts of Europe, but somehow not Italy."

"You must, Sarah. It is *il gioiello dell'Europa*. Perhaps we'll visit together!"

Before she could respond, Sarah's cell phone vibrated beside her on the sofa. With a small hand gesture, she asked Willbe to wait and took the call. The clock on her phone showed 8:11pm.

"Hello … yes … this is she … Who is this? From the Public Library?"

Sarah glanced inquisitively towards her friend.

"Yes, that's right, I was there. I visited one of the restricted sections in the morning, the rare books sections, exactly... Yes, I had a recommendation letter from Timothy Geithner, why do you ask?"

Sarah put the call on speaker so that Willbe could listen in. She pointed to her wristwatch indicating her puzzlement at the late hour of the call.

"One of the books you consulted is missing, madam."

"Excuse me? Sorry, but there must be a mistake," replied Sarah. "I consulted several books and took some notes on my laptop. I know exactly which books I took out and I returned them all."

"We are also very sorry, madam, but I have the afternoon shift and my colleague who was here in the morning left a note with your number on it. The note says that Sarah J.F. Mayer selected, among others, three extremely rare books for reading and research. One of them is missing: *Secrets of Italian Cities* by Jacques Desgranges."

Sarah, taken by surprise, straightened herself on the sofa and interrupted the person on the phone:

"The name is correct and I did request this book, but as I said, I returned it."

"Alright, if you don't mind then, could you please come back to the Library so we can sort this out?"

"I don't mind at all. I'll be there in the morning and can talk to your colleague, probably the same person I talked to before."

"Thank you very much. I will leave him a note saying that you'll be here. Around what time, please?"

"Let's say between 11:15 and 11:30am."

"Thank you, Ms. Mayer. I apologize for the inconvenience. Good night."

They hung up and Sarah, still with the phone next to her ear, looked at Willbe with an expression of distinct irritation on her face.

"I didn't take any book from the Library, that's absurd! And in any case, it would be impossible. You know that place - nobody can sneak out a book from there, let alone a rare book."

"There must be a mistake."

"Mistake or not, my heart missed a beat when they mentioned the name of the book."

"The name of the book? Why?"

"That was the book where I read about the Venetian Files."

"Ok, so?"

"After what you just told me about your family, your ancestors... I don't know, I had a feeling..."

"A feeling? What are you talking about? It's surely just a coincidence. They must have stored the book on a different shelf and are looking for an excuse to justify their own mess."

"Maybe, I don't know, Willbe."

"With millions of books and thousands of people reading them everyday, this must happen often. I didn't realize that you are superstitious, Sarah." Willbe smiled as he said this.

"It isn't superstition; it's just that I don't believe in coincidences."

Willbe continued to smile at her.

"I'm serious, Willbe. I saw your reaction when I mentioned those files. You're still not telling me everything, I can tell. From the moment I got to the Tallulah, I could tell that there is something bothering you, that there's more to what you're telling me."

Willbe's expression turned serious and he appeared embarrassed. He moved a little closer to Sarah.

"Yes, Sarah, you're right. It's not that I don't trust you, of course. It's just that I still don't know how all of these pieces fit together and if I'm perhaps just being... silly."

Under Sarah's intrigued gazed, Willbe rose, picked an old book from the shelves – a late 19th century hardcover edition of Niccolo Machiavelli's *The Prince* – and placed it on his desk, asking her to come closer.

"Before I explain, Sarah, can you just tell me whether the book you saw, the one by this Desgranges, discussed the content of these Venetian Files?"

"I don't think it did, but we can look at it together once it is found."

Willbe returned to the book in front of him. Opening it carefully, he removed two folded sheets of old paper. Sarah, still bothered by the recent phone call, followed Willbe's careful movements with attentive curiosity – and a tad of apprehension at his change of behavior.

*Why the mystery?*

"I received these papers exactly as you see them now, inside this book. The sheets were inserted at this very page, which has a few highlighted lines, as you can see. It happened during a family dinner the day I got my PhD."

Willbe laid the two pages out on the desk, with extreme care, one beside the other, as Sarah read aloud from the highlighted lines in the book:

"'*At this moment, left lifeless, Italy awaits for her sons to cure her ills, end the raid of Lombardy, end the usurpation of Tuscany, and heal the wounds that for so long have burned.*' What does it mean?"

"Machiavelli's exhortation to the Italians. From the little that I have read about him, Machiavelli was an ardent defender of Italy, a man ahead of his times, a great poet and politician. And these two sheets here are a letter, or more precisely a copy of a letter, kept as a family treasure with great care and devotion."

Sarah examined the pieces of paper with a professional eye, without knowing where this was going.

"And what is the connection, if there is any, between Machiavelli and the letter?"

Willbe grabbed a magnifying glass and offered it to Sarah.

"Look at the signature."

"It's almost impossible to read."

"True, but the initials in capital letters are quite visible."

Sarah moved closer to the document with the magnifying glass:

*Vitorio Giuseppe Fibonacci*

"A 'V', then I believe a 'G' and then an 'F', is that it?

"Exactly: Vitorio Giuseppe Fibonacci, my ancestor and one of the richest men in Venice in the 14th century – a man who loved Italy, two centuries before Machiavelli. The text you read was highlighted by my uncle, who gave me the book with this document inside. I think he wanted to draw my attention to the common ideal of a great Italy that both men shared."

Still unsure as to how all this fit together, Sarah placed the magnifying glass beside the book and, immersed in thought, returned to her seat with a sigh:

"Do you know what the rest of the letter says?"

"Yes, I translated it and keep a version on my computer."

"Then I'll read it carefully, Willbe, I promise. But before that I need to sort out this misunderstanding with the Library."

"Of course," Willbe replied.

"It's curious though..." Sarah's voice trailed off.

"What's curious?"

"I might be confused with this phone call from the Library and all, but I think that I saw this name in that same book."

"Really?"

"You said he was alive in the 14th century, right?"

"Yes, that is what I've been told."

"Hmm..." Sarah returned to the table and stared passively at the letter.

"What is it?" Willbe asked.

"I might be wrong, of course, but I think the typography used in this letter is from a later period, after the Gutenberg press."

Willbe looked disappointed. Sarah realized she had made a comment at the wrong time and backpedalled.

"We'll look into it tomorrow, I promise. After I sort out this silly matter with the Desgranges book."

# 6

*Circa 1350-60 AD*
*Vicenza, Veneto Region - ITALY*

Six oil lamps illuminated the smallest of the meditation rooms of the Franciscan friars, isolated from the main monastery building. The room could not be more than one hundred square feet in size. The only furniture was a small oak table at its centre and two oak stools against the walls.

On the wall to the left of the entrance hung a heavy wooden cross; it attracted attention not only because of its size, but also for the quality of its woodwork. Standing from the ground to almost the height of the beam across the ceiling, its imposing form contrasted with the vow of poverty made by these men. The absence of the figure of Christ hanging from the cross had already been the subject of heated discussions between visitors and the friars. Most thought that the artist, an unknown local sculptor, had refused to portray the suffering of Christ. The empty cross was instead meant to symbolize the liberation of men. Others considered the artist an apostate. Nobody knew what had happened to him, and contradictory stories about his death abounded.

Having had such discussions a long time ago, Friar Luigi moved towards Giuseppe Fibonacci with a wide smile, greeting him with a fraternal handshake and a warm embrace.

"To what do I owe the honour of this unexpected visit, when you, my friend, should be in Pisa helping your people celebrate the unveiling of such a wondrous tower?"

"I have come from Pisa, Luigi, and you are right, the tower is certainly a wonder. The people are filled with pride."

"It is impressive that they managed to raise it with the incline."

"I am also in awe, but I confess that I do not understand its engineering."

"God's miracle..." risked Friar Luigi.

"If you say so."

They both smiled. Friar Luigi motioned towards the oak table:

"Refresh yourself, please. The wine is made here in the monastery." Luigi gestured towards the table on which stood jugs of water and wine, and plates with prosciutto, cheese, nuts, and olives. "You must be hungry; the journey from Pisa is long. I'll see to it that your servants and horses are fed. They shall sleep in the monastery tonight."

"Thank you, Luigi, I am grateful to you."

Giuseppe and Friar Luigi had known each other for many years and, when talking in private, as happened often in the last few months, dispensed with formalities and talked like the old friends they were.

As he moved to close the door at the entrance of the room, Giuseppe went right to the topic that was in his mind:

"What stories are these that I hear in Florence, Luigi, and also in Venice, about royal debts not being honoured?"

"Rumors of this sort spread like wild fire, it is amazing. In any case, it may not be as you have heard."

"They are not rumors. These are true accounts. In Florence the men with fortunes at stake are angry about the situation. They want a solution. There are thousands of florins going up in smoke from one day to the next. It does not make any sense, Luigi. We cannot keep taking risks of this magnitude."

"There is always a way out, Giuseppe, don't get ahead of yourself."

"We are also involved in this. Neither you nor I can lose money like this, so unexpectedly... I had always thought that a King would honour his word, is this not true?"

"Your faith is touching," said Luigi, his eyes sparkling with irony.

"What they say and already take for granted is that the house of Peruzzi is going bankrupt, for King Roberto of Naples died and his descendants defaulted on loans made in Florence."

"Nothing insurmountable, I think."

A momentary silence descended between the two men, both absorbed in thought. Giuseppe helped himself to a handful of nuts.

"There is no way to enforce the debt of a King, Luigi, especially after his death. You know this as well as I. It is not worth our time to make these loans. Unless..."

Friar Luigi waited for the end of the sentence:

"Unless?"

"Unless we the lenders adopt more stringent rules for some loans and do what has been suggested to me by certain Florentines and merchants here in Veneto."

"Increase usury, charge for the risk..."

Giuseppe looked at his friend with a questioning frown, barely hiding a mischievous smirk.

"Strange and risky words for a God-fearing man."

"A God-fearing man who is not removed from secular problems. Nevertheless, speak of the devil and he shall appear, is it not true? It is all there, in the comedy written by the Florentine, the seventh circle of hell: usurers licked by eternal fire."

"Religious people and poets usually get along quite well, Luigi, for both live in another world. But yes, you understand my meaning: charge for risk. It is only fair. Especially for galleys crossing huge distances on the seas."

"I have not yet agreed with some of these ideas, Giuseppe. For now, I insist, these are simply rumors that reached my ear."

"Then, no doubt, your attentive ears heard the news about the English King and his war debts, not just with the French, but also with some of our countrymen."

"King Edward? No, I have not heard, what do the rumors say?"

"That he will not honour his agreements with his creditors."

"And you, my friend, think that we can interfere in these royal affairs?"

"Not now, but perhaps we ought to in the future."

"How, Giuseppe? As usual you seem to know more than the rest of us."

"No Luigi, I don't know more, I merely observe and evaluate. What if we had some wine?"

Before Luigi could answer, Giuseppe poured two glasses and offered one to his friend.

"*In vino veritas.*"

As they toasted, Giuseppe thought to himself: *What exactly did Luigi plan to do with the money that he had been amassing through the monastery?*

*************

After drinking a second glass of wine with gusto and providing a superficial explanation of his relationship with Giovanni Acunto, the English mercenary adopted by the Florentine merchants, Giuseppe decided it was time to drop the subtleties and flourishes. Since leaving Pisa four days before, convinced that he had to keep the reins of the family businesses firmly in his hands, Giuseppe had been pondering to himself whether the time was right to bring Luigi into his confidence. He was about to put in train his plan to find the ways and means of protecting the immense wealth recently amassed by Italian merchants and moneylenders – his own wealth and that of Friar Luigi's included. But was Luigi ready?

*Friar Luigi di Vicenza would not betray me. Never.*

If nothing else, Luigi had entrusted Giuseppe with his own considerable fortune. And for all his piety, he too appreciated the worldly pleasures afforded by gold. If his private dealings were revealed, the bonfire would be his inevitable destiny. Unless he had powerful allies in Rome, which Giuseppe doubted was the case. He had heard stories that Luigi, at some point in his life, had received vast amounts of gold from a Knight Templar, a distant relative. But he had never asked his friend about such stories.

To him, men like Luigi and Giovanni Acunto, who were each in their own ways masters of deceit though their positions in life had kept them separated like water and oil, were the perfect partners for secret business. Whether legal or illegal was beyond the point, for the laws – both divine and earthly – were always flexible for those with power.

Giuseppe had come to understand that he, and the men like him who conducted their business all over Europe and beyond, had to find ways to protect themselves from the risks they faced, above all, in the distant offshore lands. Piracy, storms, and simple poor judgment – all these things cost money.

"In Venice the sailors and merchants speak of unknown lands. They talk of voyages to the West, far beyond the Isle of Britannia. There is money to be made from these voyages, Luigi, but there are risks, too."

"Do you really believe these stories about lands to be discovered in the West? They seem fantastic to me."

"This is what I hear, Luigi. I have no reason to doubt those who tell me these stories. There is serious talk about it. It would be good for you to leave this monastery once in a while and talk to people in the streets and ports of Venice."

"I hear they are all impious; lovers of novelty and frivolity," Luigi retorted with a smile.

"You think so? When Marco Polo came back to Venice, with great riches incidentally, the topic of the existence of other lands was the subject of some speculation, Luigi. The number of sailors who believe in this possibility grows by the week, with each voyage. Some astronomers have conducted detailed studies on this topic."

"I am more like Saint Thomas, I need to see it to believe."

Giuseppe helped himself to prosciutto and a piece of bread. He looked at the friar with a serious expression:

"Luigi, I have been working very hard; you know this. Too hard for a man of my age, even though I expect to live for many more years. I make money, lots of it, by the sweat of my brow, as your bible says."

Luigi smiled, slightly embarrassed, and raised his wine glass in a toast to the ironic reference. Giuseppe, animated, carried on:

"I have a large family in Tuscany, all of them hard workers, it is true, but it is my duty to secure the best future for my sons that my fortune can provide. And to the grandchildren that they will give me, and great grand-children and who knows how many more generations."

"Alright, Giuseppe, what is your point?"

"Listen carefully, Luigi, as carefully as you can. I have very few true friends in Venice; even in Pisa. But you are one of those friends."

"*Grazie tante...*" interjected Luigi.

Giuseppe acknowledged him with a nod and continued:

"Not all of them work as hard as I do, from dusk to dawn, and don't get me wrong, this has given me the chance to gather a considerable amount of money."

"It is more than simply considerable, from what I hear. You are one of the richest men in Italy, I am told."

The compliment touched Giuseppe's Tuscan pride and sparked his enthusiasm even more. His voice became a notch louder:

"True, but this is all money that needs to be invested, Luigi, it can't be wasted! We buy land, purchase jewelry, gold and silver; we even help Kings. We support artists, painters like Lorenzo Veneziano, Giotto di Bondone..."

"And Lorenzo di Bicci in Florence, too."

"I personally funded a large part of the construction of the tower in Pisa and have pledged a great fortune for the establishment of the university there. Nevertheless, we are still forced to submit to the Church and royal families!"

"And what is the problem? This is how it has been for centuries."

"With all due respect, Luigi, these are people who produce nothing. And times are changing..."

Almost instinctively, Luigi moved closer to the enormous cross to his left and in a gesture that surprised Giuseppe toasted eloquently to the absent Christ:

"*In nomine patris et filii et spiritus sancti,*" recited Luigi.

"I am not joking, Luigi."

"Did I say that you were joking?"

"Then for what reason did you raise a glass to the cross? Some blasphemy?"

"Blasphemy, Giuseppe? Have you forgotten that one of the greatest miracles of the absent master here was to multiply the bread and turn the water into wine? Where is the blasphemy? You should be the one watching your words. But carry on, finish what you have to say."

"That is it, Luigi, that is all I have to say. You touched the right point, used the right words: to turn is a most appropriate verb. Not exactly water into wine, but we can turn money into something else. Multiply it and turn it into power. Not just financial power, but political power. Do you see it? It is possible to turn money into a power greater than that of Kings and Popes."

Luigi drank the remaining half of his wine glass in one large gulp.

# 7

*September 11, 2008*
*Venice – ITALY*

The municipal police of Venice had, with some difficulty, isolated the area where the black-suited body lay – an arched passageway along the Grand Canal not far from the Rialto Bridge. The two visible ends of the pedestrian alleyway and the arched window overlooking the Grand Canal were sealed off with transparent bubble wrap, letting enough light in to clean up the bloody scene, while blocking the view from prying eyes. Around the body of the unknown man, an aureole of blood blossomed out from the wound in his abdomen. A partial footprint was visible at the edge of the drying blood. It suggested the sole of either a military or a hunting boot.

The *Polizia di Frontiera* arrived at the scene following a local police speed-boat. The detective in charge of the operation, a man called Piero de Lucca – a tall and hearty fellow who was used to identifying tourists by their body language, behavior, and clothes – assured his colleagues that the dead man was Japanese, likely wealthy, judging from his suit. He appeared to be about sixty years old and no documents were found on his body. No passport, identity card, credit cards, business cards, hotel address... nothing.

The city of Venice was used to unusual occurrences and a few mysterious deaths. The strangeness of the Japanese man's death was the katana with *kanji* script printed on its handle – the weapon had in fact pierced through one of his hands and pinned it to his stomach. *Seppuku?* The position of the body, with the hand in a defensive motion, made it unlikely. There was also no indication of any ritual, and the location, surrounded by tourists, made little sense. No, suicide was not the explanation, in Piero de Lucca's opinion.

Piero's orders were to move the body as quickly as possible. The professionalism of the police was admirable. The other police officers taking part in the cleanup knew from experience that some matters were above their pay grade and it was best to keep their mouths shut. Only the earpiece of the commander, connected to a radio transmitting from the police station, could be faintly heard.

In the mechanical but unpleasant sequence of steps that followed, the body was nearly thrown in the motorboat of the municipal police and taken straight to the morgue for an autopsy. It did not take more than fifteen minutes for normality to return to the spot near the Rialto Bridge, and once the alleyway was opened to tourists again, no trace of what had happened could be found.

Though he was used to receiving orders he sometimes disagreed with, Piero was troubled by the urgency that seemed to accompany the processing of the dead man's body.

*************

## Frankfurt – *GERMANY*

The lights had just gone on inside the three rectangular blocks of exposed concrete on 14 Wilhelm-Epstein Street when a courier delivered a white plastic envelope at the reception desk seven minutes before closing time. It was addressed to the President of the Deutsche Bundesbank – the German Central Bank.

The thirteen-storey building housed one of the most powerful financial institutions in the world. Its discreet and somber architecture, with its grey tones, could be placed, somewhat charitably, between the more traditional German architecture, such as can be seen around Römer Square, and that of a more modern Germany seen in the bold skyscrapers of Zeil Gallery and its shopping malls crisscrossed by escalators in all directions.

The envelope reached its destination at the top level of the building and was placed on the President's desk at exactly 5:57pm. It was opened at 8:14pm when he returned from an exhausting meeting with the Bank's Executive Board. From inside the opaque plastic envelope, the German central banker removed a paper envelope, also white and rectangular, with the stamp TOP SECRET across the seal flap.

*Verdammt!* It was not the first time he had received an envelope like this. He knew what it signified and that he should destroy it as soon as he finished reading, no matter what the contents were. Before opening it, he took one of the three cell phones scattered on his desk and called the direct line of the President of the European Central Bank.

The effects of the possible, and some thought almost inevitable, bankruptcy of the Lehman Brothers bank in the United States would certainly spill over the borders of that country and, while it would cause complications for the European and world economies, things should not get out of control. What was necessary was to prevent a run on the banks, a panic. This was one of the most urgent problems to be faced that weekend. Crises had to be confronted and, whenever possible, defeated. Not everyone loses in a crisis; certain people even gain.

*Some say that is why central banks exist.*

"Hello... Jean-Claude?"

Axel Weber checked that the door to his office was closed and went back to sit in his rotating chair. He liked challenges, and the current crisis offered many for his logical mind. Crisis management was a touchy subject for his government. Even über-modern Germany could not erase from its collective memory the image of citizens pushing wheelbarrows filled with Deutschmarks during the Weimar era.

\*\*\*\*\*\*\*\*\*\*\*\*

The President of the European Central Bank, Frenchman Jean-Claude Trichet, calmly tapped his fingers on his desk and listened attentively on his cell phone to Axel Weber, his counterpart at the Deutsche Bundesbank.

Five years on the job, Trichet treated all such *special calls* with respect, elegance and, above all, discretion. He tended to listen more than he spoke, unless faced with a situation requiring his intervention, which was becoming more and more likely. For months the daily briefings prepared by his assistants had been warning of increasing volatility in the financial markets, imminent bank failures, and the bursting of the American housing bubble, all of which threatened to infect international markets. It was one of those times when markets downplay the risks of moral hazards and expect central banks to come to the rescue. A sensible professional, Trichet did not take long to understand which way the wind was blowing.

"Like you, Axel, I have a special team following this closely. We have direct lines of communication with Washington, London, Paris, Tokyo, and Beijing ready to be used in case of emergency. But you and I can also meet and talk in person, what do you think?"

"I think that's a good idea, let's schedule something as soon as possible then," said Weber. "You can come here now and I can order lunch in my meeting room. We will have privacy and more time to talk."

Trichet hung up and kept looking at the phone, making it spin on the table between his fingers, his thoughts on the news he kept receiving, now at an hourly rate. The most recent update had informed him of an emergency meeting between Hank Paulson, Timothy Geithner, and the heads of the largest American banks later that weekend.

*Crises, after all, can always be used for something,* he thought. *But not when they acquire tsunami proportions. Central banks had better be prepared.*

He looked again at the blueprints for the construction of the new ECB headquarters, which would no doubt become one of the most impressive and modern buildings in Frankfurt. *Part of my legacy,* he thought with pride. Under his leadership, the institution created barely ten years earlier would face its first real test in combating a global financial crisis.

*************

## Washington DC – USA

Let Lehman Brothers file for bankruptcy? Could he perhaps be missing the rationale for this? Would the Federal Reserve have the tools to stop a run on the nation's banks if that happened?

For Hank Paulson, that seemed to be a possibility contemplated by the British Exchequer, although he could not be sure about it. That did not make much sense for a country that once ruled the world economy. After all, one could always take out the bad apples without necessarily chopping down the apple tree.

But which were the bad apples at the moment? Or the "toxic assets", as the results of some of the financial alchemy of recent years had become known.

*And who had the right to call something toxic anyway?*

Perhaps that was the most appropriate expression for the state of the world economy at that moment, but it was, nevertheless, irritating that the same Wall Street boys who created these assets were apparently deciding to dump them. Assets based on high-risk subprime mortgages sold as triple-A securities, as safe as the most solid companies in the country, for example. Was this not a scam that could have been prevented? Paulson was discouraged.

*The markets should not become hostage to irresponsible traders.*

The specter of the great crisis of 1929, when financial turmoil was allowed to spread and cause havoc in the rest of the economy, always came back to haunt policymakers. In principle, the best way to make the rulers of money understand and follow the rules was to let them face the consequences of their risky bets. But a generalized panic punishes irresponsible traders and average citizens alike, suggesting that some government help was necessary.

*I did not come to Washington to be Mr. Bailout,* was Paulson's frequent complaint about the contradictions between his free market views and the role his office was expected to play in turbulent times.

The primaries were over and Washington was getting ready for November when the country would decide to elect either John McCain, and keep a Republican in the White House, or Barack Obama, giving the reins of the nation to a Democrat. From a distance, the peaceful change in government that happened every four years in the United States might seem straightforward, but it carried risks and involved complex arrangements.

Who would steer the ship of state to a safe harbor in the middle of a crisis, and how many billions of dollars would it cost? Anxiety and euphoria mingled in ever more uncertain proportions. Nobody knew how much time the world economy, and in particular that of the United States, still had to face up to the needs of a world that was growing more populated, more demanding, and more dissatisfied.

Whatever the results of the upcoming presidential election, the fact was that Hank Paulson did not envy his successor in 2009. And he envied even less the Executive Board of the Federal Reserve.

The Treasury Secretary was heading to New York the next day for an emergency weekend meeting with Timothy Geithner and the CEOs of all major Wall Street firms. The agenda was to find a solution for Lehman. He hoped that the British would come through.

# 8

*August 19, 2008*
*New York City – USA*

Sarah did not sleep well. Her conversation with Willbe and the call from the library about the Desgranges book had left her feeling uneasy, though she wasn't quite sure why. She even had a dream in which Willbe was followed by faceless members of a secret society who cornered him and made incoherent demands.

She woke up with a headache. Forcing herself out of bed, Sarah walked to the bathroom and, looking herself in the mirror over the sink, noticed the skin under her eyes slightly darkened.

*I'm useless without a good night's sleep.*

Her thoughts returned to the document Willbe had shown her the night before. Certain features of it still didn't make sense to her. The letter was printed in *Antiqua* typeface and dated 1380, written in Venice and signed by a Vitorio Giuseppe Fibonacci, whose signature not only was not handwritten, but also was the only part of the document printed in *Gothic* letters. She knew from her training that these two fonts were not normally mixed in this manner, unless it was a typographical montage.

*Vitorio Giuseppe Fibonacci. I'm sure I saw that name in one of the books I looked at. And why the different fonts? There were no printing presses in Europe in 1380; the first was at Gutenberg in 1455. Were there two different documents? Is Willbe's copy a merger of the two?*

Willbe's theory was that the original letter, written in gothic font and presumably preserved for almost one hundred years by Giuseppe's sons and grandsons, had been transcribed by a copyist. The printer had simply used a different font because by that time the Gutenberg press made it possible to do so.

Sarah knew that movable types, as they were then called, could be changed in each new typographic print. She also knew that the format of the printed letters changed, with new types contributing to the transition from ancient typefaces to more modern ones. But it was the signature in gothic script that bothered her. Was it a tribute to the document's origins and proof of its authenticity? Or did it signal a mistake or forgery?

None of these questions were reasons to worry. But they did give her the feeling, perhaps for the first time, that the profession she had chosen also carried responsibilities that she had not previously appreciated. With increasingly advanced resources and the latest technology, it would not be difficult for ill-intentioned people to try to falsify "historical documents" with great sophistication.

Speculations aside, the truth was that she had not had time to read the translation that Willbe had made from the original document yet, but she intended to in the next few days. She wanted to find out why Willbe attributed so much importance to it.

*What did it say exactly? Was there some message hidden between the lines? Why did Willbe receive it as a graduation gift? Did the person who gave it to him know the origin of the document? Was there a reason to give it to him?*

The alarm went off on her bedside table. She had forgotten to turn it off when she got out of bed, still half asleep. Her headache worsened and she looked for two painkillers that would take care of the problem in minutes. It was a quarter past ten in the morning. She had an hour to reach the Public Library and sort out the clerk's mistake. She called the office to let them know that she would arrive after lunch, telling them she had to finish a report for Mr. Geithner and she needed some quiet.

Twenty minutes later, feeling mildly better after a shower and with a cup of coffee in her system, Sarah emerged from her building in the Lower East Side. She squinted in the bright sun as she hailed a taxi, realizing she had forgotten her sunglasses.

Behind her, without her even suspecting it, an elegant black Mercedes-Benz started its engine and accelerated silently, putting itself at a close distance to the taxi.

*************

"Good morning."

"Good morning," replied the young security officer seated beside one of the lions in the lobby of the New York Public Library.

Sarah produced a small piece of paper on which she had written the name of the person she was supposed to meet and, following the instructions from the security officer, headed to the same part of the building where she had been the day before. On her way, she called the library clerk to let him know that she was coming. She arrived at his desk and took a seat in one of the chairs in the waiting area. She was anxious for some reason.

"Ms. Mayer, good morning. Could you follow me please?"

It was the same person she had dealt with the day before. Biting her tongue, she simply replied, "Of course."

The clerk led her to what was surely the office of the person in charge of that wing of the Library. She was greeted by an affable gentleman with hair parted in the middle, thick eyebrows and round glasses balancing on top of a small red nose. He asked the clerk to leave and pointed to a chair in front of his desk:

"Please Ms. Mayer, take a seat. My name is John Kaminsky."

"Thank you, Mr. Kaminsky."

"I asked you to come to my office for a very simple, albeit embarrassing, reason."

"Embarrassing?"

"Please don't be alarmed. I assure you it has nothing to do with what they told you on the phone last night. What I mean is that it is embarrassing to us. I had to see you to apologize in person, not only for myself but also on behalf of the Library. The matter has been resolved."

"I'm pleased to hear it, Mr. Kaminsky, but now more than ever I would like to know what is going on, because if it was just a misunderstanding you could have called me and saved me the trouble of coming here."

"Of course, Ms. Mayer. I will explain."

The red-nosed man pulled a piece of paper from one of the drawers in his desk and handed it to Sarah.

"The book you examined yesterday, *Secrets of Italian Cities* by Jacques Desgranges, is one of very few remaining copies in existence. One of three, if rumors are to be believed. A second copy is on display at the library of the Querini Stampalia Foundation in Venice, in every respect identical to the one we have here."

"And the third copy?"

"Its existence is uncertain. The copy we have here, therefore, must be protected."

"Naturally, I understand, but as you have discovered, I returned the book. And, as my letter of recommendation makes it clear, I'm no amateur when it comes to handling precious manuscripts."

Mr. Kaminsky pointed to the piece of paper in Sarah's hand:

"This is a formal apology, Ms. Mayer. Please read it carefully. If you accept its content, I can sign it on behalf of the Library, you can take it with you, and all is forgotten."

Sarah glanced at the paper for a few seconds. In formal and concise language, it contained an apology, explained that the book had been re-shelved by mistake in a different place, and cleared her from any future complaints regarding the matter. Boilerplate from public agencies, it was, nevertheless, the first time she had received such a thing.

"Thank you, Mr. Kaminsky. I'm still not quite sure why this required me to visit here today, but I appreciate the gesture."

"Please come back any time you want to continue your research, Ms. Mayer. You are always welcome here. If there is any problem, please come and see me."

With that, Mr. Kaminsky handed Sarah his business card and ended the visit.

\*\*\*\*\*\*\*\*\*\*

*The pledges that new members of this brotherhood had to take, above all that of absolute loyalty, conferred to each of them the autonomy to create a network of informants who did not know for what or whom they worked.*

\*\*\*\*\*\*\*\*\*\*

Sarah was circumspect when she left the Library. The apology letter confused her. It was so unnecessary. The only reason she could think for it being given was the fact that she had used a letter of reference signed by Timothy Geithner.

*Maybe they were trying to avoid being sued?*

The black Mercedes that had followed her to the Library, and which had remained parked nearby while she was inside, pulled out into the traffic moving up Fifth Avenue. Its license plate identified it as an official vehicle of the United Nations.

As Sarah walked towards Bryant Park, she pulled out her phone to call Willbe. He answered quickly:

"How did it go at the Library?"

"Alright. A bit odd, actually. Are you busy now?"

"Not really, I just need to go to the university after lunch."

"Come have a coffee with me at Bryant Park then and we'll talk about it. I can wait for you at the Park Café."

"I'll be there soon."

# 9

*Circa 1350-60 AD*
*Vicenza, Veneto Region – ITALY*

The wine and the heated conversation were warming up the interior of the monastery's meditation room.

"The only power higher than that of Kings and Popes is that of God, Giuseppe. We should not even be discussing this. Is it with such diabolic spirits that you come to a servant of the Lord to try to convince him that there is a higher power than the Creator? Now that would be a blasphemy."

"What do I care about blasphemies? You know very well my opinion about gods and religions, Luigi. Life is too short for such fears and fantasies."

Luigi pointed to the enormous cross without a Christ.

"Believe it or not, Giuseppe, only He could have made us friends."

"He? He who?"

"Don't play with serious matters, Giuseppe."

Luigi returned the glass of wine to the small oak table and walked towards Giuseppe with a serious expression. He politely took the other glass from the hands of his friend and, holding him by the arm, made him sit on one of the wooden stools.

"Giuseppe, our friendship has survived our many disagreements, but I never imagined that you would be capable of saying words like these."

"Don't be so dramatic, Luigi."

"*Va bene*, but listen, how can you think that there is a power higher not only than that of Kings and Popes, but also above Christ himself, the Son of God?"

"Why not, what is the problem? I am talking about money, Giuseppe, the same money that you value so much. Money is and will continue to be the greatest power that men fight for. That is what I am referring to: money.

Which, I might add, has also kept our friendship alive, regardless of what you might think."

The two friends looked at each other for a few seconds. Giuseppe continued:

"Remember the parable about rich men entering the Kingdom of Heaven, Luigi; it is easier for a camel to pass through the eye of the needle. You are a rich man too, my friend."

"There is a difference between wealth and avarice, Giuseppe. Greed is a sin. You are putting me in a very difficult position. We could both end up in the bonfire."

Giuseppe found the warning strange:

"And who would condemn me? You? No, you wouldn't dare. Remember that we are in the same boat."

An uncomfortable silence filled the room. Giuseppe looked at Luigi with a puzzled expression, a mix of commiseration and doubt. More than ever, he needed the approval of his friend:

"I didn't come here to argue, my dear Luigi, I tell you that most sincerely. We are living in changing times. For men like us – merchants and traders – there is the opportunity to build connections with the rest of Europe and far beyond. We are going to make a lot more money, Luigi."

"But where does it take us? Are there no bounds to wealth?"

"Luigi, open your eyes! Leave the monastery for a bit: the world is not going to be divided as it is now, between Kings and subjects, or Popes and churchgoers, noblemen and serfs, rich and poor. These times are creating a new type of man, more forward looking, more ambitious, less fearful of God. One who will make money his new God, and in that way be better at using his wealth."

"I never thought I would hear you say such things, Giuseppe. May God forgive me, but from what I understand you are suggesting that the two of us should join this new caste."

"Not only join it, Luigi, but lead it."

"How? I can see that these are the ideas that this Giovanni Acunto has put inside your head. He and your other friends in Venice."

"Nobody put ideas inside my head, Luigi. These are my own ideas, based on what I see going on around us. And I have many more ideas that I haven't yet shared with you. Perhaps you should take some notes."

"Are you out of your mind? Put down in writing your heresies? We might as well surrender to the Inquisition now!"

"Calm yourself, Luigi. You could write in code – you religious men are skilled in concealment, aren't you?"

"I will listen to what you have to say. That's all I can promise at the moment. No notes for now."

Giuseppe, in a gesture designed to defuse his friend's evident discomfort, put his two hands over Luigi's shoulders and looked him in the eyes:

"Banking houses, Luigi. What do you think?"

"What about them, Giuseppe?"

"For what reason, Luigi, should we not create one? I ask you to give me just one reason. Others are doing it, but they lack vision. And we have enough money to fund our own businesses and to lend to others, which we already do here and in neighbouring towns, am I wrong?"

Circumspect, Luigi looked at his friend thoughtfully:

"A banking house... our banking house? Are you being serious?"

"I have never been this serious in all my life, Luigi."

"But how can a servant of God own a banking house?"

"Where there is a will there is a way, especially for a servant of God."

Not knowing how to respond to the irony, Luigi searched for his glass of wine. Giuseppe stood up, examined the contents of the bottle and, before Luigi could say anything, poured what was left into their two glasses, raising his and declaring:

"*Per Bacco*, Luigi, like this, that's the true way to toast. *Auguri!*"

"You have some nerve toasting the pagan gods in front of the cross, Giuseppe." As Luigi said the words, though, he was aware that his own faith was not as strong as it once had been. Giuseppe, reading Luigi's expression, understood that he should not rush things.

"I'm sorry, Luigi. Before I try to convince you that we are about to start the greatest business of our lives, I want to amuse you with a game invented by my granduncle, Leonardo Pisano, the great Fibonacci, as he became known. Here, help me a little."

Giuseppe moved the food from the small oak table to one of the stools and, grabbing one of the round loaves of bread from the basket, asked Luigi to help him make more than two dozen small balls out of its soft interior. When they finished, he gathered all the small bread balls on one side of the table, swallowed the last of his wine with a gulp, and held some of the balls in his hands:

"Now pay attention, Luigi. If I put down one ball here and another beside it, how many balls are there?"

"Two, from what I can tell," Luigi replied and laughed, feeling the effects of the wine.

"Very good," continued Giuseppe. "Now let's pretend one of the balls is you and the other is me, alright? Now I take this other little bread ball and put it next to us two: a Venetian merchant, say our common friend Cristaldi. How many are there now?"

"Three little balls," said Luigi, wondering where this was going.

"And now, beside these three balls - the two of us and Francesco Cristaldi - I'll place two others, let us say new business partners from Florence. Therefore?"

"Five little balls."

"Now let me show you the curious side of this with another group of little balls. Keep paying attention."

"One little ball plus one little ball equals two little balls. One little ball plus two little balls gives three little balls. Are you still with me?" asked Giuseppe with a broad smile.

"Yes," replied Luigi, his patience wearing thin.

"Two plus three gives five. Three plus five? Eight."

"Hold on," interrupted Luigi. "Are you playing with me or being serious? Anyone who has studied some mathematics inside or outside the monastery can recognize this, as you put it, game of yours."

"It is not strictly a game, of course, but it does teach us how to reason, to think about growing something in a safe and harmonious way. Nature gives us many examples of this."

"And so what? Just because one of your ancestors stumbled upon these numbers by chance..."

"We don't know if it was by chance, but in any case, it doesn't matter. Just imagine that each of these numbers represents a type of business, say one of my businesses, for example, or one of yours. A third is a business from one of our Florentine or Venetian friends, and so on and so forth. If we invest in each of these businesses, they in turn will generate further opportunities and more businesses. Here in the Veneto, in all of Italy, in Europe, and beyond. It is a way of seeing things, of thinking, of acting. Money is like the land that we harvest, Luigi. If it is cultivated well, it yields even more money. Think about it."

"And what are we going to do with so many businesses and so much money, Giuseppe?"

"That's the point, Luigi. We have finally arrived at the point that interests me and for which I need your support."

Giuseppe paused theatrically to check whether his friend followed his line of thought. He continued in a solemn voice:

"It is here that the banking house comes into play - our banking house."

"The banking house," repeated Luigi.

"We create our banking house, manage our own fortune with reasonable safety, and we begin to receive proper compensation for the risks we are exposed to in our businesses. For example, suppose we stock a ship with a large quantity of goods and it is attacked by pirates in the high seas, or hit by a storm that makes us lose half of the shipment. What can we do?"

"Against Satan or the forces of Nature, there's nothing one can do. Only God..."

"And that's where you are wrong again, Luigi. It is precisely here that you are wrong. We have arrived at one of the key points, if not the central point, that I am trying to make. But perhaps we need a little bit more wine, no?"

"Any more wine and I cannot be held accountable for my actions or my thoughts."

"*Va bene*. Let's pause and take a wander through the monastery's garden, shall we? A little bit of fresh air is always good; it reanimates the spirit and opens the way for new ideas. Let's go."

# 10

*September 12, 2008*
*Ardennes Forest – BELGIUM*

The breakfast table was set in the small office next to the bedroom. It was a small meal as usual: a slice of papaya with granola, cottage cheese spread on toast and seasoned with oregano and olive oil, and a glass of grapefruit juice.

Discipline extended to all aspects of Monsieur Henry's life. He opened the laptop on the table and logged in to the secure mailbox that he used to conduct the organization's affairs. A single message informed him that the incident in Venice had been handled. The replacement for Hideo Akashiro, the Japanese industrialist, would be inducted into the group later that day .at a ceremony in Iguaçu Falls, Brazil.

Having ascended to the very top of the brotherhood, Akashiro had also pledged to obey orders with unquestioning loyalty. Their centuries-old organization operated under a deceptively simple principle: money equals power; more money equals more power. It did not tolerate betrayal; nor was it concerned with political disputes or local traditions, let alone national pride.

The fact was that Japan had been suffering from the aftermath of a bubble for nearly two decades. The warning signal back then came when a Japanese businessman bought a painting by Vincent Van Gogh, *Portrait of Dr. Gachet*, for 90 million dollars, a sure sign of how easily money was flowing.

At the time, prompted to send a report to Monsieur Henry, Akashiro demonstrated an unnecessary degree of sympathy for the easy credit fueling consumption in his country. His report expressed confidence in the Japanese market, noting with patriotic pride that Mitsui Real Estate had recently made a 625 million dollar offer for the Exxon Building in Manhattan. So exorbitant was the amount that a malicious contemporary commentator suggested that all the Japanese wanted was to enter the Guinness World Records.

To end the prolonged recession, Japan had to be more daring and less conservative. Akashiro had not been firm enough on the tiller. He had disobeyed the brotherhood for some time – and he had to have known that he would eventually pay a high price for his insubordination. That time had finally come. In recent weeks, in what Monsieur Henry assumed was an act of desperation, Akashiro had compromised the organization's secrecy. For this, he paid with his life.

*************

The 50 kilometers between his castle in the Ardennes forest and the medieval town of Dinant normally took Monsieur Henry forty-five minutes to travel, for his driver was not allowed to exceed the speed limit. Used to the trip, Monsieur Henry paid no attention to the beauty that passed by his window as they drove.

He had learned to live in isolation since the death of his wife in the summer of 2000. Childless, he had been a partner in an accounting office as a young man, when he inherited a considerable fortune from his father, largely in the form of shares in the Swiss Commercial Bank – one of the largest European banks at the time, with Swiss, Belgian and French capital – in addition to just over three million Swiss francs deposited into his personal bank account. The inherited shares paved his way to becoming President of the bank just before his fortieth birthday.

Back then, in the late 1980s, his bank had been facing serious problems due to rapid expansion and dubious investment decisions. He had managed to save it from bankruptcy by isolating the portfolio of toxic assets and preventing the problem from spreading to other banks and financial markets.

*It was a masterful play*, thought Monsieur Henry as he headed to his cardiologist's clinic in Dinant. *Money changes hands. It's a question of knowing how to move the pieces on the board.* But for how long would he remain the most experienced player, or at least the player with most power?

Similar problems faced him now, but on a much greater scale. The mounting crisis in North America threatened to spread across the world. Bear Stearns, Fannie Mae and Freddie Mac, and soon Lehman Brothers – the list of teetering financial institutions was growing. He was not surprised that most people didn't see the parallels between what was happening now and what had happened in 1929.

*We have become blind to the lessons of history*, he thought to himself.

Ever since he had become part of the brotherhood, and especially after he became its leader, Monsieur Henry had worked to preserve and increase its power, following the invaluable advice of the founders and their successors in the art of lending and receiving money. It was all there in the archives. He always smiled to himself when he saw the Middle Ages referred to as the Dark Ages.

Leading one of the largest and most secretive financial empires in history had its price, and Monsieur Henry knew this well. He was predisposed to abstract thought, and enjoyed both mathematics and the tricky financial challenges he had to handle. Apart from leaving him the inheritance, his father had taught him how to face adverse situations.

As he approached seventy, Monsieur Henry knew that it was time to start looking for someone to replace him at the bank and also at the helm of the organization. For the more public role, his staff in the human resources department at the bank, and headhunting agencies in London, Zurich, and New York, provided him with reports on possible candidates. For the other role, he had his own sources. One report he had received a few weeks earlier caught his attention. The information in it made him think that he might have found someone he could groom to succeed him. It called for an accurate investigation and extreme care.

*************

## Iguaçu Falls – BRAZIL

The five businessmen from different parts of the world met for breakfast in a private conference room in their reserved wing of the Belmond Hotel. As the staff left the room, the men helped themselves to fruits, juices, cakes, and breads with exotic jams, accompanied by a traditional dish from the Northeast called *beiju* – thin tapioca pancakes served with savory and sweet sauces – and the best Brazilian *cafezinho*.

Their first topic of discussion was the previous day's successful punishment of Hideo Akashiro. News that he was on board of the as-yet-unrecovered airplane had reverberated around the world in the hours since the story had broken. The crash was being reported as an accident and the search for debris from the plane would continue for many days. There had been no mention in any newspapers, or on radio or television networks, about the incident in Venice.

The replacement of their Japanese brother had been one of the reasons for the meeting. Their newest member, the Brazilian, would be formally inducted into the inner group of the organization later that day.

The other reason was the need to develop a strategy to deal with the crisis that was emerging in international markets – the topic they moved to next.

The American representative asked to speak first. He explained that the economic crisis had its origins in the out-of-control optimism of certain markets, particularly in his country, and had to be stopped immediately. It risked affecting the fragile economies of Iceland, Ireland, Greece, and Spain. To stop it, they should use all methods at their disposal.

The South African spoke next, calling attention to a new element: the move by China, Russia, India, Brazil, and potentially South Africa, towards creating a new economic bloc. There was nothing to be criticized in the economic and commercial strategies of these countries, he said; they each had the potential to become an independent pole of wealth accumulation and warranted the organization's close attention.

The Frenchman, trying to find a point of convergence in the conflicting views of his European counterparts, in particular his colleagues from England and Germany, agreed that the crisis had already been allowed to go too far and that measures had to be taken as quickly as possible to prevent panic taking hold in European markets.

The Australian spoke next. He explained that even though most of the affected financial institutions were headquartered in the U.S. and Europe, Asian economies were, nevertheless, exposed because of trade and financial channels. He expected the effects of this crisis in the region to be comparable to those of the Asian crisis of the previous decade.

The Brazilian spoke last. As the host of the meeting, he expressed his pride in ascending to a position in the brotherhood not hitherto reached by any other South American, and his hope that his appointment would contribute to the goals of all present in the meeting, consolidating their power to influence the economic destiny of the entire planet. He described how Brazil, a nation whose rich lands and subsoil attracted the attention of forward-looking and ambitious eyes, was not likely to be immediately affected by the crisis, although caution was necessary in the months to come. He moved on to list the Amazon forest, the Guarani aquifer, huge oil reserves, voluminous meat and soy exports, and the largest production of niobium in the world as indicators of Brazil's likely prominence in the near future.

When the Brazilian had finished speaking, the Frenchman, as the most senior member present, motioned that the group commence the induction ceremony.

*************

The two doors leading to the conference room where they were gathered were locked from the inside and two security guards positioned themselves outside, one in front of each door. The inner parts of the curtains on the three large windows were drawn. The thin fabric still let the sunlight in, but blocked the gaze of curious eyes in the gardens of the hotel.

Secret societies survive through the imposition of dogmas and rituals. By tradition, the initiation ceremony for a new member of the Guardians of the Venetian Files - the highest rank of the organization - always took place in his country of birth. It also had to involve a total number of participants equal to one of the Fibonacci numbers, in this case five.

The four men who were already inducted members of the group had in front of them a black leather folio, closed by buckles attached to leather strips and containing a brief report on the qualities of the new member, his credentials for the position, and a sealed envelope confirming the name of the chosen person.

The Frenchman placed a wooden box at the table in front of him. It contained a hunting knife, serrated and with a sharp narrow tip, alcohol, iodine, and sterilized gauze. At the centre of the table, in a lacquered box inlaid with velvet, sat a 14th century gold coin, a priceless florin bearing the face of King Edward III of England. It symbolized to these men a triumph over what they considered to be the first default in financial history: Edward's refusal to repay his war debts to Florentine bankers in 1345.

Their rules required that existing members read the report prepared on the initiate in his presence, and then confirm the name of the member who had been selected. At that point, the most senior member present at the ceremony would carve the letters V and F into the left bicep of the initiate. Once the grisly task was completed, the five men joined hands and declaimed in unison: *Absque argento omnia vana*[*].

---

[*] Without money, all is in vain.

# 11

Willbe kept his word and arrived within minutes at the Bryant Park Café, where he found Sarah seated at one of the covered tables in the garden with a worried look on her face.

"I'm guessing the meeting didn't go well?"

"I have the same strange feeling I had when I left your apartment last night."

"Judging from your expression they must have done something to upset you."

"Not really. It was all very odd, actually. I was taken to the office of a Mr. Kaminsky... John something Kaminsky."

Sarah was ready for lunch and a stiff drink. She passed the envelope she had received from the clerk at the Public Library to Willbe, who arranged himself in the chair opposite her.

"Check this out."

Willbe quickly read the letter, then placed it on the table and signaled to the waiter.

"Don't worry about this, Sarah."

Sarah stared distractedly at the other side of the street. Willbe followed Sarah's gaze and noticed two men in black suits emerging from a Mercedes parked across the street. Both men were wearing earpieces.

"Try not to worry, Sarah. Can I tell you the stories that my Uncle Emiliano told me when I was in Pisa about what happened to the fortune amassed by my ancestors in Pisa, Venice, and Florence?"

"I want to hear about it, Willbe, but not now, please. Let's leave it for when I'm more focused, ok?"

"Sure. On a different note, then, am I right in thinking that you want to conduct a more rigorous test on the document that I showed you?"

"Yes, please don't take it the wrong way. It's a normal procedure in this kind of situation. Also, I didn't have a chance to read the translation properly."

"It's no problem at all. I'd like to hear an expert opinion and confirm that the document is authentic. We can go together, right?"

"Yes, I have two friends who can help us. One is a professor who taught me at university. The other works at the library. I'll contact them."

"At Columbia?"

"Yes, you can come with me and speak to them and explain how you came to have the letter."

"I think the content alone suggests that it's authentic – it's nothing more than a letter from my ancestor Giuseppe to his sons. Who would keep such a document other than a family member?"

"I see your point, Willbe. I'll read it again more carefully."

"You can do it now if you want."

"Do you have it here with you? What about walls having ears and all that?"

A little embarrassed, Willbe replied:

"We're in a park, there are no walls here."

"I'll pretend I didn't hear that," retorted Sarah, her mood improving.

Willbe opened his laptop, circled the table and sat beside Sarah.

"I carry a digital copy with me. The original is safely stored."

As Willbe and Sarah re-read the letter from Giuseppe, the two men who had emerged a few minutes earlier from the black Mercedes walked into the café and headed to a table several metres away, close enough to have Willbe and Sarah in sight, but far enough as not to draw their attention. At least that's what they intended. One of them spoke into his cell phone. Willbe pretended not to notice.

\*\*\*\*\*\*\*\*\*\*

*Maius, anno 1380.*

*Ai miei amati figli Gianpaolo, Vitorio e Luigi, che un giorno mi sostituiranno negli affari di famiglia, vorrei lasciare l'esempio e la testimonianza di un uomo che ha sempre creduto nella forza del lavoro come la spinta del progresso e dell'impegno dell'uomo verso nuove conquiste.*

*Insieme a tanti studi che ho fatto con il mio sforzo e con lo sforzo dei nostri antenati, vi lascio in eredità una banca a Venezia e una seconda banca più modesta a Firenze. Inoltre vi lascio una Compagnia di Navigazione in possesso di sei navi per il commercio di merce di qualsiasi specie che si possa fare, nei porti d'Europa ed anche nei porti d'oltremare.*

*Di tutte e tre chiedo che vi prendiate cura con l'astuzia dei lupi e la forza dei leoni.*

*Mantenetele vive e sane per i vostri figli, nipoti e bisnipoti, in modo che il nome Fibonacci arrivi non soltanto a terre e mari già conosciuti, ma anche nei nuovi posti da conoscere.*

*Troverete nella cassaforte della banca di Venezia note varie di lavoro scritte da me e dai miei soci che probabilmente vi saranno di aiuto nei momenti di difficoltà economiche e finanziarie molto comuni in tempi di guerre e di trasformazioni sociali, visto che un anno non è mai uguale all'altro.*

*Con l'amore del vostro padre,*
*Vitorio Giuseppe Fibonacci.*

*May 1380.*

*TO MY DEAR SONS Gianpaolo, Vitorio, and Luigi, who shall one day substitute me in the family business, I want to leave the example and the testimony of someone who always believed in hard work as a source of progress and in the determination of man towards new achievements.*

*As a result of my efforts and those of our ancestors, I leave you to inherit a banking house in Venice and a second one, more modest, in Florence, as well as a shipping company with six ships for the transport of merchandise of all kinds to the ports of Europe and the far seas.*

*I ask you to take care of all three enterprises with the cunning of wolves and the strength of lions. Keep them alive and healthy for your sons, grandsons, and great-grandsons, taking the name Fibonacci to other lands and seas that you might come to visit.*

*Inside the main safe at the banking house in Venice, you will find notes written by myself and other partners that ought to be useful in times of financial trouble, especially those arising from war and social transformation.*

*With fatherly love,*
*Vitorio Giuseppe Fibonacci.*

\*\*\*\*\*\*\*\*\*\*\*\*\*

Sarah sighed pensively as she looked up from the screen.

"Willbe, please don't take this the wrong way, but I'm still not convinced that a document this old would use two different typefaces, even taking into account the invention of the printing press in the second half of the fifteenth century." Sarah looked at Willbe with narrowing eyes, as if apologizing for her continuing doubt. "I'm not being tiresome, am I?"

"No, you're being professional and I appreciate it. What did you think about the text in the letter itself?"

"A will, that much is clear. A man worried about maintaining his wealth in the hands of the family."

"Just that?"

"Did I miss something else?"

"Aren't you interested in whether this wealth was actually maintained?"

"To be honest, the question didn't occur to me when I was reading. I suppose it might be important to someone in the family."

"Read this last paragraph again, please."

Sarah turned her attention to the laptop screen and slowly re-read the final paragraph in a low voice:

*Inside the main safe at the banking house in Venice, you will find notes written by myself and other partners that ought to be useful in times of financial trouble, especially those arising from war and social transformation.*

"So?" pressed Willbe.

Sarah did not know how to respond:

"The whereabouts of advice on how to administer the business..." she offered.

"Yes, advice from Giuseppe and his partners."

"And?"

"Notes for moments of economic and financial difficulty. But what could they be, knowing that banking was only beginning to take shape at the beginning of the fourteenth century?"

"I have no idea, Willbe."

"Don't you see? Giuseppe left notes on how to deal with economic difficulties. Advice on how to keep an immense fortune from disappearing just as the world was about to fundamentally change through the discovery of new lands in the West. With money circulating among European peoples, increasing trade in the Far East, and advances in science and technology, they had the perfect conditions for accumulating wealth, provided they knew what they were doing. And the notes were stored in Venice..."

Sarah was having difficulty following Willbe's line of reasoning, even taking into account that he could be a distant relative of a wealthy ancestor.

"Are you trying to suggest that those Venetian Files have something to do with this?"

"It's a possibility."

Sarah raised an eyebrow.

"It seems a bit of a stretch to me, Willbe. The pieces don't quite fit together for me at this point."

Willbe sat back in his chair with a sigh.

"Ok then, let's go talk to your friends at Columbia."

The tone in his voice bothered her.

"You don't like what I said?"

"No, Sarah, it's fine. I understand what you're saying and you're right to ask this sort of questions. I know it sounds crazy but... well, what if it's true? One day I'd like to take you to Pisa to meet my Uncle Emiliano. He has some interesting theories about this topic, and many stories to tell. Perhaps he can even convince you with some of them."

They kissed in public for the first time. A common enough occurrence for thousands of young couples in the parks and squares of New York, with only one difference: this young couple was being closely watched. One of the men in black took a cell phone out of his suit pocket and keyed a few numbers.

*************

The black Mercedes with United Nations license plates parked next to an imposing building on the banks of the Hudson River. The driver walked around the front of the car and opened the rear door. A young, elegantly dressed man carrying a briefcase emerged. He informed the driver that he would not be long and walked to the main entrance of the building. Answering his phone before going through the doors, he gave instructions to the security agent on the line:

"Don't lose sight of them."

He identified himself at the reception desk and was given authorization to proceed to his meeting with the Belgian representative at the UN. As vice-consul, he followed orders from the Belgian Consulate in New York. He was not inclined to question orders, but he was beginning to feel a measure of irritation that his diplomatic services had, for days now, been reduced to following two ordinary U.S. citizens inside their own country.

*This is not what I signed up for when I became a diplomat.*

# 12

*Circa 1350-60 AD*
*Vicenza, Veneto Region – ITALY*

Giuseppe Fibonacci was uneasy as he left the monastery in Vicenza. Friar Luigi had clearly drunk more wine than he was accustomed to, and Giuseppe had had to help his friend to his sleeping quarters at the end of the evening. Excess of this sort was unusual for Luigi, who was generally a man of moderation. Giuseppe's proposal had obviously unnerved the friar, presenting as it did a conflict between faith and material progress. As Giuseppe rode towards Venice, he wondered whether he had been mistaken in raising his idea about the banking house with Luigi. He trusted him implicitly - they had known one another for decades and Luigi had saved Giuseppe's wife's life when their first son, Gianpaolo, was born prematurely. His youngest son was even named Filippo Luigi in his honour. Nevertheless, the fear he detected in his friend concerned him. He wondered whether Luigi would be able to cope with the stress - physical and metaphysical - of setting up a banking house.

*On the other hand,* he thought to himself, *Luigi has amassed quite a considerable fortune for himself over the years – his religious scruples clearly have their limits. If he does join me his involvement shall remain secret, of course. The Pope and the other cardinals in Rome will not tolerate a competitor like Luigi,* he thought with mischievous irony. *And what will Luigi do with his money if he refuses my proposal?*

In addition to the money that Luigi had made through his work for the monastery, it was rumored that many years before he had received part of a fortune in gold from a legendary Knight Templar, a distant relative of their maternal grandfather. As far as Giuseppe knew, Luigi was childless, and all of his relatives were either dead, or their whereabouts were unknown. Giuseppe's heart missed a beat at the thought of Luigi leaving his considerable fortune to the Church.

*Rome, or the Papal State to be precise, was already filled to the brim with riches.*

Giuseppe decided that he would return to Vicenza shortly and continue his conversation with Luigi. He would propose a contract between them setting out their responsibilities, and emphasizing that Luigi's role was a private one, unknown to the rest of the world.

*But what if Luigi did not agree to sign the contract?*

He would have to proceed alone. His beloved Pisa, not to mention Florence and Venice, with the Adriatic Sea on one side and the Tyrrhenian Sea on the other, were certainly big enough to have more than one banking house. He had to act.

*And act fast, before the whole situation slipped away between my fingers.*

*************

It was already dark when two Franciscan monks awakened Luigi in his bedroom. He had disheveled hair and was disoriented as he stared blearily at the younger men.

"What are you doing in my bedroom this early in the morning?"

"We were worried by your absence during dinner", replied one of the friars.

"Dinner, what do you mean?" Luigi demanded.

The two friars looked at each other with awkward smiles.

"I'm fine, I assure you. I will be with you in the meditation room in ten minutes."

Luigi watched as the monks left his bedroom, his thoughts still confused by the previous evening's discussion with Giuseppe.

*How could I possibly involve myself in a banking house? What about the vows of poverty I took so many years ago?*

What would those young monks, some still beardless, think if they discovered the truth about him? That Luigi de Vicenza was a fraud. That he betrayed his God, not for thirty pieces of silver like Judas betrayed Jesus, but for several thousand florins.

After washing his face and arranging his thinning hair, Luigi chewed on a few leaves of mint, crossed himself in front of a small crucifix, uttered the words of the *Pater Noster,* and headed to the refectory, where a plate of his favourite soup of corn with cauliflower awaited him.

*I have gone too far*, he thought. There was no way he could accept the challenge from Giuseppe Fibonacci. Or was it exactly what he should do?

# 13

*September 12, 2008*
*Venice – ITALY*

The next morning, with the sun no more than a small orange stain on the horizon, the unidentified body, already autopsied, was wrapped in hospital sheets, awaiting removal to the indigent section of the cemetery in San Michele Island.

Inspector Piero de Lucca, a member of the forensic squad of the *Polizia di Frontiera* in Venice, observed all that was happening around him, his hand occasionally running through his uncombed hair.

*How can we bury someone without even attempting to identify him? Especially since he might not even be Italian? And a man dressed in a suit like that was no indigent. Perhaps he's a Japanese intelligence agent?*

The case would be officially closed in a few hours. The short autopsy report – which was missing the coroner's signature – mentioned that the body exhibited, apart from the fatal wound, a small incision on the right bicep with the letters V and F. At that point in the investigation, there was no reason to think the tattoo had any significance; nevertheless, Inspector de Lucca recorded the detail in his pocket book, noting that the letters were in Roman script, not Japanese characters.

Thus, far in the investigation Inspector de Lucca had followed all instructions and orders given to him, but he was becoming increasingly dissatisfied with the way the investigation was being handled.

*Why should the body be sent to the pauper's grave in San Michele cemetery? Who was giving these orders?*

He suspected the silence surrounding the investigation might have something to do with international organized crime, high finance, or government corruption. Even so, he could not ignore what he felt was his duty to seek justice for the murdered man. During the autopsy, Inspector de Lucca discreetly asked the coroner to examine the clothes as the corpse was being undressed: tuxedo, shirt, tie, socks, underwear, shoes – anything that could offer a clue, however small, that might help him identify the man. Stitched on the inside of the tuxedo jacket, the policeman found the name of the store from where it had been bought, and recorded the detail in his book. He thanked the coroner, and repeated his request for discretion. Before he left, he took a picture of the face of the dead man with his cell phone.

*VF... Letters formed by the scar on the skin, the result of a cut made with a small sharp knife. Were these his initials?*

# PART 2

*... other times, an illusion constructs reality.*

# 14

*September 13, 2008*
*Brussels - BELGIUM*

It was a Saturday like many others for the majority of the billions of citizens of countries around the world, except perhaps for the less than promising expectations of financial analysts, who feared that the burgeoning economic crisis would amplify to levels not seen since 1929. Apart from that, all was fine in the best of all possible worlds, as Candide's old Professor Pangloss would say.

The same could not be said for the men meeting that evening in a boardroom at the Brussels branch of the Swiss Commercial Bank on Boulevard Pacheco. For them, this was not a regular working day. All appearances led the bank employees believe that this was an emergency meeting called in reaction to the sudden drop in the value of the bank in European markets. But there was more to it than that.

M. Henry's brothers in the organization ascended to the third floor through a side door of the building, under a strict security protocol that prevented outsiders from identifying them. Five of them had participated in a meeting the day before in Iguaçu Falls in Brazil and were expected to bring a worked out plan. They were not in Brussels to *save* the Commercial Bank per se, but to give this impression of purpose. Rather, they were there to *rearrange* the global economic crisis that had dragged on since the previous year and which could veer out of control in the next few days if urgent measures were not taken. Such was the unknown, secretive and discreet manner in which these men, together with M. Henry in his castle in the Belgian Ardennes, for years dealt with the economic fate of the world.

But who were these men (and up to this point they had been all men)? How did they come to occupy their positions? Many of them were well known, at least in business circles, occupying directorship positions in famous financial institutions and large corporations; others were heirs to immense fortunes. They were chosen by tradition and went through the most rigorous evaluation of their competencies and skills in economic and financial matters, beginning when they were still students in the most select universities. Collectively, they controlled around two-thirds of the world's wealth.

The number thirteen was an integral part of the tradition. Not by superstition, but by pure mathematics, thirteen being the sixth prime number and part of the Fibonacci sequence, named after Leonardo, the mathematician, whose grandnephew Giuseppe was one of the first to codify the practices of banking.

Their secret was a simple one, for no human being, even the most imaginative, could possibly believe that thirteen people could control such large proportion of the financial wealth in the planet. Impossible? Fantasy? Too much imagination? Nothing is really impossible in the world of money.

*And if anything were impossible*, M. Henry used to say with conviction, *one only needed find more money.*

Confident as they were in the powers of markets and competition, the men in the brotherhood saw themselves as planners, directing the broad movements of the world's economies. Their decisions were collective, and this was precisely their strength. Decisions made by the group were final, and their oath of fidelity permitted no deviation.

Theirs was a history constructed on centuries of trial and error, full of intricate twists, intrigue, power struggles, and death, all kept quiet whenever it was necessary, and without leaving any trace that could betray the impenetrable security barrier built around it. A secret society, as one usually calls these groups, most of them formed in the Middle Ages and the beginnings of the Modern Era. Some were ancient and achieved the status of legend, such as the Knights Templar, the Knights of Malta, or the Illuminati. Others are more recent, like the Rosicrucian Order and Opus Dei, and some are explicitly connected to illegal activities, like the mafias in Italy, Russia, and Japan. Religious or not, most of these societies did not give themselves public names, as a matter of security. This was the case with these Guardians of the Venetian Files. Some of its founding members were the creators and first guardians of the knowledge contained in notes and procedures on how to transform the wealth originating in a variety of investments, and how to consolidate power and influence.

These notes – the Venetian Files, as they came to be known – were first organized in medieval Italy as simple archives. With time, they grew in content and became a type of manual, a code of how to deal with economic crises.

Nearly all of the annotations in these files fit within this category. Despite their age, they remain remarkably insightful. To this day, there exists no comparable document with such a richness of details. Sequences of historical facts, social and religious events, power struggles in or between countries, experiments with money invested in different businesses, patronage and revolutions, research funding and support for scientific and technological advances – the collective opinion and study of those who, from the Low Middle Ages onwards, tried to identify the origins of economic crises and, over time, patiently helped to create the mechanisms to combat them.

Money stood at the centre of all they did – whether in the form of gold, silver, nickel, precious gems, or paper. Each in its own time was exchanged for goods and services, or as backing for other types of promises such as stocks, which are just parcels of participation in the capital of large corporations.

In its essence, money is simply a promise capable of creating a world of progress, realizations, ways of acting and thinking. Or, put differently, an illusion to be permanently confronted with the naked reality of an increasingly complex life on Earth. The reality of survival, of accumulation of wealth and the many advantages and maladies it brings. But the mechanisms, the paths, and above all the shortcuts, for accumulating wealth can also become an illusion, or else reality playing a sick joke. Greed and power; command and obedience.

*One cannot do anything without money.*

*************

While the other members of the organization met in Brussels, M. Henry remained ensconced in his castle, invisible to the world around him. This anonymity was part of his power. As soon as he had received the bulk of his inheritance in the form of stocks in the Swiss Commercial Bank, some thirty years ago, he renounced his former name and became M. Henry. Before that, he had been a brilliant employee on his way to partnership in one of the largest accounting firms in Brussels. He carried out his duties with great competence in three adjacent offices in the firm's headquarters in the historical city centre. His daily work put him in contact with executives and lawyers of the most powerful European companies, and he quickly earned their trust in conducting large-scale deals and investments.

By then almost thirty-five years old, with a degree in business administration and specialization in commercial accountancy, he was assigned as a financial analyst to a large multinational pharmaceutical company established with French, Belgian, and Swiss capital. His task was to examine the company's books for the last ten years. His final report, the result of eight months of sleepless nights and extensive, meticulous work, led to the discovery of one of the largest accounting frauds of the time, equivalent to around half a billion Euros in today's money. As a result, he was poached from his accounting firm and hired by the pharmaceutical conglomerate on a permanent basis to help administer a multibillion-dollar global business.

Now the oldest member of the organization, it was unknown by the other brothers exactly when M. Henry had been recruited by the Guardians of the Venetian Files, thought it was assumed to have been in the 1960s or the first half of the 1970s.

In about half an hour this gentleman, in the quietude of his living room in the Belgian Ardennes, would contact his brothers in Brussels. By now they had all taken the necessary measures and began to act, making sure that central bankers of major economies around the world received their directives on how to proceed. Panic, this time at least, would not take hold of the world's financial markets.

And M. Henry, with good reason, took pride in that.

*************

Almost ten years earlier, on December 15th and 16th, 1999, the finance ministers of nineteen countries and the finance commissioner for the European Union, together with representatives from the World Bank and the IMF, gathered in Berlin to take one further step in strengthening the relationship between the world's most advanced economies, something that was felt to be necessary after the successive economic crises of the 1990s. At its Cologne Summit earlier that year, the G7 – the powerful group consisting of Canada, France, Germany, Italy, Japan, the United Kingdom, and the United States – was formally enlarged by the addition of twelve other countries and the European Union.

M. Henry had followed closely the trajectory leading to the formation of the G20. More than just followed, he actively helped the organization to become a reality, both directly and through his allies.

A decade later, with another G7 summit scheduled for the following month and a G20 meeting expected to take place soon after, M. Henry found himself pleased at once again to be facing a situation that required his help. After listening carefully to the opinion of his twelve peers in the brotherhood, he had to make a decision that was going to impact the fate of many financial institutions, some of which had been undeniably irresponsible, led by gamblers who took unnecessary risks.

Two months earlier, several banks around the world announced losses of hundreds of billions of dollars. The fire sale of Bear Stearns to J.P. Morgan, orchestrated by the Federal Reserve back in March, had bought policymakers some time, but did not stop the avalanche of bad news from the housing market that mounted during the summer months.

The new integration of major economies, now nearly a decade old, was about to be tested for the first time, and it was unclear whether the G20 central bankers had the right ammunition to stop the imminent panic.

Banks, insurance companies, stock markets, and other financial institutions were being closely monitored by regulators, governments, the financial press, and millions of small investors who were part, directly or indirectly, of this volatile world. It was not as if there were no safeguards in place, but the memory of each new generation of actors in the financial markets tended to be very short. And everyone had to be reminded of certain rules from time-to-time.

Satisfied with the success of the Akashiro operation and his immediate replacement by a new member of the brotherhood, M. Henry was ready to begin a new rearrangement of the world economy: deciding on whether or not to save Lehman Brothers, finding a buyer for Merrill Lynch, making sure that AIG did not tumble.

Nevertheless, after each crisis he managed as the years went by, he became more preoccupied in finding a replacement for himself, someone even more cunning than he had been, if that was possible. He was sure he would find someone though. Maybe he had already found him, as the list of potential names was already impressive.

He had to gather more information about the top three names whose dossiers were encrypted in his computer. One of them, in particular, caught his attention because of a peculiar coincidence in background.

# 15

*August 19, 2008*
*New York City – USA*

Still a bit insecure about where they had left their conversation, but intent on preventing it from interfering on how they felt about each other, Willbe and Sarah said goodbye with a prolonged embrace and a discreet kiss, standing beside a small kiosk near the entrance of Bryant Park, and agreed to meet again the following day at Columbia University. They wanted to obtain information on how to verify the authenticity of the letter they had just read.

Sarah knew a few places that did such evaluations, but wanted to double-check with her friends and let Willbe choose one. That was a measure of how taken aback she had been at his reaction to her raising the possibility of the document being forged or adulterated.

She walked in long strides towards her office, as she only had half an hour left to check all the material that her boss was going to take to Washington. There were two meetings in Timothy Geithner's itinerary for that trip: one with Secretary Paulson and another with Chairman Bernanke.

When he arrived home, Willbe put the laptop on his desk, poured himself a glass of lemonade and sat comfortably in his armchair to think about ways to avoid what was looking like a looming conflict between him and Sarah. That was the last thing he wanted. Sarah had, after all, discovered something incredibly important: the reference to the Venetian files in a rare medieval book.

The truth was that the research topic he had chosen for his postdoc had a clearly stated academic goal, namely the detailed study of "systemic risk measures" during financial crises, but also a hidden personal goal. He would never forget the dinner with his Italian family when he received the document containing the letter from his ancestor. It was an objective letter that carefully laid out the bequest of Vitorio Giuseppe Fibonacci and advised his heirs on how to take care of the many and varied family businesses.

His Uncle Emiliano, about whom curious narratives abounded, was considered the strange one in the family, but Willbe did not think he possessed the imagination to invent some of the stories he told. Where did he hear them? Willbe would like to find out.

*What happened to the fortune acquired by Giuseppe Fibonacci and apparently administered by at least four or five successive generations of his ancestors? There was good chance that it was even enhanced during the 15th and 16th centuries. Could it have been swallowed by the economic crises of the following centuries?*

These were recurrent thoughts for Willbe. With Sarah's help he could find the material to refresh Uncle Emiliano's memory and find out where the rest of the information came from.

The celebratory dinner for his PhD in Pisa, earlier that year, was a recollection still vivid in his memory, not only because of the number of family members he met and for the delicious Tuscan dishes served, but above all for the surprise gift: a copy of a letter from Giuseppe Fibonacci to his sons, carefully placed inside one of Nicolo Machiavelli's books. He held in his hands, filled with awe and understandable pride, a document that was almost seven hundred years old – a relic. It meant a lot to his future ambitions.

There was also the intriguing and very private conversation he had had with his oldest uncle, whom until then he did not know. Emiliano Augusto Fibonacci, Uncle Emiliano, with his full head of hair and vast white moustache, for no apparent reason other than sincere fondness for the nephew who chose Pisa to pursue his doctorate in mathematics, decided to make him aware of some historical facts that accompanied the Fibonacci family saga. Facts, both ancient and contemporary, which were either unknown or largely ignored by most of the family, as Uncle Emiliano emphasized several times in their conversation.

Most of their relatives did not attach any significance to certain events or characters from the past. For example, who was this Franciscan friar named Luigi, allegedly a business partner of Giuseppe Fibonacci? Who took control of the family business in the second half of the 15th century after the death of Giuseppe's youngest son, head of a bank in Florence and another in Pisa?

After all, genealogical research was common among Italian families with a rich and noble past. They were generally proud of their ancestry, and many remained rich to this day, especially in Florence.

*Why not his family?*

It was difficult to believe in information preserved only through oral tradition, especially with so many puzzling details. The most intriguing of which, especially for Willbe, was the mysterious disappearance of a Fibonacci couple, residents of Venice, after the end of World War II in 1945. Nobody in the family had any information about the couple and their infant son after that.

*Could it be that Uncle Emiliano was indeed the crazy one in the family?*

He did not get that impression from his uncle. There were no signs of any type of paranoia. Willbe had confirmed with other family members that the couple had in fact disappeared in 1945, though they didn't like to talk about the subject.

There must have been a reason for that conversation with his uncle, and probably new facts to be uncovered sooner or later, he was sure of that. The way things were progressing, months after he had returned from Pisa, there was no reason to hide the entire story from Sarah.

He had exchanged two or three emails with his uncle after returning to New York, but he noticed that, at least on the questions that interested him the most, the old man didn't open up in writing.

*I must return to Pisa as quickly as I can.*

*************

On the way from Bryant Park, Sarah could not think about anything other than the looming scenario of disappointing Willbe with her insistence on finding out whether the letter signed by Giuseppe Fibonacci was potentially a fraud. Even though Willbe tried to hide it, it was obvious that the document was more to him than a mere family relic. It was, nevertheless, her duty to warn him.

Arriving late in her office on Liberty Street, Sarah noticed a peculiar sense of excitement, beyond the usual scramble before an official trip. Timothy Geithner, the 9th President of the Federal Reserve Bank of New York, was a man in high demand. She was, nevertheless, surprised by the rush of her colleagues moving around gathering documents that could be useful for the boss to take him to Washington. His flight was scheduled for the end of the afternoon.

Sarah's presence seemed to ease the tense atmosphere in the office, as everyone knew the trust that Geithner placed in her, in particular her prodigious memory when dealing with archival material.

"Did I miss something?"

"He's been asking for you..."

Geithner's executive assistant, a young red-haired woman who dressed like the hippies of another era, signaled to Sarah to come closer to her desk for a more private chat.

"Can you tell him I arrived?"

"Sure. You know, some people here in the office have been saying that he might be part of the next administration if the Democrats win. What with all these frequent trips to Washington and all."

"You had better not mention this to him. You know how he hates gossip."

"Calm down, Sarah, I'm just letting you know what people have been talking about. But if it did happen, it would be great, don't you think?"

The eyes of the assistant had an extra spark in them.

"These meetings have been booked for a while now, Vicky. Don't you start daydreaming, imagining things."

"You like to be contrarian, don't you?"

"Can I come in then?"

"Yes, as soon as he finishes talking to Washington."

Sarah returned to her own desk with a foggy mind. She let her hair down, placed her bag on the leather sofa where she helped screen journalists and other visitors, and popped a sugary chewing gum in her mouth. She sat down, took off her shoes and stretched her legs in an attempt to relax a bit. She liked Vicky and her sincere ways, but she thought she was still a bit green and naïve about politics.

*But what if Geithner were invited to be part of a potential Obama administration? He had worked in the Treasury when the last Democrat was in the White House, so the idea was not that farfetched. What if he invited me to come to Washington to work with him? How would I continue the research with Willbe?* No, she was not going to start speculating like that.

With Geithner travelling to Washington she would have a break for a few days. More than enough time to right things with Willbe, beginning the next day, when they would meet at Columbia.

# 16

## *Circa 1355-65 AD*
## *Venice, Veneto Region – ITALY*

The Piazza San Marco was unusually busy on this festive Sunday. Despite the drizzle at sunrise, hundreds of early risers flocked around the square for the celebrations of Venice's patron saint.

In front of the majestic Basilica of Saint Mark, a small group of performers entertained the public just before midday. The group staged a traditional play for this date about the legend of Tancredi, lover of Maria, daughter of the Doge of Venice. Tancredi died young, fighting in the army of Charlemagne in the war against the Turks and Arabs in Spain. Within the same tradition, beautiful young girls offered rosebuds to the families watching the play, accompanied by the delicate sounds of flute and the vibrant and passionate beats of drum and tambourine. According to legend, Tancredi was mortally wounded and fell by a rose bush near the battlefield. Before dying, he coloured a rosebud with his own blood and entrusted it to his friend Orlando to take back to Maria. The day after she received the news of Tancredi's death, on the 25th of April, Maria was found dead with the rosebud resting on her breast.

Used to the festivities and the annual performances of the legend, Giuseppe Fibonacci paid little attention as he walked around the square with his family: his wife Marinella, their sons Gianpaolo, Vitorio, and Filippo, and two servants.

That night he would receive a visit from Signor Francesco Cristaldi, a merchant and good friend in Venice, as well as Friar Luigi de Vicenza, who had finally agreed to discuss the opening of a banking house.

*************

After dinner, during which wine was served and consumed in moderation, Marinella and the children excused themselves and left for their bedchambers

74

while the three gentlemen moved to the great hall, better suited to unravelling the topic they were there to discuss.

"Friends," announced Giuseppe's deep voice, "let us toast this meeting: to the future of our businesses, to the progress of Venice and the Veneto."

He handed to each of his visitor a small crystal chalice with plum liquor, which they all raised, repeating in unison:

"To the first banking house in Venice... *Auguri a tutti noi!*"

Giuseppe continued:

"I brought you here, my friends, to formalize what we have been discussing in the last few weeks, making official the preparations for the founding of the first bank in Venice. In about three months, at most, we can start the *battle*, as Luigi puts it, with the grace of God. We are here to sign a contract, a definitive agreement regarding our decisions."

Friar Luigi was not entirely comfortable yet, even though he knew that Cristaldi and Fibonacci were like brothers in blood. To begin with, for obvious reasons, he thought that his name should not figure publicly as a partner of the banking house.

Giuseppe, barely hiding his elation, carried on:

"My good Luigi, I can still see some lingering worries in your gaze. Calm yourself. Don't be so pessimistic, everything will work out the way we planned."

Luigi outlined a smile.

"To make sure of that, we would like you to write down notes about this meeting, making our intentions clear and the amounts to be invested explicit, as well as setting out the partnership terms for me and Francesco, our rights and obligations..."

Luigi nodded in agreement. Giuseppe continued:

"With the understanding that I will represent you, as we will sign a separate private contract, between friends and to be left at the bottom of a drawer, but whereby the weight of our word has more value than the regal seal and the ecclesiastical authorities in Venice. As you see, you should not be so worried."

Luigi thanked him with a bow, lightly bending forward with his hands crossed over his chest. A new toast was raised, this time by Signor Cristaldi.

Luigi began to speak:

"I put my trust in you, my two good and loyal friends – I am in your hands. It would not be improbable, in the days we are living, that someone could be taken to the Inquisition for this. Even though I should not need to remind you, I urge you never, under any circumstance, to give any sign of my participation in this partnership."

Giuseppe and Francesco shook hands with Luigi and embraced each other in a demonstration of trust and loyalty.

"I believe I speak for myself and for our friend Francesco: Luigi, we give you our word of honour."

Luigi continued:

"As I do not have relatives, neither close nor distant – or if I have them I do not know them – let alone heirs, I ask that the private contract that we sign stipulate that I will leave my portion of the partnership to the three sons of Giuseppe and the two sons of Francesco, in equal parts. This is the least I can do in exchange for your confidence."

Francesco Cristaldi effusively shook hands again with Luigi and Giuseppe, visibly moved, and cried out:

"*Lunga vita per noi...*"

To which Luigi and Giuseppe answered:

"*Troppo lunga!*"

*************

Giuseppe Fibonacci owned two warehouses near the port of Venice, which was still extremely busy, despite the drop-in activities brought on by the plague and the few peasant uprisings caused by hunger and poverty. He used them to store the products he imported and exported, and thought they would be ideal locations for the banking house he envisaged.

In one of the warehouses, he built an imposing foyer with walls of dark wood and a dividing counter made of lighter wood. The foyer faced the street walked by most people heading to or coming back from the port, where they conducted their businesses or simply strolled through the busy docks. It was a strategic location for people who, having large quantities of florins, gold, and silver at their disposal, might be interested in lending them to merchants and sailors for a fee. Giuseppe was intent on opening his banking house before the end of the decade, or at the very latest in the first few years of the 1360s.

In the central and northern regions of Italy – Liguria, Piedmont, Tuscany, Veneto, Emilia-Romagna, and Umbria – the tribulations of daily life were met with great sacrifice and stoicism. New work and trade relationships were being forged between the cities. And new institutions were needed to replace the older banks – the *bancas* or benches in open markets and squares – used by grain merchants for some time now to help finance their trade.

Instead of operating under the open sky, the new banking houses would provide a secure space where financial transactions could be protected from inclement weather or the greed of onlookers and robbers.

Merchants, sailors, noble families, landowners, clergymen, artists, and scholars were beginning to gain awareness that their professional and financial activities were changing before their eyes. While some demonstrated enthusiasm for new developments, others began to try to protect their interests in novel ways. Money started to take new forms in feudal society, not only in the form of metal, mostly gold and silver, but also the novelty of bills - *billettes* – signed letters promising delivery of physical products, primarily grains, sometime in the future in exchange for borrowed funds.

Hope and uncertainty moved all - winners and losers in each transaction, even when they were not fully conscious of it - towards a world that could no longer exist solely between heaven and hell. Between Kings and Popes imposing rules and dogmas. Between the cross and the sword. Life blossomed in the squares of villages and cities that grew beyond the liturgy of the church and palace deals. Streets bustled with activities outside of religious processions and celebrations of Queens and Kings.

Underneath it all was the nascent idea that progress, the future, was in the hands of common men and not in the cold grandiosity of chancels or the ostentation of gold embroidery in royal ballrooms.

**************

When the opening day for his banking house finally arrived, with characteristic duplicity of purpose Giuseppe invited Friar Luigi to bless the premises. He was not slightly bothered by the cynicism of the act.

For one thing, he figured that this way Luigi could attend the proceedings without raising any suspicion of his participation in the partnership. Apart from that, even though he was secretly agnostic, seeking the blessing avoided complications with the Church, often concerned by the wealth of others.

After receiving authorization from the head of his monastery in Vicenza, Friar Luigi agreed to accept Giuseppe's invitation, despite his initial discomfort with the idea of making a speech and giving a blessing to the new bank. A few delicate contradictions still existed and had to be resolved between the religious and secular spheres in his mind.

The guest list for the event was small, but Giuseppe, Luigi, and Francesco were surprised by the number of people who showed up for the opening, most of them relatives and close friends. Novelty and gossip always walked hand-in-hand.

The space, encompassing around one thousand square feet, was not large enough to accommodate all those who were curious and interested in the new business, and many had to stay on the street in front of the warehouse.

Flowers and strips of silk in blue and white decorated the walls of the enclosure, well-lighted by candles and oil torches. The small party attracted the attention of those who had to walk by the strategically located premises.

*News would soon reach Florence,* thought Giuseppe. *I hear another banking house just opened there, and one in Sienna too.* It was the beginning of a new era, as he had predicted.

With the sound of a small bell, rung with enthusiasm by Cristaldi after Friar Luigi finished his prayers, the guests were asked to approach a table placed in front of the counter, upon which lay two roasted pigs, breads, cakes, sweets, fruits and – most importantly – several bottles of wine and grappa, as the cold could already be felt with some intensity.

Giuseppe asked for silence and improvised a small speech:

"Dear friends. This is a moment of happiness and celebration for us all, and I will not take too much of your time with laudatory speeches. Most of you here know that I am not a man of words, but of action."

A few giggles could be heard.

"Everything around us makes me believe that we are entering a new era for business. Times of prosperity, for sure, despite doubts, and threats. I, hereby, declare open the first banking house of Venice, the House of Fibonacci and Cristaldi, in the service of Veneto and Italy. Thank you!"

Applause and cheers were mixed with the sound of a vocal quartet accompanied by Marinella Fibonacci, who played a small piece on the lute. The music was of unknown, but doubtless profane, origin – clearly a small provocation on the part of her husband.

In good spirits, Giuseppe and Francesco followed the sounds with small head movements, while they chatted with guests and answered questions about how the new business was going to work.

Events like these were beginning to change the world in profound ways.

# 17

*September 13, 2008*
*Venice – ITALY*

Inspector de Lucca disembarked the ferry at Saint Angelo Terminal on the Grand Canal unaware that he was about to begin one of the most complicated investigations in his long career as a police officer.

In the Calle degli Avvocati, not far from Piazza San Marco, a small and sophisticated formal wear boutique distinguished itself by the charm of its premises: marble flooring, dark wood walls, well-arranged shop windows, tasteful lighting, and two impressive chandeliers hung from the ceiling.

The shop was empty at this morning hour. Agent de Lucca, his own attire contrasting with the elegance of the boutique, introduced himself as a police officer to the striking shop attendant who greeted him as soon as he stepped inside. After a few questions he was able to establish that the tuxedo had been ordered by a guest of Hotel Danieli two days earlier, a Thursday, normally a very busy day at the boutique. As each weekend approached, a stream of celebrities - real and wannabe - bought outfits for a variety of parties, banquets, festival celebrations, and other events.

*Hotel Danieli! This was no ordinary tourist...*

An employee of the hotel had come to pick up the tuxedo that had been fitted for a Japanese customer whose measurements were taken the previous night, on Wednesday. He had been given instructions for it to be charged to the hotel, as it was customary for some of the wealthiest guests.

"When he came to choose the tuxedo, was the customer alone or accompanied by someone?" asked Piero.

"Alone," answered the attendant.

"Was there a name for the delivery?"

"Not a full name, just a room number, 131, written on a hotel card, next to the letters 'H.A', but I can't tell if that was the customer's initials.

When he was here he tried to speak Italian, but I told him that we could probably understand each other better in English."

"Did he mention where he was going to wear the outfit he was buying?"

"No, he didn't say anything about it, but I could tell he was a bit nervous."

"What made you think that?" asked Piero with an imperceptibly raised eyebrow.

"He kept glancing at the entrance of the shop."

"Could he have been waiting for someone, a female date also in need of an outfit perhaps?"

"I didn't get that impression."

"May I ask, why?"

"He had a worried look, even some fear on his face, I might say."

*Beautiful, observant and intelligent…*

"Fear? That's interesting. I wonder what makes you say that."

"When I sell formal outfits, it is important to observe all the details about the customers, who tend either to be very rich already or are people trying to make it in the world of business or entertainment. The manner of speech, their way of expressing themselves, can let you know whether they are trying to give the impression of being someone important, or whether they are shy but need to appear otherwise in public. All the little acts that people play in these kinds of circumstances, whoever they happen to be."

"I'm impressed. From what I can tell you would make an excellent police officer. But I'm still not sure why you say he was in fear."

"Well, he had a handgun that he discreetly touched under his suit jacket when he first came in."

"Did you suspect it was a gun or are you certain about it?"

"After he tried on the tuxedo, one of the shop assistants asked him to take a few steps around the fitting area to see if it needed any more adjustments. As he walked away from the fitting cubicle I saw the underarm holster hanging from one of the hooks inside."

"Very observant of you."

"I do my best to increase sales, Inspector. I work on commission."

Piero could not hide his attraction to the sales assistant.

"I'm very grateful for your help, *signorina.*"

"Please call me Claudia," replied the smiling attendant handing him a business card.

*Una bella ragazza.*

He carefully stored the card in his wallet to indicate that it was not going to be thrown away as soon as he stepped out.

"You have been very kind. *Arrivederci.*"

"Please stop by and try some of our clothes. I think they would suit you."

Piero, with his large suspenders and unbuttoned jacket, registered her move. He had a hunch that his investigative skills and good memory, always the subject of praise from his colleagues, would bring him back to that store, even if the clothes they sold were far beyond his modest policeman salary.

He searched again for the business card she had just given him, as if to show that his interests went beyond the investigation, and read it in silence. With the card still in his hand he made a gesture of goodbye.

"Just one second, Inspector..."

"Yes..."

"I believe I still have the card from the hotel, I don't think I threw it out."

The attendant went to the cashier counter and searched for the card inside a drawer.

"Here it is. You can see what appears to be the guest's initials written on the back."

"It looks like it. Thank you very much for this."

"My pleasure. If you need anything just give me a call. We are open on Sundays..."

*Claudia Celestini Sforza, a name to remember.*

He smiled to the shop attendant and exited completing the goodbye gesture he had started.

*************

*Why on Earth would a Japanese businessman, around sixty years of age or older, dressed in black tie and staying at the Hotel Danieli, not be reported as a missing person? And why did he have no identification on him when he was murdered?*

*Even assuming that news of his death in the Italian press was being censored by the same powerful people who had kept him unknown until now, much still made no sense. How could someone unsheathe a katana and plunge it into someone else's abdomen by a busy Venetian canals and get away with it?*

With these thoughts, and feeling a bit perplexed, Piero de Lucca arrived at the Hotel Danieli on Riva Degli Schiavonni - one of the most luxurious hotels in the world - just before lunchtime. The gothic columns, marble staircases and chandeliers of Murano crystal made an impression on any visitor. Piero had always admired the luxury and sophistication of the place. It was not his first time there, but he had only ever visited for work reasons; it would be unthinkable for him to stay in such a hotel for pleasure. He had heard that the presidential suite could cost five thousand Euros per night, while the "simple" rooms were at about one tenth of that price.

*An obscene amount, even for rich people,* he thought.

He walked to the reception desk and showed his police badge to the hotel clerk, while at the same time he pulled out the notes he had taken at the garment store.

"Good morning."

"How can I help you, sir?"

The front desk agent examined the man in front of him, certain that he was not looking for a room for the night.

"Piero de Luca, *Polizia di Frontiera,*" announced the inspector while he studied the reactions of the clerk. So far, none.

*A man accustomed to hiding what he thinks from the hotel guests.*

"Were you working the reception desk yesterday morning?"

"No sir, it would have been my colleague Nino yesterday morning."

"*Va bene.* I'm here to ask you about a Japanese guest staying at the hotel..."

"Do you know his name? We have a Japanese delegation in town for a marketing event..."

"No, but I know he is staying in room 131".

"Room 131? That's curious. You are not the first person looking for a guest in room 131. On Thursday afternoon a couple came here looking for him, saying they were expecting to meet him here, but the room key was up in the keyboard and nobody was answering the phone."

"A couple?" said Piero, more talking to himself than asking a question.

"Young couple, looked like reporters, although they were dressed quite formally, perhaps going to cover some event. The guy had a camera and the girl was carrying a small notepad. They had a coffee at the bar, waited for about half an hour, and left."

"I see that the key is still up on the board. Has the guest left for the day?"

"The key was there when I started my shift, so he either left very early in the morning or didn't come back last night."

"Can you check his name on the guest list?"

The hotel employee hit a few keystrokes on his computer.

"I'm sorry, sir, but some of our guests request not to have their names included in our list."

"But surely he had to show some identification when he checked in?"

"It says here that a diplomatic passport was checked and returned to the guest."

"But you have no record of his name?"

"No sir, sorry. Our hotel is frequented by many important guests – politicians, lobbyists, diplomats, even police officers like yourself..."

Piero ignored the jab but changed his expression as he faced the clerk more sternly:

"What do you mean by that?"

"Nothing, sir, it is just that the staff is instructed to provide the highest level of service to our guests, including, in some cases, respecting their requests for discretion."

"I'd like to see the room, please."

"I need to talk to my manager, sir, but I suspect this will not be possible without a warrant."

"Yes, please, talk to your manager. It appears that your very important guest has gone missing."

"Just one moment, sir."

The clerk used his two-way radio to contact the hotel manager and inform him of the presence of the policeman and his request to see one of the rooms.

*A diplomatic passport. Now that says something. And a young, elegantly dressed couple.* He would have to look up any gala events the previous day.

In a few seconds a man with grey hair and a well-trimmed goatee introduced himself to Piero.

"How can I help you, Inspector?"

*************

## Brussels – BELGIUM

The digital clock strategically situated behind the head of the boardroom table indicated 10pm on an agreeable, almost autumnal, evening in Brussels. For many in the financial industry, it was going to be a sleepless night.

The meeting that was taking place on the third floor of the Swiss Commercial Bank was already at an advanced stage. Nobody was allowed to enter or leave the room without authorization. Telephones with direct lines to London, Washington, Paris, Rome, Frankfurt, and Tokyo shared space with folders, papers, coffee cups, glasses and bottles of mineral water, and small triangular sandwiches.

Each of the participants provided information, opinions, suggestions, and criticism for the task at hand: to build a policy of intervention to contain the economic crisis in a way that protected the interests of the group.

Most of what had to be done in the next few hours had already been decided, but they still had to review the implementation details related to bureaucratic nuances that such difficult and delicate policies required. It was important not to offend the sensibilities of any of the officials involved, and above all not to give any impression that a group was behind their actions. For that secure and untraceable location in Brussels would soon instruct the finance ministers and central bankers of all major economies on what steps to take to save their financial systems. They had all been secretly notified that these instructions would follow in the next few hours.

Economic commentators in major newspapers, magazines, and television networks, including some renowned economists, had been calling attention to investment banks such as Goldman Sachs, Morgan Stanley, Merrill Lynch, and above all Lehman Brothers, who depended heavily on short-term borrowing but had none of the guarantees provided to commercial banks. Bear Stearns was also in that category before its hurried sale to J.P. Morgan six months earlier. Part of the international media, as usual, helped to stoke the fire in an attempt to defend the corporate interests of one bank or another in their own countries, as well as their own interests.

Without government intervention, Lehman Brothers was likely to declare bankruptcy in the next two or three days, and the insurance company AIG had just asked the Federal Reserve for a forty billion-dollar loan.

Should they allow the onset of a panic? No, this possibility should be avoided. Everything ought to return to normality within the next few weeks. Without some collateral damage, however, it was hard to maintain the grip of fear in the general public. If a crisis could always be avoided, people might start to question whether banks really need all the special guarantees and protections they receive.

Therein lay the problem faced by the brotherhood from its inception. Let a crisis run its course and the entire system can collapse. Control it too tightly and the public begins to question the special status conferred on banks because of their inherent fragility.

Sacrifices were, therefore, necessary. In this particular crisis, the choice of which major bank should fall was made easier by the refusal of both Bear Stearns and Lehman Brothers to participate in the LTCM bailout in

1998 – another of M. Henry's masterful moves. Their defiance would be punished sooner or later. Bear Stearns' time had come in March. Now it was Lehman's turn.

The decision not to save Lehman from bankruptcy had been already approved by twelve of the members of the society. Only M. Henry's final vote was missing.

At fifteen minutes past ten, several cell phones scattered around the table rang at the same time, mixing the text message chimes of different manufacturers. A single message appeared in all of them:

*Gentlemen: you are authorized to send the instructions according to the approved plan. Good luck, H.*

# 18

*August 20, 2008*
*New York City – USA*

Professor Donald Pfeiffer, one the most respected mathematicians in the world, was taking his usual after-lunch stroll across campus at Columbia University. A couple times a week he ate at Tom's, an inexpensive restaurant on Broadway, a few blocks south of the entrance leading to the Mathematics Department, where he had his office.

A scholar with an extensive curriculum, Professor Pfeiffer was a renowned probability theorist specializing in financial mathematics, with dozens of articles published in academic journals, and four books. He was a member of the National Academy of Sciences and taught at Cornell and Princeton before accepting a position at Columbia.

His quiet gait was in complete dissonance with his brain, where formulas, equations, numbers, and concepts raced at lightning speed, together with less abstract thoughts, many of which were somewhat out of ordinary.

What was most curious to his colleagues, students, and close family members was that Donald Pfeiffer was an enthusiast of conspiracy theories, capable of telling impassioned stories about the assassinations of John F. Kennedy and Martin Luther King Jr., or the incongruous circumstances around the September 11th attacks, the true motives of the Bush family for declaring war against Iraq after the invasion of Kuwait, and many other facts of recent American history.

Hundreds of eccentrics paraded through the paths, gardens, and above all classrooms of Columbia University, and Professor Pfeiffer was one of them.

"Professor Pfeiffer..."

Without realizing that he was being called, the professor continued walking until, just a few steps away from the entrance to the building, a gentle touch on the arm that carried his inseparable leather briefcase stopped him:

"Excuse me, Professor Pfeiffer."

Upon hearing his name, Donald Pfeiffer turned and, recognizing his interlocutor and noticing his beautiful companion, immediately replaced his surprised look with an amiable smile:

"William Benjamin," exclaimed the professor, "what an incredible coincidence! I was just thinking about you and some of the conversations we had in Pisa, do you remember?"

"I will never forget those conversations, Professor. Attending one of your special lectures around the time I finished my doctorate is one of my fondest memories of my time in Pisa."

"Ah, Italy, isn't it a fantastic country? And who is this enchanting young lady?"

"This is Sarah Mayer, Professor. A good friend of mine and a collaborator in some of the research I'm doing for my postdoc."

"Italy, dear Sarah, is a wonderful country. If you haven't been yet, you should take advantage of your friend William here and ask him to show you Florence, Rome, Milan, Venice, and all the little towns in between.

"I hope to visit Italy soon," replied Sarah with a glance towards Willbe.

"You will fall in love with it, Sarah, I'm sure of that. And do you know why I was thinking about you, William Benjamin?"

"I have no idea, Professor."

"Because of some documents, if I remember correctly, that had something to do with your ancestors, and your wishes to know more about your family history, especially about your famous relative Leonardo."

Sarah and Willbe looked at each other. She had a mischievous expression, while he appeared a bit embarrassed.

"That is true, the family members I met in Pisa had many stories to tell. I must confess that some of them fascinated me."

"Let's have a drink one of these days and pick up where we left off. Let our imaginations go wild, so to speak."

Willbe and Sarah smiled.

"I would love that. Could I bring Sarah along?"

"It's all over between us if you don't," replied the professor with a charismatic smile. He handed them a personal card with a residential address. "If you'll excuse me, I need to finish an opinion piece for the *Financial Times* today, but let's book something for next weekend at my place, what do you think? Send me an email, please, William."

"Sure thing, Professor."

"It will be a pleasure," Sarah replied.

With that, Professor Pfeiffer waved goodbye and entered the building.

"He is a character," commented Willbe. "It will be worth your time getting to know him. Always funny, as you just saw, but very serious when it comes to mathematics."

"And by the looks of it he knows more about your family documents than I do," stated Sarah with a hint of jealousy.

"It's not like that. I just made reference to the possibility that more stories existed, and perhaps, however unlikely, of there being some lost documents belonging to an old family member, forgotten at the bottom of a drawer or something. The only document I know of is the one I showed you yesterday."

As he began to walk again, Willbe remarked with a smirk:

"I didn't know you were the jealous type, though."

Sarah felt wooed, but could not stop thinking about the reason they had come to Columbia: the possibility that the document Willbe had was a fake.

*************

At Columbia University's Rare Book and Manuscript Library, Sarah and Willbe listened attentively to the curator of Medieval and Renaissance Collections, Samuel Oliver, a friend of Sarah's from her undergraduate years at NYU.

In his opinion, the document he examined could be authentic, but to be sure he would need to make a more rigorous evaluation, exactly in the same way that his department did with the rest of their archive whenever there was any doubt about authenticity.

His staff at the library could do a preliminary evaluation; there was no question about that. But the peculiarity of the document showing two very distinct typefaces demanded a more rigorous examination, the opinion of a specialist.

This observation made Sarah worry again about frustrating Willbe's expectations, but the next phrase from Sam reassured her.

"From what I can tell, Sarah, this is an authentic copy of an older document. This should be the simplest explanation."

"What makes you say that?" inquired Willbe.

"You see, Italy was one of the countries that contributed the most to typography around the end of the 15th and the beginning of the 16th centuries, which led to a bit of a fashion in convents, universities, and even among private citizens around that time: the desire to update older documents, some still written on papyrus, and transcribe them into newer and cheaper paper.

Willbe was excited by this observation from the curator and keen to secure a professional evaluation:

"Can this investigation be done here in New York?"

"Absolutely," responded Sam, "but let me tell you a bit more first. It is also known that, around that same time, some rare books were reprinted in larger numbers, say works about historical facts of the Roman Empire. One example is Virgil, whose reprinted works could be called the first pocket-books, the first bestseller, one might say. But it didn't stop with Roman or Greek books. Reprints of religious and philosophical teachings, contracts, accounting records, even recipes, became quite common."

"For a document like this, which looks like a will, would it be necessary to have some sort of signature on it?"

Willbe nodded, agreeing with the question posed by Sarah.

Looking at it one more time through his magnifying glass, Sam replied:

"This might explain the need to preserve the original signature of this gentleman, this Vitorio Giuseppe Fibonacci. The signature might have been handwritten on the back of the original document and then merged with the full text once it was reprinted. That's actually a very plausible hypothesis."

"And you are sure that we can find someone who could make this evaluation right here in New York?"

Willbe sensed a bit of apprehension in Sarah's question.

Samuel Oliver was categorical:

"Absolutely sure!"

Willbe and Sarah asked at the same time:

"Who?"

"I'll give you the address of a most wonderful character, Mr. Carmona, who works for a rare-book dealer near Central Park. He has quite the work-space at the basement of the shop, where he keeps all of the instruments that he needs to examine old books, some of them very high tech. Just don't come off too strong, as he can be prickly sometimes."

"How do you mean?" asked Sarah a bit puzzled.

"Try not to appear too anxious, that's all."

Willbe could tell that Sarah was a bit upset that her friend had detected her unease.

"You're right Sam, I am a bit anxious. Could you perhaps give this Mr. Carmona a call to introduce us?"

"I could, but I don't think that's necessary. He doesn't care for little formalities like that. Just say I sent you there, he knows me personally. Besides, if it doesn't work out with him, there are other options. He is not the only rare book evaluator in New York City. You could also try some of our professors, Sarah, or other academics interested in this period."

"Any recommendations?"

"You could reach out to Robert Langdon, for example. His group in Harvard has been doing some work on uncovering hidden symbols that were 'lost in transcription', so to speak, during this period."

"That's not a bad idea," agreed Sarah. "He's very busy though. In any case, thank you very much Sam. We will pay a visit to this Mr. Carmona first."

*************

The young diplomat, who had been reporting to the office of the Belgian representative at the UN for days, showed signs of a bad night's sleep. He returned to the parking garage of the majestic building and took his habitual seat at the back of the black Mercedes.

He asked the driver to take him quickly to Columbia University, where the two security agents who had been assigned to observe Willbe and Sarah were stationed.

On the way, he kept reexamining his thoughts. The most recurrent was his desire to return to Belgium and, if possible, redirect his career. He was tired of playing a fake spy and thought that he was qualified for more noble diplomatic missions.

When he arrived at the arranged spot at the university's parking lot, the two agents approached the car. One of them opened the back door and, to appear efficient, started babbling:

"The two lovebirds have been going around kissing and hugging, calling more attention to themselves for public displays of affection than for any other suspicious activity."

The older agent, grizzled and with a Bronx accent, seemed to enjoy the assignment of following a harmless couple through the streets of the Big Apple. His younger colleague added in a Californian accent:

"If they got themselves in some kind of trouble, they sure know how to play the part of a romantic couple oblivious to the world around them."

The short report, without any significant information, did not please the young vice-consul:

"Is that all you got?"

The two agents exchanged embarrassed glances.

"The girl seems a bit distracted," risked the younger agent.

"Could you put that in language I can understand," quipped the diplomat.

"Well, after you gave us her name, we ran the search you asked and found her cell phone number. We then called to try to pinpoint her location. She picked up the call and left her cell phone on without realizing it. We could hear them talking about an old document, something to do with the professor's family."

"I'm listening..."

"He said the *F* in his name stands for 'Fibonachi' or something, I couldn't hear it well. Sounded like someone trying to impress his girlfriend with talk of his important family."

"What about this old document then?"

"Something from the Middle Ages, or some old junk like that. Nothing will come of it," concluded the older agent.

"We'll see about that."

"You know, I have never been assigned to follow someone interested in books. I'd think that's normal, him being a professor and all, no?"

"You should do what you are being paid for. Anything else?" asked the diplomat with a hint of impatience.

The agents looked at each other again, less than amused.

"Well, they chatted with an odd looking man, who might have been a math professor too, given that they were in front of the Mathematics Building, but who knows? Then they entered the building, stayed there for about half an hour, exited, and headed to the library."

"Ok. Keep your eyes open. I'm going to the library to find out what is going on."

"Want one of us to escort you?" asked the West Coaster.

"No, thank you, there is no need. I'll draw less attention if I go alone," replied the vice-consul, trying to picture either one of the agents inside a library.

"But we were officially assigned as your security detail."

"That's ok, really, there's no threat here. Ask the driver to use that spot over there near the exit, reserved for official vehicles. I won't be long."

"You'd do us a favour if you are," muttered the New Yorker under his breath.

The other raised his thumb in agreement.

"This guy doesn't get the whole spy thing at all. He keeps going back and forth like a chicken with its head cut off."

"The worst thing is that I still don't understand what we are doing here, you?"

"I don't care, as long as they pay well and on time."

*************

## Ardennes Forest – BELGIUM

M. Henry, having successfully controlled the strings of the world's economy for the past thirty years, felt a hint of apprehension as he reread the last couple of reports sent by the Belgian vice-consul in New York to one of his associates in Brussels.

Nothing that would make him lose sleep, just a small feeling of weariness brought on by the responsibility that rested on his shoulders: to pass the baton to his successor with dignity and without major problems to be solved.

The reports explicitly mentioned that a Miss Sarah Judith Frances Mayer, an archivist currently working for the New York Fed, had recently consulted the book *Secrets of Italian Cities* by the French author Jacques Desgranges at the New York Public Library. Moreover, her research was connected, as far as they could gather, with the work of a William Benjamin F. Hubbard, a postdoctoral fellow in financial mathematics at Columbia University.

There was nothing wrong, in principle, with someone consulting that book, but its rarity and the description of some ritualistic ceremonies – one in particular – contained in the only three copies in existence, necessitated further scrutiny of this Sarah Mayer.

M. Henry knew the book well. One of the remaining copies was carefully stored in his immense private library, and he kept a careful watch on the other two copies – one in New York, the other in Venice.

The additional information – that Sarah had been referred to the Public Library by a letter from the President of the New York Fed, Timothy Geithner – was enough for M. Henry to order a more detailed, and at the same time more discreet, investigation about her.

*And who was this Dr. Hubbard?*

Probably he was just another academic looking for new ideas in the strangest places, a rising star trying to advance his career. Nevertheless, the investigation should also include this young scholar, but with even more discretion.

*Unpleasant surprises seldom travel alone.*

Even if this was just academic research, where did young Sarah find the information about this obscure book? Chance? Unlikely. He needed more information about the pair.

*William Benjamin F. Hubbard, financial mathematics, rare books — something of out of place in this equation.*

M. Henry opened the locked drawer where he kept the passwords for some of his encrypted secrets and pulled out an address book. It was an object that could as well be from the Stone Age compared to his electronic gadgets, but still safer than many other ways to store information.

*Hackers... Hackers... They charge a fortune, but money was not an issue. Let's see what the web has on our two researchers. It's worth a try.*

# 19

## *Circa 1355-1365 AD*
## *Venice, Veneto Region – ITALY*

After the New Year celebrations, with some of the excitement and apprehension around the opening of the banking house behind him, a restless Giuseppe Fibonacci, his dream now a reality, walked in the gardens of his villa holding hands with his wife Marinella.

His feelings were entangled. He could not separate his enthusiasm with the new banking business from his fears that it would not prosper the way he wanted.

The fights and disputes between Genoa, Venice, Florence, and even his beloved Pisa, all involved in commercial and political conflict, much of it avoidable, put him in a delicate situation. The only reason his own business had not suffered from these feuds yet was his conciliatory nature and, of course, the fact that he was already one of the richest men in Italy, which meant that he could protect his interests better than most.

Thoughts ricocheted inside his mind like a gulp of swallows, moving from one direction to another in the hope of finding the best way forward. At the centre of his whirling cogitations stood a preoccupation with his family, above all his sons Gianpaolo, Vitorio and Luigi.

"You have been a very understanding wife, Marinella, and a dedicated mother. I really ought to count my blessings."

"Why the sudden compliments, Giuseppe?" asked his wife, a little suspicious.

"Because the life of a man of business, a merchant like myself, is full of risks. Without them one cannot achieve anything, but because of them one can lose everything that is achieved. Where do you think I stand right now?"

"You stand in your garden, holding hands with me", responded Marinella, "which is what you do when you are happy."

Giuseppe smiled and pulled her a little closer to him:

"You know very well what I mean, but I enjoy your playful mood."

They kissed.

"It will all end well, Giuseppe, do not worry. Nothing in the world is worth more than the love, respect, and admiration of our sons."

His marriage to Marinella, the youngest daughter of a rich Florentine merchant, had brought to him not only good luck, but the bliss – that was the word he liked to use – of three sons in the first six years of being married.

They met very young – he was twenty-three, she sixteen – and could have had more children if not for the difficulties she experienced giving birth to their fourth son, who lived for only two days. The complications left her sterile, but Giuseppe, unlike other men in the area, did not seek to father children outside of wedlock. The three they had fulfilled him and were the object of his unbounded affection.

He wished to live for many years to come, but he knew that he had to start transferring responsibilities to his eldest child.

"I have been thinking of asking Gianpaolo to be my personal secretary and start grooming him for the business."

"You can be sure he will be the happiest boy in Venice if you do that. He cannot wait to start working at your side."

His three sons, whose ages ranged from twenty-three to eighteen, received a good education from tutors, two of them recommended by Friar Luigi, not only in religious matters as their mother insisted, but also teachings already containing some of the humanistic ideas that would lead Italy to its Renaissance. The three young men were also often witness to their father's tirades against what he called the *obscure world of religion,* sometimes under the critical gaze of their mother, who had not abandoned her own religious upbringing. It was hard to believe in an omnipotent and omniscient God, argued Giuseppe, who symbolized love and had created mankind in his own image, but nevertheless punished his rebellious or nonconformist creatures with eternal damnation.

*What kind of love was that? I would not be able to do that to my own children.*

Marinella made his decision easy: from that day forward Gianpaolo would accompany him in all his business dealings and would be asked to give his opinions about them.

With time he would find a role for Vitorio and Filippo Luigi. Maybe one of them could lead the bank in Florence, why not?

*Dreams were part of the game.*

\*\*\*\*\*\*\*\*\*\*\*\*\*

Used to arduous work, from dawn to dusk, as he was fond of saying, Giuseppe was not the kind of man to feel dispirited for no reason. Seated in his small and neat office near the port of Venice, he assessed the results of the first three years of the new business with an air of triumph. He had come to realize that owning a bank was not at all comparable to being an importer and exporter of fabrics, foods, or spices, or even accumulating gold, silver, and precious stones. He could have anticipated some of the difficulties in the new trade, but only practice would teach him how to address them.

Fabrics, foods, and spices, for the most part, were merchandise to be traded in the short to medium term, provided they were properly stored for local trade or packed for longer trips. Money, on the other hand, could last much longer. At least that was the initial impression that Giuseppe got from running a banking house. Money only went bad if it stayed still.

Relationships, management, and commercial practices in the new banking business were distinct, demanding different skills and timeframes to carry them out. The ledger to keep track of transactions was similar to the books he used in his other business, but it obeyed a different logic. There were still two entries to record each transaction, just like when buying or selling any product, but what they recorded were promises between borrowers and lenders.

New challenges and difficulties, that is, was what he expected to face from then onwards.

*How to set the interest to be charged for each loan, for example? How to avoid bad borrowers, or defaults? Could the money raised by the bank in Venice be used to lend to people in Florence or other parts of Italy? What would happen if all the Venetian merchants demanded their money back at once and he couldn't make the Florentines pay back their loans quickly enough? But surely that could only happen if the Venetians thought the bank didn't have enough money in its vault to begin with. If they all believed the bank had enough to pay back when needed, then it would have enough. But what if they didn't believe?*

Giuseppe was a practical man and acted according to the needs of the moment, without trying to devise miraculous theories or being paralyzed by fear. But the implications of what he was beginning to grasp as the foundations of his new business were tantalizing.

*Belief, trust, power, panic, control.*

His practical instincts led him to back a group of noblemen in Florence who opposed Salvestro de Medici, a member of the patrician class who in a few years would become the *Gonfaloniere di Giustizia*, the highest post in the government of Florence, the *Signoria*. Younger than Giuseppe, Salvestro had allied himself with textile workers and other lesser guilds and became an enemy of powerful merchants and early bankers.

Giuseppe's own power and influence was the object of envy and antipathy from many of his competitors, especially now that he owned a bank in Venice. This alone would be enough reason for rumors about him to begin to spread across Northern Italy. He knew his people well.

One of these rumors, reported to him by his younger son Luigi, had it that the Fibonacci family would soon open a bank in Florence.

*That's good – I helped spread the news myself.*

As the House of Fibonacci and Cristaldi approached its third anniversary, Giuseppe was convinced that power was the best protection against uncertainty. It was one thing to be a landowner or a merchant. Being the owner of a bank was something else altogether. The power it yielded was something that he was learning day by day.

*Blessed the day I took the risk in this direction, alongside two of my friends, two honoured men.*

One of them was seated across the room from him at this very moment, working at his desk. A Florentine living in Venice for many years, he had a frown on his forehead.

"What is wrong, Francesco? Books not balancing?"

The frown was gone from Francesco Cristaldi's face as he stood up to stretch his legs:

"Actually, I was thinking about Florence, Giuseppe. I'm not sure we should have Salvestro de Medici as an enemy, especially if we are thinking of opening a branch of our bank there. He's a man capable of anything to increase his influence in Tuscany, Veneto, and the rest of Italy. We need to be careful with men like that."

"What is the problem with that? Don't we behave in the same way? We are capable of using the same means."

"Not all, Giuseppe, not all. We are not dishonest, for example. Besides, he has a large family and some of the younger ones are being prepared to take on the family business. They are ambitious and do not hide their intentions from anyone. At this pace they'll have the power they want in a few years."

"Over my dead body, I tell you," responded Giuseppe. "I swear to you and to our good friend Luigi de Vicenza that it won't be easy if they try. You and I have our own small army. Salvestro had better not meddle with our businesses in Florence."

Cristaldi, their friendship notwithstanding, did not like the bravado coming from his business partner. He respected Giuseppe and knew him to be sincere, but that attitude was worrying in a man who was good at leading, but not so good at sharing responsibilities.

# 20

*September 13, 2008*
*ITALY – Venice*

As they entered room 131 of the Hotel Danieli, Inspector de Lucca could not hide the surprise from the manager and the front desk clerk who escorted him:

"*Cazzo mio!*"

The room was in disarray, chairs upside down, the bed unmade, on one of the paintings on the wall, part of the frame and the glass broken as if a heavy object had hit it. By the side of the bed, there lay an open suitcase with clothes scattered around it.

Without attempting to disguise his sarcasm, Piero shot at the two:

"So, you gentlemen were completely unaware of what took place here? No hotel maid or room service person informed you of what they probably heard or saw?"

Embarrassed, the front desk clerk mumbled looking at the manager:

"Privacy here is absolute, Inspector, if you know what I mean..."

What caught the attention of the trained police officer next was an open bottle of wine next to two glasses, one of them overturned with its contents spilled over the cloth covering a table in the contiguous sitting-room.

The scene indicated an altercation and possible fight between two men, as nothing suggested the presence of a woman in the room. There was no indication of any wild party either, something not uncommon in hotels of this sort.

Turning to the manager, Piero requested that the room be sealed off and that nobody be allowed to enter it from that moment onward.

"Most importantly," added the inspector in a tone that tolerated no disagreement, "you should not let anyone, inside or outside the hotel, know about my visit here."

The severe stare of Inspector de Lucca met the alert but suspicious eyes of the manager.

"Certainly, Inspector. I would say that we are more interested than anyone else in preventing this strange story from casting a shadow over the hotel. You have my word."

Counting on the understanding, sincere or not, of the manager, Piero began to think of how he could advance this investigation without alerting his superiors.

"Did the couple identify themselves?"

"No, because they did not come to the room, it was not necessary."

*It is impossible to take the manager at his word. Not that he gives any indication of being dishonest, but his position obligates him to silence. Celebrities abounded among the guests. I will have to conduct this investigation alone. First, I need someone to analyze the fingerprints on the wine glasses, someone I trust, even if I have to deviate from normal procedures.*

"I'll send someone from my team to collect a few objects."

Before leaving the room, Piero noticed a small rectangular piece of paper on the floor between the bedside table and the bed. Carefully, he approached the bedside table and tested the lamp, as if this was of some importance, bending to follow the cord to the back of the bed. This allowed him to pick the piece of paper from the floor as he was rising and put it inside his pocket.

As he was leaving, he told the hotel staff:

"I'm counting on your understanding and discretion, gentlemen."

They knew from his tone that this was an order rather than a suggestion.

\*\*\*\*\*\*\*\*\*\*\*\*\*

Being a superstitious man, Piero de Lucca exited the Hotel Danieli through the same door he had entered. Outside, he felt his cell phone vibrate inside his pocket. He looked at the screen and was surprised by the caller's name – he had to think quickly how to proceed.

The death of the Japanese man had to remain out of the news; there was no question about it, even if he disagreed with the decision.

He hesitated on whether or not to pick up the call, but his well-trained instinct made him answer without any trace of apprehension in his voice:

"*Ciao. Sono io, Piero.*"

On the line was his *questore*, the officer above him in the hierarchy of the Border Police. Because of his competence, de Lucca had the respect of the force all over the Veneto region, especially because of his good rapport with tourists and with his superiors.

"Hello sir, what can I do for you?"

"We need to talk, Piero. Come and see me on Monday afternoon, please. I just got a call from Rome about a serious matter."

"Certainly. Is 4pm suitable?"

"Yes, see you then. Now have some rest and enjoy your weekend."

*No doubt this is a serious matter. Phone calls like that are only placed if the matter transcends Italian borders.*

He considered returning to the hotel to show the front desk clerk the picture he had taken at the morgue. Just to be sure. He examined the piece of paper he had collected from room 131 -the stub of a ticket for the Querini Stampalia Foundation in Venice – and decided to keep it safe until he had other clues about this strange death.

When the clerk saw Piero approaching the counter again, he welcomed him with a smile and some forced familiarity:

"Hello, Inspector, back so soon? You have the situation under control already?"

Piero thought the informality was out of line, and simply motioned to the clerk to move to the end of the counter, out of sight of other guests, and discreetly showed him his cell phone:

"Was this the guest in room 131?"

Initially unsure, the clerk inspected the morbid picture for several seconds and replied with confidence and a more serious tone:

"Yes, that was him for sure, Inspector."

"*Grazie,*" said Piero while he shook the clerk's hand as a goodbye gesture. He knew these small pleasantries could come in handy when necessary.

The inspector left Hotel Danieli for the second time with a worried look, knowing exactly what kind of conversation he was going to have with the *questore* of Venice on Monday.

He knew his boss very well and was determined to show him that he had not disobeyed orders for no reason; that it was more prudent to gather a modicum of information about the Japanese gentleman than to proceed blindly.

What if someone else with knowledge of the case accused the Venice police of not investigating it on purpose? It was better not to be caught in the crossfire. Power games tended to be merciless with the unwary.

*Which orders should be obeyed? Nobody is above the law, right?*

\*\*\*\*\*\*\*\*\*\*\*\*\*

## Ardennes Forest – BELGIUM

*Central banks offer a great service to their countries, regardless of what some radicals might think,* M. Henry reflected alone in his library.

He tended to dismiss the opinion that central banks should not intervene in the economy. All that was necessary was to show that they played a positive role. Granted, central banks ought not to become a club to protect bankers. They should appear to be impartial in their decisions.

Most people accept that a functioning economy needs a lender of last resort. It is easy to understand that banks need the confidence of depositors and that, when this confidence is gone, even the most solvent ones can crumble.

The trick has always been to know to whom to lend, when, and how much. The golden rule, or the Bagehot rule as it is sometimes called, counsels that, in a panic, central banks should "lend freely, at high rates, to solvent banks".

*But who is to say which banks are solvent?*

The history of central banking is littered with episodes of commercial banks being rescued one year, only to fail the next, or banks that could have been rescued but were left to fail for no apparent reason other than the caprice of whoever was making the decision. Conspiracy theories abound, for example of Protestant central bankers punishing banks run by Catholics. M. Henry knew better.

*The rule is that there is no rule. Central banks would always eventually step in to save the system, but they should keep everyone guessing about the fate of each individual bank.*

Preventing moral hazard was the usual justification. If every bank expected to be rescued, the idea goes, they would become reckless and take on excessive risk. But again, M. Henry knew that there was more to it. For people who think moral hazard is a real problem actually tend to argue that the best way to prevent it is not to rescue any bank. Abolish central banks altogether, let the markets decide the fate of failing banks!

*Let a financial crisis run its course. What a silly concept.*

The truth is that we don't know what would happen if a financial crisis were allowed to run its course because this has never been allowed to occur. Public opinion has no stomach to see a crisis through, even if the end result is to reduce the chance of future crises. The pain is too great.

*Present reality always wins over future planning.*

No, preventing moral hazard was not the reason behind letting some banks fail. The key was to cause enough havoc to remind the public how ugly a financial crisis can become. Remind them why they have a central bank to begin with.

*But, which failures would do the job? How long to let a crisis develop before pulling all the stops and rescuing the survivors?*

That was for him to decide. It had been the self-proclaimed prerogative of the brotherhood for centuries. The accumulated knowledge of countless experiments, some successful, some less so.

Lehman Brothers was the one left to fail this time, and that would do the trick. The massive crash in stock markets around the world that day, the Monday after Lehman filed for bankruptcy, was already prompting desperate calls for action in all the advanced economies.

Those at the helm of central banks and finance ministries of G20 countries had already been instructed on how to act. It was a good time to remind them who was in charge, who had the deciding power. Other firms would receive the help they needed, starting with AIG the following day. Lehman Brothers paid the price for their own irresponsible behaviour, and for their arrogance in believing they were above the rules ten years earlier.

*Most importantly, the case for central banks had been made again. The system still needed its custodians. And as for* quis custodiet ipsos custodes*, well, I know who.*

---

* who will guard the guardians?

# 21

*August 20, 2008*
*New York City – USA*

Willbe and Sarah decided to take the subway from Columbia to Midtown and arrived half an hour later at Columbus Circle stop. As they walked towards the bookstore recommended by Sam Oliver, Willbe peered around him trying not to draw Sarah's attention. For a split second he had the feeling of being watched.

*Nothing to justify such absurdity. Watched by whom, and for what reason?*

He kept the impression to himself, for he could already tell that Sarah was in an agitated mood.

Two flights of stairs took them to the basement of the Argosy Bookstore, one of the most traditional in Manhattan, where they would find Mr. Carmona.

The basement was itself an extension of the bookstore, where Carmona had organized a space to receive, select, and evaluate the authenticity of the many rare books to be displayed to the public, in addition to the odd document that from time-to-time landed on his desk.

He was a self-taught appraiser, but he had a degree in Italian literature from the University of Bologna, his birthplace. He came to America when he was five years old, accompanying his parents and an older sister, who had fled Italy to escape Mussolini. He had a soft spot in his heart for Italy, especially Bologna because of the years he spent there as a young man when he returned to Italy to study. His aptitudes and professional rigor made him something of a celebrity in the non-negligible community of rare book aficionados and collectors of printed relics.

When they located his desk at the end of an array of bookshelves, Sarah grabbed Willbe's arm trying not to laugh as she turned her back momentarily to the person seated behind a pile of books.

"What is it, Sarah?"

"Look at what an odd character he is!"

Willbe glanced towards the man, who had to be Carmona, then looked at Sarah who was trying not to laugh, and finally back at the man at the desk.

"What's so funny?"

"Who does he remind you of?"

Willbe did not know what to answer.

"I'll give you a hint," whispered Sarah, "Carlo Collodi... childhood book."

"Geppetto!"

"Shush, be quiet, remember what Sam said, he can get angry."

"I'm pretty sure Sam didn't mean that..."

Composing themselves, Sarah and Willbe approached the desk covered in books, tweezers, a pair of gloves, magnifying glasses, paperclips, and a small flag holder with miniature Italian and American flags spiked in it.

"Mr. Carmona," attempted Sarah in a gentle voice.

Looking at them over the rim of his rectangular glasses, without raising his head, the man emitted a hoarse sound of agreement.

"You were recommended to us by Samuel Oliver, from the Rare Book and Artifact Library at Columbia. Do you have a moment?"

Carmona examined the couple in front of him, focusing on Sarah:

"Certainly, if I can be of any help to you."

"I'm sure that you can," replied Sarah, trying to remember Sam's advice about not coming off too strong.

Willbe placed an envelope on the desk:

"We need to determine the authenticity of a document, allegedly from the 15th century, that I received from my family in Italy."

*************

Mr. Carmona, wearing his binocular magnifying glasses, had been examining the document handed to him by Willbe for several minutes without saying a word or showing any sign that he was displeased by the task.

The respectful silence among the three people around the desk created a wall between them and the surrounding background noise in the bookstore, inaudible to Mr. Carmona because of the concentration on his work and to Willbe and Sarah because of the expectation of confirming whether they were in the presence of a medieval relic.

Before Mr. Carmona began his examination, Willbe briefly told him how he had obtained the document, the reason for his stay in Pisa, and a few other details of his academic life. Mindful of Sam's advice to Sarah, he wanted to speak just enough to gain the old man's sympathy, hopeful that their common ancestry would take care of the rest.

Mr. Carmona read the document with a degree of focused attention that seemed excessive even to Sarah, who was used to these procedures. He gave the impression that he was examining each letter of it, perhaps looking for some flaw, a smudge that could reveal a cheap falsification.

"There is no doubt this is an old document. I have seen this type of paper before. If you allow me to speculate, I'd say it is a typed copy of an earlier handwritten version, a custom that spread through Europe after Gutenberg. Taking this into account, I can almost guarantee that the document is authentic."

Sarah was so relieved that she grabbed Willbe's arm without realizing it. But the real surprise came when, after moving the magnifying glasses to the tip of his nose, Mr. Carmona told a mesmerized Willbe that he had already seen the name Vitorio Giuseppe Fibonacci in a book he had examined for the library of a museum in Venice.

"Are you sure, Mr. Carmona?" asked Willbe trying not to give away his excitement.

"Positive, young man. I have a very good memory for small details, something very handy in my profession, don't you think?" said Carmona as he winked at Sarah. He proceeded to explain that he remembered the name in part because of the famous family name. Sarah immediately noticed the expression of pride in Willbe's face.

"But not only that, I also remember the occasion because this very prestigious museum, which could have used an appraiser from anywhere in Europe, instead decided to call me, here in New York. I felt very honoured by the choice, as you can imagine."

"And what was the name of the book?" Willbe's heart was thumping as he asked the question.

"And the museum?" added Sarah, no longer able to hide her anxiety as she remembered the words of the man who gave her the apology letter at the Public Library the day before.

"I know the answer to both of your questions, but before I tell you let me confirm with what I have written in my notebooks. Please give me a moment."

Mr. Carmona put the magnifying glasses beside the document he had just examined and pulled a thick hardcover notebook from the shelf behind his desk. Colour-coded tags divided the notebook in groups of pages corresponding to different years.

"You must forgive me, but I have not had time to transfer all my notes to the computer. I'm a rather old-fashioned person, I'm afraid."

Sarah and Willbe looked at each other recognizing the professional pride of the charismatic appraiser.

"Let's see, this was a few years back, 2005, I think. That's it, here it is."

Willbe and Sarah peeked over Mr. Carmona's shoulders as he went on:

"Querini Stampalia Foundation in Venice. And the book was called *Secrets of Italian Cities*, by the illustrious yet little-known French author Jacques Desgranges".

Sarah exclaimed at once:

"I can't believe this. There's another copy of this book in the New York Public Library, and possibly only a third copy, but nobody knows where. It's an extremely rare book."

"That's correct, young lady, and exactly what I was told by the person who asked for my evaluation, the director of the museum himself. A very erudite person, though a tad superstitious."

"What makes you say that?"

"He told me that the book was surrounded by some sort of legend, known only by a handful of late Middle Ages aficionados."

"A legend?" inquired Sarah with renewed interest.

"Something related to creeds and curses having to do with a secret society. And since I don't believe in this sort of nonsense, I cut that conversation short."

Sarah looked at Willbe with a surprised expression.

"Do you happen to recall the context in which this Fibonacci gentleman was mentioned?" asked Willbe.

"Nothing special," responded Carmona. "Although, from a certain point of view, in the most special context of all."

"Most special context?" asked a puzzled Willbe.

"Yes, you see, this book, the first edition of which came out in the first half of the 16th century, opens with a dedication *in memoriam* of this gentleman, who belonged to a very rich family in Tuscany – a patron of the arts and sciences at the end of the 14th century."

"Was all of this mentioned in the book?"

"Right underneath the name we see here in your document."

Sarah looked at Willbe with affection and relief. She could sense his pride. His obsession, as she had come to think of it, was founded on something after all.

A satisfied Mr. Carmona returned the notebook to its place on the shelf.

"This is helpful for you, then?"

"You have made us very happy," responded Sarah.

"How much do we owe you for the appraisal, Mr. Carmona?"

Willbe asked the question a little embarrassedly.

"A good pizza at Il Corso, that will do! It's a restaurant not far from here and I'm quite hungry. What do you think?"

"It would be a great pleasure!" answered Willbe.

"A little courtesy between Italians, don't tell anyone."

"Where in Italy are you from?"

"From Emilia Romagna, Bologna more precisely."

"I've not had the pleasure of visiting Bologna, but I'm sure there will be opportunities, right Sarah?"

They continued to talk animatedly as they headed to the restaurant.

*************

Despite the good news delivered by Mr. Carmona that afternoon, Willbe had trouble sleeping that night.

After the dinner with Sarah and Mr. Carmona, he went home with the sensation that something groundbreaking was about to happen. Unlike Sarah, he tended to reflect quite a lot on the meaning of coincidences, trying to read them for guidance on how to proceed when he was undecided about something. He didn't think this was superstitious, but viewed it more as a method to solve problems, as in mathematics.

For example, his choice of going to Pisa for his doctorate was a decision he took after a conversation with his parents about his intention to study in a university with a tradition in mathematics. Two or three days after this conversation, his mother received a call from one of her Italian relatives - her brother Emiliano, whom she hadn't seen in many years - inviting her to spend part of the summer in Tuscany and suggesting that she bring her son with her, as he wanted him to know more about the University of Pisa and the history of the family. Was it a mere coincidence? The youngest of five children, Willbe's mother Anna had moved to America with her husband John Hubbard before Willbe was born and, although she tried to stay in touch, had not remained close to her Italian family.

And now, as Willbe was about to begin his teaching at an American university, some of the occurrences of the last few days, marked by coincidences, put him on high alert: the document received in Pisa was authentic and the Venetian Files were not a figment of his imagination. They existed; they were real.

*Uncle Emiliano did not make up stories after all.*

He had also discovered that the same book that mentioned the Venetian Files was dedicated to his ancestor for his help in supporting the arts and sciences with the fortune he had amassed from his banking activities.

*Was there any other link between Giuseppe Fibonacci and the Venetian Files?*

He would have to return to Pisa and he felt it would not be hard to convince Sarah to take a week off from work and come to Italy with him. Pisa and then Florence; and of course, Venice. He imagined that one week, maybe ten days, would be enough.

Before that, however, he would visit Donald Pfeiffer's house with Sarah. Under these circumstances, it was an invitation he could not refuse. For one thing, Professor Pfeiffer's enthusiasm for Italy would likely make a good impression on Sarah too. His deep knowledge of the history of finance had already been influential in Willbe's understanding of the role of money from feudal to modern times. Finally, with his penchant for conspiracy theories, he might also help them to connect some dots.

Most urgent, though, was a visit to the Public Library. The book by this Frenchman Desgranges had more information to give them, he was certain.

\*\*\*\*\*\*\*\*\*\*\*\*\*

Mr. Carmona said goodbye to the young couple after dinner and returned to his workstation in the basement of the Argosy Bookstore. He browsed through his notes again until he found the number he was looking for and proceeded to make an international call to the private line of Hideo Akashiro.

# 22

*July, 1367 AD*
*Venice, Veneto Region - ITALY*

Friar Luigi de Vicenza had felt restless ever since waking up. A merciless summer was putting him in a bad mood.

What bothered him the most was that he did not know the true reason for feeling unnerved. He had an inkling that the piece of paper slid under his bedroom door two days before had something to do with it, as it suggested circumstances beyond his control and potentially harmful to him.

*Revenge? Retribution? Envy? The Devil taunting him?*

While they enjoyed his unwavering dedication, he never heard a murmur about his work coming from his brothers at the monastery. Not even about his friendship with Giuseppe Fibonacci. He was not a suspicious person and was not about to interpret the behavior of the Franciscans as evidence that they saw him as an unusual clergyman; perhaps someone more orthodox in appearance than substance. He didn't think it was a criticism of the way he took care of the finances of the monastery.

As a member of the Order of Penance of Saint Francis, he believed he was far from having committed any type of heresy, that much was clear in his head. He had also never practiced usury in his personal dealings at least up until now.

*What about now?*

He noticed that ever since the opening of the banking house he had become less patient, less caring about spiritual questions and more distant from the young novices, who nevertheless, remained ready to listen to his advice or admonitions. He also felt less secure in his faith in Christ.

*Being a secret partner in a bank, was this not an indirect way of benefiting from usury?*

Giuseppe Fibonacci had had the best possible intentions when he had asked him to manage the financial books of the banking house. He had no doubt about that. This activity, which looked easy at first, was taking up more and more of his time, including frequent trips to Venice, often once or even twice a week. And it was precisely in doing this that he had to face the truth that was consuming him from inside: the accounting of interest. It tormented him, for it confirmed that, for all practical purposes, he had become a direct beneficiary of usury.

Francesco Cristaldi, like Giuseppe, had to take care of other businesses. They had agreed on a division of responsibilities in which he, Luigi, would participate according to strict rules of discretion.

*Discretion? What discretion? How exactly were they being discreet?*

To travel to Venice every week, covering the distance in a cart pulled by two mules, often without any goods to trade, was not the sort of behavior one would expect from a monk. One of the novices told him in confidence about the rumors that were circulating within the walls of the monastery. It was not prudent to simply ignore them or declare them unfounded.

*How did Giuseppe and Francesco not take this into account?*

If only his task was to maintain the *secret book*, as they had come to call the record of deposits and loans made by the bank. But no, he also had to record the profits and losses, whenever they occurred. And in that task he felt unsure, embarrassed, a sinner.

Trade among Italian cities had grown in such a manner that the circulation of money between them led to the appearance of new and profitable businesses. The Church itself took part in many of these deals, so his superiors were also taking advantage of the many opportunities.

*Everything would be fine in due course. Or would it?*

Setting the interest to be charged to each merchant who borrowed money from the bank, taking into account the varying times agreed for repayment, demanded an effort unforeseen by the three partners when they decided to open their banking house. And the number of merchants who came to the bank was increasing, some even returning to complain about incorrect calculations. He carried these problems and challenges with him to the bank and back to the monastery, where he locked himself up in his room searching for solutions.

How to come up with different values for what was essentially the same service: lending money? Was money to cultivate a field, for example, different from money used in a sea voyage to India? The risks were different; some of them incalculable.

*If accumulating wealth was a sin, why were cardinals and bishops not guilty of it? Or the Pope, even?*

Doubts and uncertainty prevented him from sleeping well, sometimes even eating well.

Luigi was predicting another sleepless night. The following morning, he would return to Venice, this time intent on discussing the frequency of his visits with his partners and the problems they were creating. Problems like that anonymous note passed under his door.

He consoled himself with the thought that greed, although linked to avarice by Saint Thomas, was not formally a capital sin. But this exception would not redeem him to himself, much less before an Inquisition tribunal.

And he was not even greedy, for he did not accumulate wealth for himself, but to help his fellows. He envied no one and led a simple life.

The truth was that he did not know what to think anymore.

He picked up the piece of paper and read it again, his heart beating a little faster now.

*************

The port and its surroundings were quiet at the evening hour when the partners met. The Fibonacci & Cristaldi banking house had closed its wooden front door and two torches were lit inside. Outside, the lazy light of a summer evening was losing strength.

Giuseppe looked at Luigi with a troubled expression on his face, a mixture of sincere worry shown in the rhythmic nodding of the head with what appeared to be internal turmoil at the anticipation of new difficulties.

In his hands he held the piece of paper received by Luigi, which he and Cristaldi had already read. The silence after each partner read the note separately, although brief and tense, seemed like an eternity.

"We can't ignore these rumours, and much less the warning in this note."

Of the three partners, Francesco seemed the least worried:

"*Con permesso…*"

Taking the note in his hands, he read it a second time, aloud now:

"*Strange conversations can be heard in the corners of this holy house dedicated to the Lord and to His humblest servants. The Bible says, Exodus 22, verse 25: If thou lend money to any of my people that is poor by thee, thou shalt not be to him as a usurer, neither shalt thou lay upon him usury.*"

Giuseppe stood up and walked towards the front door of the bank, opened it and watched the few people walking by the street for a while. The sea air coming from the port comforted him. With his hands behind his back in a reflexive attitude, it was not hard for him to understand the magnitude of the problem contained in the note. He had to make a quick decision to help his friend.

He closed the door again and walked resolutely back to the inner part of the office. As he approached Luigi he put a hand on his shoulder and with a firm and encouraging gaze began to speak

"We have made a pledge of loyalty, Luigi, which will be honoured by me and Francesco, don't you worry about it. Nobody can prove any association between you and this banking house, if that's what this piece of paper is suggesting. If anyone in Veneto, Emilia Romagna or Tuscany dares to accuse you of that he shall face my objection and the strength of my power – our power, the power of our money."

Giuseppe paused and looked at Francesco and Luigi sternly. He asked Francesco to give him back the piece of paper and burned it in one of the torches.

"I can guarantee you that this will be just one of many problems that we are going to face in our future. But these rats better not provoke the ire of Vitorio Giuseppe Fibonacci."

Worried, Francesco urged prudence.

"Calm down, Giuseppe, calm down. We should not get ahead of ourselves. If we become embroiled with either the Church or the political affairs of Florence we will have troubles with other businesses too. Tact would be wise. We have allies here in Venice, but also in Florence, Siena, and Pisa. We must act, I agree, but with calm and intelligence.

"*Va bene*, Cristaldi, *va bene*. I will take your words into account. Luigi will spend the night at my house and rest after we eat a good fish soup with the bread he brought from the monastery. And some wine from the last harvest. If you'd like to join us..."

Cristaldi agreed with a head gesture.

Embarrassed, Luigi listened to the conversation without being able to hide his preoccupations, for everything indicated that he, rather than the business, was the problem.

"*Sono proprio io*," he exclaimed.

"What's that?" asked Giuseppe.

"I am the problem here, and I don't feel comfortable about it."

"Don't worry, Luigi, we will find a way out."

# 23

*September 14, 2008*
*Ardennes Forest – BELGIUM*

The exhausting meeting at the Swiss Commercial Bank in Brussels ended in the early hours of the morning, and the participants showed signs of fatigue and discomfort. Nevertheless, they left the building with the sense of a job well done and above all with the conviction that, even though the embers were still hot and could spark a flame here and there, the worst of economic crisis would subside in a matter of weeks and they would be able to return their attention to longer term planning.

*For how long, though?*

M. Henry agreed with the many scholars who argued that instability is an inherent feature of financial markets. Everyone familiar with finance, either as an academic or a practitioner, a trader or a journalist, an accountant or a lawyer, is fully aware that unexpected surprises are part of what generates the fluctuations observed in the markets. Fundamental uncertainty, as many liked to put it.

Regardless of how many sophisticated mathematical models try to shoehorn finance and economics into calculable expressions, every player in this attractive money game should become familiar with the possibility of facing truly unexpected situations – the unknown unknowns of Donald Rumsfeld – and be prepared accordingly.

But this type of fundamental uncertainty can create fear and self-doubt, however fleetingly, even in the most powerful man. M. Henry was less willing than others at the organization to declare the crisis conquered.

One of his cell phones vibrated on the desk in front of him. Used to receiving calls from all corners of the world, he nevertheless, thought it strange that this call was coming from Rome. He answered.

*Mailbox number 3.*

The coded message was reserved for emergency situations.

M. Henry turned his desktop computer on and looked for the address indicated by the message.

*************

## *Venice - ITALY*

The sausage *panino* with a side of *risotto ai funghi* and two glasses of wine were not quite enough to satisfy Inspector Piero de Lucca. He was a tall man used to large lunches, which resulted in the prominent stomach that he tried to hide with loose trousers held up by a collection of colourful suspenders.

He was an unusual policeman, but one who had the sympathy and admiration of his colleagues. Somewhat obsessive, which made him appear rude and impatient sometimes, Piero valued the most minute, often seemingly insignificant, detail. The petal of a flower, for example, or a shirt button, the pit of a fruit left in the wrong spot, an unused match thrown out at random, crumbled pieces of paper, fallen cigarette ashes, a lone ten cent coin - everything was important in an investigation.

This time around he fixated on the ticket to the Querini Stampalia Foundation. In it, across the place where it had been torn, one could still read that it had been used on Thursday, September 11, the same day the dead body was found in a passage leading to one of the city's famous canals.

What events led to the gentleman's death after visiting the museum? Was he there alone? Did he go there to meet someone? Was it the same person with whom he had a difference of opinion in the hotel room? The young couple who had been looking for him? Or was it all a big and fatal coincidence, just chance?

*No, chance would not put a katana in the crime scene. This was a premeditated crime, planned for that day and hour.*

He had to organize his thoughts and hypotheses very well for the meeting he was about to have with his superior. If he contradicted himself in his reasons for not following orders, he would be reprimanded and, if he insisted, likely punished with a suspension, the first in his long career. He recalled the clerk at the Hotel Danieli saying that the guest had a diplomatic passport. That was interesting. And where was this passport now? What information could he gather from the Japanese consulate?

It should not be too difficult to convince his friends at border control to go over the records of entry in Venice in the last ten days, whether through the airport, the Ponte Della Libertà, or the cruise ships terminal.

*Even diplomatic passport need to be recorded.*

And if that led nowhere, he could still try his contact at the Japanese consulate in Milan. If he tried the one in Venice someone in his unit would certainly find out, which could complicate his investigation.

*The man was dressed in black tie to visit the museum? Had there been some kind of ceremony at the Querini Stampalia that day? If so, they ought to have a guest list.*

He expected to hear back about the fingerprints on the wine glass from room 131 later that afternoon. And he would pay a visit to the Stampalia museum before long.

## 24

*August 22, 2008*
*New York City - USA*

Summer was showing that it meant business that year. Willbe opened the windows of his living room to let the early morning air in and headed for a cold shower. He was not fond of air conditioning. The nippy water fell voluminously on his head, making his body shiver and waking him up fully.

Suspecting that he heard his cell phone ringing, he turned off the shower in the expectation to continue to hear the Laurel and Hardy tune that he chose as a ringtone. False alarm. Minutes later, as he was getting dressed, he searched for his phone to check whether he had any messages or missed calls. He saw a missed call from Donald Pfeiffer and a new voice message from an unknown number.

He prioritized the former and called the number back:

"Hello, Professor Pfeiffer? This is William, how are you?"

*"Hello William. I was hoping you would call me back."*

"Anything I can help you with, Professor?"

*"Yes, yes. I was hoping we could confirm a time for you to come over this weekend, as we discussed. What do you think?"*

"I think that would be great."

*"Wonderful. I want to pick your brain on this economic crisis. I know it's a topic that interests you, and I must finish that op-ed for the Financial Times before going to London next week."*

"It would be my pleasure."

*"I have one condition, however."*

"Sure, Professor, what is it?"

*"That you bring your delightful friend, as we had agreed."*

"You haven't forgotten about Sarah, then?"

*"Who could forget such a radiant person?"*

"I'm sure she will be delighted to come."

*"Alright then, so I'll see you on Saturday evening, or is Sunday better?"*

"I think perhaps Saturday will work better for us."

*"Excellent, I'll see you then."*

Elated by the invitation, Willbe thought once more about the conversation he had had with Sarah about coincidences – the seemingly random juxtaposition of interests that sprout out of nowhere in certain moments of our lives – for which she didn't care much at all.

Next he returned to the second missed call and voice message from the unknown caller and was shocked when he heard it.

"Young Fibonacci, this is a warning: stop looking for trouble in old books. We are watching you. You and Miss Mayer can't hide from us."

He was paralyzed for a few seconds and then played the message again, paying close attention to the mangled deep voice for any clue that could identify the caller.

*What can it mean?*

It was clearly meant to be a threat, but from whom? The two men watching them at Bryant Park immediately came to mind.

*But how could they possibly know anything about the old book?*

*************

As they waited for the vice-consul to begin another tedious day of surveillance of the young couple, who seemed entirely harmless, the two security agents laughed as they hung up the phone.

"What do you think he is thinking now?" asked the younger one.

"It's going to drive him crazy."

"You want to make a bet?"

"Go on," encouraged the older one still laughing.

"From now on the love birds will walk around looking out in all directions."

"I liked the voice you made, horror movie stuff."

The agents continued to laugh.

"What's so funny," asked the Belgian diplomat who had arrived without them noticing.

The agents swallowed hard and stopped laughing at once.

"Any news?"

"Not yet," responded the more talkative young one, still a bit flustered, not knowing if the vice-consul had heard any part of their conversation.

"Did you make the call?"

"Yes, sir."

"Left a message with the exact words I told you, untraceable?"

"Affirmative."

"Sir," interjected the older security agent, "we are not really going to follow up with anything if they just keep going in and out of libraries, are we?"

"That's up to them."

\*\*\*\*\*\*\*\*\*\*\*\*\*

Young Fibonacci!

Willbe's immediate reaction to the message was to call Sarah. But he stopped dialing before completing the call, having second thoughts.

*What if I am just going to make her even more nervous?*

No, he had not asked Sarah to help him just to leave her frightened and anxious. He would keep the message to himself for now.

Willbe searched his mind for times when he had had a reason to tell anyone, either in private or in public, that the letter F in his name stood for Fibonacci. He had certainly told people when he had been in Pisa for the first time. Apart from that, he could think of only very rare occasions, the last of which three days before in his own apartment, when he was explaining to Sarah why he chose to do his doctorate in Italy.

Willbe wondered whether the mysterious phone call would be a good conversation topic for the dinner at Donald Pfeiffer's place – but that would mean he would have to tell Sarah first.

*Uncle Emiliano, just like Professor Pfeiffer, was fond of conspiracy theories. He got carried away by fantastic stories, like the ones he told me in Pisa. How much truth was in them? Perhaps only a little, given that most of the family questioned the old man's mental health.*

He was beginning to think he was getting carried away himself.

With the towel still wrapped around his waist, Willbe flopped down onto the sofa and did what any normal person who wanted to know the origin of a phone call would do: call back. The number was unsurprisingly blocked. He decided to save the voice message, just in case.

\*\*\*\*\*\*\*\*\*\*\*\*\*

At the library, Willbe and Sarah found themselves acting defensively towards each other; in the last few days it seemed that something was off-kilter with them for the first time since they had met earlier in the summer. Self-consciously, they walked in silence towards the rare books section, after Willbe made a quick comment about being anxious to see the book with the dedication to his ancestor. This was not the right time to tell her about the voice message.

Sarah seemed calmed by the thousands of books, and she began to show her familiarity with the imposing surroundings. She asked for the same employee who had helped her the first time. It was his day-off, she was told, but they were courteously greeted by his substitute.

"Good morning," said Sarah extending a hand to the young man.

"Good morning, how can I help you?"

Sarah pulled a folded piece of paper from her bag and handed to him:

"We would like to see this book, *Secrets of Italian Cities*, by Jacques Desgranges. I looked at it a few days ago."

"One moment, please," said the employee and unexpectedly left the room in the direction opposite to the collections.

Not impressed, Willbe and Sarah passed the time by observing the grandiosity of the room around them, without knowing exactly what to say to each other. Willbe attempted to break the silence:

"Does it always take this long?"

"Not really, but I guess because of the incident with me the other day they must be *verifying* something," responded Sarah with air quotes.

"Here he comes."

"Please follow me," said the young man as he started to walk back away from the books.

*************

Sarah introduced Willbe to the man who had given her the apology letter on behalf of the New York Public Library a few days before.

"Mr. Kaminsky, this is Dr. William Benjamin Hubbard, with whom I'm collaborating in my research."

"Pleased to meet you Dr. Hubbard, it's good to have you here. As I already told Miss Mayer, she is always welcome at the Library, and I hope she has forgiven our little contretemps the other day."

"Don't worry, it's water under the bridge, as far as I'm concerned. I'm researching the rare book collection at Dr. Hubbard's request, for research that is part of his work at Columbia, so I thought you should meet him."

"Very well. How can I help you then?"

"Thank you Mr. Kaminsky. We were recently informed by an expert in rare books that the book by Jacques Desgranges, the one that nearly disappeared," added Willbe with a touch of irony "was actually dedicated *in memoriam* to one of my ancestors."

Without any irony of his own, Mr. Kaminsky exclaimed:

"An ancestor of yours? From the 16ᵗʰ century?"

His surprised reaction suggested that Willbe had said something absurd, as if he didn't know how old the book actually was.

"Actually, Mr. Kaminsky, this ancestor of mine is even older than that. From what we know he died around the end of the 14ᵗʰ century. He was one of the first European bankers of the Middle Ages, in Italy more precisely, a respected patron of arts and sciences. He was one of the founding donors of the University of Pisa. Two of his sons also became bankers and were contemporaries of the Medici in Florence and Venice in the 15ᵗʰ century."

"I don't think Mr. Kaminsky is quite so interested in your family history, Dr. Hubbard," said Sarah.

"Not at all, Miss Mayer. I have never met someone with such a distinguished family tree."

Willbe continued without missing a beat:

"But surely you have heard of the Fibonacci numbers, Mr. Kaminsky, a sequence where each term is the sum of the two previous terms?"

"Now, now, Dr. Hubbard, let's not get carried away," interjected Sarah.

"I'm sorry, Mr. Kaminsky, I tend to become overly enthusiastic about this topic, I hope you can understand. In any event, do you think we can have another look at the book? There is apparently a dedication made to this ancestor of mine in its opening pages."

The librarian avoided the gaze of the young couple in front of him for a few seconds and struck his chin in an expression of disappointment.

"It is funny how certain things happen. I'd be happy to let you spend as much time as you wish reading any other book we have here, but this particular one, right now, is impossible."

"Impossible?" exclaimed Sarah. "What do you mean?" she added with a hint of irritation.

"Please sit down."

Willbe and Sarah exchanged a look of disbelief at what they were hearing.

"Mr. Kaminsky, you said a moment ago that I would always be welcome here."

"And that is absolutely true, Miss Mayer, and this has nothing to do with what happened before. It is not at all personal. I can briefly explain and you will no doubt agree that this is just an unfortunate coincidence."

Willbe avoided looking at Sarah.

"The book you are looking for," continued Mr. Kaminsky "was requested two days ago to be put on display at the Morgan Library and

Museum for the next six months. I am certain that, with your background in library sciences, you are aware of the protocol around the public display of a rare book like that, all the security measures involved."

Sarah stared sternly back at the impassive face of the librarian.

\*\*\*\*\*\*\*\*\*\*\*\*\*

Willbe and Sarah left the Public Library and walked a few blocks towards Madison Avenue and 36th Street.

The Morgan Library and Museum is one of the most elegant museums in the world. Created at the start of the 20th century to house the private library of the legendary financier J.P. Morgan, the building, located in Murray Hill, was turned into a public institution by his son, John Pierpont Morgan Jr., in 1924.

Sarah had visited the museum for the first time when she was still a student, and had come back a few times afterwards, most recently for an exhibition of drawings by Renaissance artists. It was Willbe's first visit, but he knew it as the site of the famous "Drama at the Library", when, on a fateful November weekend in 1907, J.P. Morgan summoned the heads of other New York banks and locked them in his library for hours until they agreed to join him in committing funds to bail out some of the banks that were failing as a consequence of the panic that had started a few weeks earlier. It was not the first time that Morgan singlehandedly saved the nation's financial system, but the high-stakes drama highlighted the acute need for a better way to handle financial crises. Indeed, the episode is credited with setting in motion the creation of the Federal Reserve System a few years later.

They entered through the Madison Avenue entrance and were informed that the book they were looking for was on display in the East Room. This magnificent room, lined by three-story walnut bookshelves with painted hexagonal spandrels on the ceiling depicting the twelve signs of the zodiac, displays a selection of rare manuscripts and printed books from Morgan's original collection as well as items acquired by the museum after his death or on loan from other libraries and museums. On permanent display is one of Morgan's three copies of the 1455 Gutenberg Bible.

On their way to the East Room, Willbe asked to stop for a few minutes to admire the Rotunda, an opulent anteroom complete with marble columns and mosaic panels that was designed to impress and intimidate visitors in Morgan's day and which must have played a role in cementing the perception of his almost mythical powers. When they reached the East Room, they found the book lying on a table, enclosed by a rectangular glass case, and opened at random with two of its central pages on display.

Willbe was impressed by the dimensions of the book, with its hard cover and more than four hundred pages covered with text in fonts of legible size and with the peculiarity of being bilingual – each page had two columns with the same text, one in French, one in Italian.

"Was this the book you saw at the Public Library?"

"Given that there are only three of them in existence and apparently only one in New York, I'm sure that's the one," responded Sarah in a tone that surprised him.

"You didn't mention it was bilingual," he continued, trying to ignore her tone.

"Honestly, Willbe, it didn't catch my attention."

"Really? I wasn't aware that there were old books written in two languages."

Sarah shrugged, not hiding her discomfort with his questions. Willbe again pretended not to notice.

"It seems curious to me..."

Sarah kept her eyes fixed on the book that had been in her hands only a few days earlier and was now behind thick glass.

"Six months on public display? I have never seen something like that. It's almost like someone does not want us to read this book."

Hearing this, it was hard for Willbe not to think of his Uncle Emiliano and Professor Pfeiffer with their conspiracy theories. Or the anonymous threat warning him to stop looking for trouble in old books.

"Do you want to grab a coffee before we leave?"

"Good idea, although what I really need is something a bit stronger. This book is making me more nervous than curious."

"Nervous?"

"Yes. There's something about this whole project that is unsettling me. I seem not to be able to organize myself, I can't make a schedule for my readings. All because of an old manuscript that is apparently real and a rare book that appears to be bewitched or something."

Willbe realized that he needed to tread carefully if he wanted to keep Sarah engaged in the project, or interested in seeing him at all.

They headed to the modern-styled Morgan Café and sat down.

"Don't be upset, Sarah. We will find a way out. And besides, no matter how important, one book alone does not determine the entire outcome of a research project. We can find other sources, shortcuts for information. We're just at the beginning.

"Sure, but why on Earth has this book become so inaccessible all of a sudden?"

*************

As they were about to finish their coffees they were surprised by the friendly face of Mr. Carmona approaching their table with a broad smile.

"I thought I'd find you here," said the old man pulling up a chair. "Do you mind if I join you?"

"Not at all, please sit down Mr. Carmona," replied Willbe cleaning up some space on the table for Mr. Carmona to place his own cup of coffee.

*Mr. Carmona at the Morgan Library, how's that for a coincidence.* Willbe kept the thought to himself.

"When I heard that *Secrets of Italian Cities* had been suddenly put on display at the Morgan Library, given our conversation the other night, I imagined that you'd come here to have another look."

"Indeed, but it is going to be locked away for the next six months," observed Sarah with frustration.

"And that's why I came looking for you. As you know, there is another copy of this book permanently on display at the Querini Stampalia Foundation in Venice."

"True, but I imagine they'll have the same restrictions on seeing the book as there are here, or more, if we are to believe the reputation of Italian bureaucracy."

"You are right in that, Sarah, but I also heard that they have been digitizing a portion of their vast collection of rare books and manuscripts, and with any luck this book might be part of it."

"That would be great, but how can we find out? Should we try to contact the museum?" asked Willbe with renewed hope.

"Ah, I'm afraid in that respect Sarah's impressions of Italian bureaucracy might be true. I doubt very much that anyone there will reply to a random request from someone in New York. Your best bet would be to turn this into an excuse for a little field trip and visit the museum in person. Use some more of your Italian charm, Willbe," winked Mr. Carmona.

"That's an idea, Italy is lovely this time of the year," answered Willbe, barely disguising his excitement.

*************

They said goodbye to Mr. Carmona, who wanted to stay at the Morgan Library a bit longer, and exited the building on Madison Avenue in search of a taxi to take Willbe back uptown. Sarah was going to take the subway to the office, where she had to finish some work before the weekend.

When the traffic lights turned green and a bus left the stop where the couple was standing, a black Mercedes coming out of nowhere accelerated towards the void in the road. Willbe and Sarah instinctively jumped backwards and tripped on the metal bench, almost falling over as the car climbed onto the sidewalk, coming to within a hair's breadth of hitting them. Trying to regain balance, they watched as the Mercedes veered off back onto the road, sparkles coming off its bottom as it hit the curb in high speed, and disappeared into traffic.

"Are you alright?" asked Willbe holding Sarah's arm as she steadied herself.

"I think so... What the hell was that?"

"I have no idea," answered Willbe, aware that he was lying, but not knowing what else to say.

Some passersby who saw the whole thing stopped to ask if they were okay and remarked that New York drivers were becoming more and more aggressive each day. The couple sat at the bench for a few more minutes to let the shock pass and decided to carry on as planned, Willbe going back to his apartment and Sarah heading for work at the office.

From inside the Morgan Library, Mr. Carmona watched them through the glass doors. He dialed a private number in Japan again to report on what he had just witnessed.

# 25

## *July 1367*
## *Venice, Veneto Region – ITALY*

The next morning, after spending the night at Giuseppe's home, Friar Luigi began his journey back to the monastery in Vicenza. He was moved and comforted by Giuseppe and Cristaldi's reassurances about the threat he had received, but could not shake the anxiety that had taken hold of him. Dreams, recollections, self-pity, and guilt mixed together in his mind like a crestfallen sea breaking against cliffs. He was well aware that over the years he had placed himself in a conflict between faith and money.

*Am I a greater sinner because of this? Could one quantify sin?*

He could not comprehend how his Church, or part of it at least, could still fiercely oppose usury while being the recipient of great sums from Kings, noblemen, and rich merchants in exchange for indulgences for their sins.

*Was it possible to cover the costs of an institution like the Catholic Church merely with the offerings, donations, and proceeds from sales of artisanal and rudimentary products? How much did the Crusades cost? The wealth of the Papal States was immensurable.*

Luigi no longer knew how to respond to his own doubts. He was not in a hurry to return to the monastery. He let his mules pull the cart at their own pace. The heat was oppressive and the breeze against his face helped lessen the discomfort caused by his sweat.

*Where had the anonymous message come from? Was it from inside the monastery itself, from one of the younger monks? What was really behind it?*

He still had a few hours before arriving in Vicenza, enough time to think about the best way of confronting the situation. Suddenly, Friar Luigi pulled the reins and stopped the mules. A sharp pain in his chest forced him to do so. With effort, he managed to drive the cart to a shaded area under a tree off the road. He jumped to the back and arranged a few rags where he lay down to rest and fell asleep almost instantly.

He awoke a few hours later, disoriented under the unforgiving sun at its zenith. After composing himself he recalled the pain in his chest and realized he was halfway between Venice and Vicenza. The mules looked tired and Luigi felt bad for the animals, but demanded that they walk faster now. He had to reach the monastery in daylight.

Some six hours later Luigi arrived at the monastery, just before the sun began its retreat from the day. His mind was in such turmoil that the silence of the place unnerved him. He unharnessed the mules and brought them to stable. Their bodies were coated in sweat and foam ringed their mouths. He liked these animals and, before he returned to his room, filled two buckets with cold water and poured them on the mules' bodies. He then took them to the feeding trough and gave them alfalfa and a bit of salt.

He walked back to his room with the sensation that he was being observed, and each step he took increased the disquiet that was taking hold of his soul. He stopped at the small meditation room with the huge cross without a Christ and made the *signum crucis*. He could hear the sounds of the *Magnificat* coming from the chapel and his spirit relaxed. In his agitation, nervous for not knowing what he would face back at the monastery, he did not realize that he had arrived back in time for Vespers. As he was not expected at the service, he headed directly to his bedroom. He would pray the *Complines* before going to bed.

Convinced that he was going to find another written message passed under the door, he entered his room and lighted two candles to inspect it. All appeared normal. Although his anxiety persisted, Luigi was beginning to calm down given that his return had thus far been uneventful. Nevertheless, he decided not to join his brothers for supper.

*************

Contrary to his expectations on the ride from Venice, Luigi slept deeply that night. The fatigue from the journey, the two glasses of cold water drunk with ardor, and his relief from finding no new letters upon his return afforded him a night devoid of unpleasant dreams.

The following morning, the burning red of the horizon was slowly transformed by the rise of the yellow circle of the sun, which covered the shrubs and walls of the Franciscan monastery in an almost golden hue. The early morning silence was broken only by the chirping of birds.

A hard banging on his door woke Luigi.

"Friar Luigi, open the door!"

He did not recognize the voice, which sounded more like an order than a wakeup call. Because of that, still half asleep, he asked for a few moments to get dressed. As soon as he opened his bedroom door he was surrounded by two inquisitors.

"Friar Filippo Luigi Scoppi Minardi, come with us. We have orders to take you to the presence of the Tribunal of the Holy Office."

*************

With his head covered by a black hood with two holes through which to see, Luigi was escorted out of the monastery, walking with his hands tied in front of him and led by the horse of one of the inquisitors. He had some idea of where they were taking him, for some of the few Inquisition processes in the region had been the topic of conversation during meals at the monastery, and the rumors pointed to the dungeons of one of the churches in Vicenza.

Rituals necessitated pomp and circumstance. Not by chance, the inquisitors walked very slowly, allowing the local population to gather alongside and form a small procession behind the possibly condemned man.

Despite his sunken heart, dry mouth, and buzzing ears, Luigi still managed to walk with some dignity. This time, however, his thoughts were not aimed at his God, but his earthly friends Vitorio Giuseppe Fibonacci and Francesco Cristaldi.

## 26

*September 15, 2008*
*Ardennes Forest - BELGIUM*

M. Henry woke up early as usual and had his breakfast in the peaceful company of his cell phones and laptops, as well as the newspapers and magazines he received every morning. He was also joined by his old desktop computer, which was strategically positioned beside the breakfast table and with which he maintained a special friendship through many years and innumerable upgrades.

He tried to keep up with the pace of technological change, much of it funded and supported by the economic empire he led. But he was also beginning to feel left behind by some of the most sophisticated new developments. He refused, however, to waste time familiarizing himself with every piece of new equipment.

*Wealth and knowledge don't necessarily go together.*

For his group, wealth should always come first. His intelligence was not artificial and required physical health, wholesome habits, medical monitoring and, above all, the reclusive environment where he chose to live.

It was clear, though, that he needed to find someone younger to lead the organization. Someone brought up in the new technology, the new world; someone, as he often joked, who could think like a machine.

Among his twelve peers there was nobody under the age of fifty. The change in leadership would be a calculated yet, necessary risk.

*I'll take care of this soon.*

What was making the news that morning? In a brief synopsis, the New York Times reported on the events he had helped set in motion:

*"In one of the most dramatic days in Wall Street's history, Merrill Lynch agreed to sell itself on Sunday to Bank of America for roughly $50 billion to avert a deepening financial crisis, while another prominent securities firm, Lehman Brothers, filed for bankruptcy protection and hurtled toward liquidation after it failed to find a buyer.*

*But even as the fates of Lehman and Merrill hung in the balance, another crisis loomed as the insurance giant American International Group appeared to teeter. Staggered by losses stemming from the credit crisis, A.I.G. sought a $40 billion lifeline from the Federal Reserve, without which the company may have only days to survive."*

Most major newspapers and morning TV shows around the world covered the fall of Lehman Brothers, focusing on the fact that the bank had been left to face its own fate and was not rescued by the Federal Reserve. Many analysts considered this to be a grave error. Other suggested even more draconian measures against unscrupulous bankers.

*If nobody is punished, respect for the rules of the game disappears.*

M. Henry sat back at his comfortable chair and savored a piece of Belgian bread with myrtle berry jam.

*William Benjamin and Sarah Mayer have just left Italy this morning. Very interesting. Both so very young.*

He continued reading the Belgian and French newspapers. And he was still waiting for news from Venice.

# PART 3

*Nevertheless, nothing is more deceptive than reality itself.*

## 27

*September 15, 2008*
*Venice – ITALY*

The *questore* of Venice, Giustino Bertolli, was a professional with an extensive career in the police and justice system. His resume even boasted a stint in the security division of the *Ministero dell'interno* at the start of the government of President Carlo Ciampi. He was someone who executed his state duties with dedication and solemnity. He was approaching sixty years of age, and it was not hard to see that he took care of his appearance, with an elegant and firm posture and civilized habits that were evident as he wiped his mouth on a linen napkin before sipping from a crystal glass containing Poggerino Chianti.

Piero de Lucca did not refuse the wine on offer.

Bertolli ate locked in his office to avoid interruption. He savoured his *salmone al forno con verdura,* ordered from a nearby restaurant.

*Un uomo cortese,* thought de Lucca.

"My dear Piero, I don't have to tell you that this is another one of those delicate moments in the life of a magistrate or career officer, like you and me, where politics becomes mixed up with the interests of individuals. Times when we cannot tell at first which are the best ways forward, or when we don't really have the option to choose what we think is best."

"Mr. Bertolli, I appreciate your courtesy in inviting me for a face-to-face conversation, but I must say that it wasn't too difficult for me to figure out the reason for this meeting. Please feel free to say what you have to say."

"Of course, I know that Piero, and I thank you for your candor. I'm aware of your professionalism, your dedication to the security of Venice, and above all your sagacity. I did not call you here to give you a warning, if that idea crossed your mind."

"*Grazie tante.*"

"I called you here to let you know about an informal conversation I had with someone from the Ministry of Foreign Trade, who said that the person found near the Rialto Bridge, the Japanese fellow, was a distinguished businessman in the naval engineering sector. Apparently his business was in trouble and from the looks of it he was embarrassed and decided for the *seppuku*, you know," he paused and gestured with his knife near his abdomen.

De Lucca listened attentively to what the *questore* was saying. He had known from the first words that he was up for a good duel. And he still had no idea who was really behind the arrangements being made to cover up this case.

"And that Japan would appreciate if we could keep absolute silence about what happened," concluded Bertolli.

"Naturally, I can well understand the concerns of the Japanese government. But for him to come all the way to Venice to disembowel himself? With all due respect, sir, it seems unrealistic."

"Any other theory, Piero?"

"Hypotheses for now, Mr. Bertolli, but ones that suggest something more complicated than suicide."

"Please, Inspector, tell me your hypotheses," said Bertolli, emphasizing slightly the final word.

"It seems to me, sir, that Venice was chosen to settle some unfinished business. Why come from Japan to end one's life near the Adriatic? From what I know about Japanese culture, this doesn't make any sense. And why is the Japanese government so intent on hiding this death, especially if this was a well-known person?"

Mr. Bertolli took another sip of his Chianti while staring directly at Piero, who had now paused.

"Please continue, Piero."

"The very attempt to get rid of the body as quickly as possible, as we were instructed to do, is also typical of organized crime, of whichever origin. The facts that no documentation was found with the body and that a diplomatic passport is missing are also suspicious."

Faced with Piero's reasoning and without wanting to argue, Bertolli came up with the first platitude he could think of:

"Documents go missing all the time."

"And you, sir, have just added a new motive to my suspicions."

"I have?" a surprised *questore* perked up in his chair.

"Involuntarily, of course. But do you really think that a rich businessman in the Japanese naval industry would be in such troubles?"

"How on Earth would I know?"

"In Japan of all places, an island cut off from the rest of the world if not for air or sea travel?"

The inspector paused again, as if expecting an answer from his superior, who seemed unconvinced by the arguments he was hearing while finishing his glass of wine. He carried on:

"I could be wrong, but I don't buy this suicide story. If there's an industry that could be considered strategic for Japan I would say it is the naval industry, don't you think? And if their government is so concerned with hiding his death now, wouldn't it be easier to have helped him out of his troubles?"

Giustino Bertolli was forced to admit to himself that Inspector De Lucca's line of reasoning was compelling. However, he was there to give a message to his subordinate. He poured a little more wine in the inspector's glass.

"I'm not talking to you in an official capacity, Piero, but you must understand that it is a delicate situation that we have here."

"I understand, sir. I assure you that I will conduct my work with the utmost discretion. All the same, Venice cannot allow a murder to go unpunished, if that is what has occurred."

Bertolli nodded affirmatively.

"Agreed. I hope I can count on your understanding and cooperation, though, Inspector. We have managed to keep this from the press, so far, and I'd like to keep it that way, especially if there is a foreign connection."

"I'll do my best, sir."

*************

Piero returned to his office after his meeting with the *questore* convinced that his intuition about the Japanese man's death was well founded, and that he had to tread very carefully if he wanted to avoid jeopardizing the comfortable retirement that he was expecting in the not-so-distant future. On the other hand, if he was successful in proving that no Italian citizen had anything to do with the death of a Japanese businessman, this could make him a candidate for some honourific post in the police hierarchy of Venice or even nationally.

He had spent the weekend going through papers, materials, and his own notes about the investigation that he decided to carry on by himself if necessary. The result of the tests he had ordered on the fingerprints lifted from the wine glasses in Room 131 of the Hotel Danieli was that they did not match any records in either the local or the national electronic databases. They must belong either to a resident with no previous convictions or to a foreigner.

He could ask to have the prints checked against the Interpol database, but a request of that nature was bound to be noticed by someone in the department. He decided instead to send a photograph of the dead man, the one he had taken with his cell phone during the autopsy, to the personal email of a trusted friend at the Interpol in Milan, asking that any information on the identity of the man in the picture be sent directly to him and deleted immediately afterwards.

*************

Fifteen minutes later he received a response: an image of the same man when he was still alive, accompanied by the Interpol's file on the man. Piero locked the door of his office to read the entire document. It made reference to a diplomatic passport shown at the Venice International Airport on September 10. Something about that name - Hideo Akashiro - looked familiar.

*Of course! The initials written on the back of the Hotel Danieli card that the beautiful sales assistant at the formal wear store gave to me: H.A.*

He folded the printout, placed it inside a random book on his shelf, and wrote another email thanking his Milanese friend, emphasizing again the need for discretion and promising him a good bottle of red wine.

Piero kept the door locked and typed the man's name into his search engine. The list of suggested sites was not long, and one immediately caught his attention. There, in bold face, a news item announced **"Japanese businessman killed in airplane accident"**, with the follow up snippet: "Hideo Akashiro, one of Japan's wealthiest men ..."

*What is this about? Why are these newspapers spreading false information? Could the man have died twice?*

He laughed at his own thought.

Two other articles in the *New York Times* and the *Financial Times* reported on the crash of the Malaysian Airlines plane and illustrated the pieces with photos of the Japanese businessman. Asian newspapers covered the story in more detail.

Used to confronting the darker corners of criminal minds and investigating acts of brutal violence, Inspector de Lucca nevertheless felt a shiver run down his spine.

*What is going on here? This case is becoming stranger by the hour. These articles must have been planted to hide the truth of Akashiro's death here in Venice.*

He remembered that the guest staying at the Hotel Danieli had been planning to attend some sort of gala event on September 11, the end of the summer, when such events abounded in Venice. A simple phone call was sufficient to confirm that Querini Stampalia Foundation indeed hosted a vernissage that day for a new exhibition of Italian Renaissance painters.

Maybe the staff at the museum could identify the Japanese guest. He wrote down the address of the museum on his notebook: Campo Santa Maria Formosa, 5252.

# 28

*August 22, 2008*
*New York City – USA*

Concerned that their work together might be having an effect on their feelings for each other, Sarah and Willbe decided to take a break from research that Friday night. Timothy Geithner's trip to Washington afforded Sarah a relative respite for two or three days in the office. It was the opportunity she needed to, among other tasks, write down a timeline for the research work with Willbe.

By his turn, Willbe was becoming convinced that he needed to return to Pisa, preferably with Sarah. Mr. Carmona's suggestion about the museum in Venice only reinforced his conviction.

*The sooner the better.*

They would not have another opportunity for at least another year, for the holiday season in December was not the best time to navigate the narrow streets of Italian cities on foot or travel the roads that, incomparably beautiful in the Spring or Fall, were much less impressive in Winter, with some even closed for traffic because of heavy snowfall.

*This is an ideal moment in every respect.*

A short but irresistible trip, for Sarah would no doubt like to meet the rest of his Italian family, in particular his Uncle Emiliano with his secrets and intriguing stories.

*Does Sarah have a valid passport?*

He called, excited at the possibility of surprising her:

"Sarah?"

*"Yes"*

"Do you have a passport valid for immediate travel?"

*"Yes, I do."*

"Then let's travel to Italy!"

*"Seriously?"*

"Yes, we can go next week, what do you think?"

*"I don't know, Willbe. I need to check with work. I do have vacation time, but I can't just drop everything and travel to Europe all of a sudden."*

"We can come up with a reason. Tickets are on me. My family would love to meet you. We can plan during the weekend."

*"You academics sometimes don't get it, do you? I can't just come up with something... They need to authorize me or I can lose my job."*

"Alright, we can talk about it tomorrow after our visit to Professor Pfeiffer, remember? He was adamant that you come too, I was even a little jealous..."

*"Oh please, don't be silly."*

"I know, I'm just joking. But he is expecting us tomorrow evening. I told him I'd confirm with you. Can I pick you up around five thirty?"

*"Yes, that's fine. We'll talk more about this trip then."*

"Great, see you tomorrow."

Willbe hung up, his heart racing and a smile on his face as he imagined Sarah looking puzzled at her desk at work, still with the cell phone in her hand. Surprised with his own proposal, he let himself fall on the sofa and began daydreaming about romantic nights and wonderful sex on the Adriatic coast.

*American Air Lines or Alitalia?*

His maternal ancestry spoke louder. He opened his laptop and searched for the Alitalia website. The next available ticket at a reasonable price was for Wednesday, September 3.

He then dialed Professor Pfeiffer's number.

*Something tells me this trip will change my life.*

# 29

*July, 1367*
*Venice, Veneto Region - ITALY*

Giuseppe could not fathom the news of Luigi's arrest.
*How will my friend defend himself before the Tribunal of the Holy Office against accusations of heresy and usury?*

Different types of currency had circulated in Europe for centuries now. Money changed hands and was routinely used for a variety of purposes, sometimes even donated to the Church, which kept accumulating wealth as time passed. Borrowing and lending had become common practice and he could not recall anyone in Vicenza who had been accused of usury in living memory.

Despite its power, and perhaps because of it, it would be prudent for the Church to stop torturing and murdering people for these practices, considering how much the world was changing. Individual confessions, remission, indulgences, the invention of purgatory, these were all innovations of the Church intended to lighten its burden and help it adapt to new times.

*On what grounds did they arrest Luigi? Do they have any proof of heresy? Surely not. Proof of usury? Hardly, as Luigi did not sign any documents for the bank. Was his crime to be friends with bankers? How many other clergymen were, too?*

It was common knowledge in Italy that the Franciscans and Dominicans were ardent defenders of the Inquisition, and the way Giuseppe saw it, the arrest of Luigi had all the markings of a treacherous plot inside the Vicenza monastery.

*Luigi's partnership in the banking house was kept strictly secret.*

His pledge to defend Luigi was now being put to the test, and Giuseppe was a man of his word. Everybody knew the methods used by the Holy Office when they wanted to extract a confession from an accused person. Especially when there was no concrete proof, as in cases of witchcraft and demonic possession.

Luigi was not a heretic in either words or actions. He was a believer and practiced his religion with dedication, especially the tasks that were given to him at the monastery.

Giuseppe recalled the day he travelled from Pisa to Vicenza to talk to Luigi about the possibility of opening a banking house. He thought about the concerns and doubts he raised about the new role of money in commercial relationships in Europe and overseas.

*And to think how different our lives are now, only a few years later. Man was not created to live imprisoned, and much less to have the sword, or worse, the cross of the Church, hanging above his head.*

The news of the arrest and execution of the Knights Templar in France under the reign of Philip IV had shown that not even the defenders of the Inquisition were safe from accusations of heresy, most of them baseless.

*How can one prove or disprove a person's faith?*

The subjectivity of this question often resulted in sentences of imprisonment, torture, and death.

Rumored to be a descendant of a Knight Templar himself, Luigi could not count on any benevolence from the Holy Office, despite being a Franciscan. Sin was unpardonable whether or not it was committed by men of the Church.

In time, heresy would no longer be considered the most severe crime against the Church. Nevertheless, a taste for purity and the temptation of the power to control millions of souls had taken hold of the most reactionary factions of Catholicism of the day, resulting in a surge in torture and public executions.

*Was this in the interest of an institution that preached love and charity? The discourse of humility did not go hand-in-hand with the practice of violence and arrogance.*

Giuseppe was readying himself to defend Luigi. He had to be prepared for a duel of ideas. Was he afraid of the Inquisition? Not at all. With his hundreds of thousands of florins, land, and property spread through Tuscany and Veneto, ships moving in and out of the port of Venice, he had learned the real meaning of money. And the power it conferred on those who had it in great quantities. Not even the Church was above this power.

He knew what to do and the path he had to follow. First, a frank conversation with Cristaldi, during which it would be agreed that the former mercenary would officially come forward as a witness in defense of Luigi.

*What risks do we face before the greedy eyes of the Church?*

He would put into practice his theory that money wields the real power.

Next he would have to gather details regarding the accusations leveled against Luigi. Finally, and no less importantly, he would need to discover which ecclesiastical authority was in charge of the trial.

Though he was not the only banker in Italy, much less in Europe, Giuseppe knew that his fortune was a valuable trump card in what was ultimately a game of power and intimidation. He was not afraid of the Holy Office, and did not believe in Heaven or Hell.

Nevertheless, he thought it prudent, and let Cristaldi know this, to search the drawer of his desk at home for the contract signed by Luigi and burn it without leaving any trace of it.

*You can never be too careful with the Inquisition. Besides, my word is worth more than any piece of paper.*

# 30

*September 15, 2008*
*Ardennes Forest – BELGIUM*

M. Henry felt relieved by the plan put into motion to tame the crisis that threatened to spiral out of control that weekend. He was also a vigilant man, though, and spent his Monday reading news reports on how the world was reacting to the measures taken.

The message from Rome that mentioned "mailbox number 3" referred to two topics of distinct origins. The first indicated a low level threat that could be resolved in a couple of hours with two or three phone calls and emails. The second topic was potentially more serious. The message simply showed copies of the identification pages of American passports for two passengers who had entered Italy through the Bologna Airport exactly ten days before and who had just left the country through Venice. He saved the image in an encrypted file and deleted the message.

The fallout from the Lehman Brothers bankruptcy would take up most of his time in the next couple of weeks, but he was convinced that the worst was over, even though markets would continue to be turbulent for many months to come.

*Although there is always the chance of a reawakening of the factors that led to disaster in the past, it looked like this was not the case now. One should always remember 1929 and its lessons. The world was different now, but ... and there was always a 'but' waiting around the corner.*

In the chess game running inside his head, he was already calculating many moves ahead, particularly concerning the U.S. presidential elections coming up in November. In Washington and around the country there was considerable tension, for this was no ordinary election. Voters were optimistic about a change in leadership after eight years under President Bush, but there was also fear around the deteriorating economy and the lack of clarity in what the two rival candidates would do about it. Barack Obama seemed to have a lead with his "Yes, we can" message, but John McCain could not be dismissed. What exactly each candidate would do about the economic downturn remained unclear.

Strictly speaking, M. Henry did not have a preference for either candidate. He had no doubt that whoever won would do what was necessary to protect the economy, and he had ways to ensure that this included protecting his interests. A prolonged recession seemed to be the worst possible outcome.

*But how much money would be necessary to pull the country out of a recession?*

Money begets money, and both McCain and Obama knew that. All that the president-elect would need was sound advice to let him know at short notice the amount that would be necessary to stimulate the economy, and where to find the funds.

The brotherhood would have all the numbers ready. It was part of their preparations for election years in the countries most important for the world economy.

M. Henry was prescient, meticulous, and patient.

*Rapid transformation, rapid solutions. Was contemporary society ready for this? Was the world economy ready?*

He returned to the computer and searched for the encrypted message with the image taken from the passport of William Benjamin Fibonacci Hubbard.

*What would be the best way to make contact now that he was back in New York? Perhaps he could use the Belgian vice-consul again.*

# 31

*August 23, 2008*
*New York City – USA*

Donald Pfeiffer lived in a comfortable apartment on the top floor of a building on the corner of 3rd Avenue and 83rd Street, with a view of Central Park from the balcony.

Sarah and Willbe were punctual and carried with them a bottle of a Tuscan wine - a 2007 Barbi Brunello - to give to their host.

"Do you remember this wine, Professor? You were introduced to it in Pisa in a restaurant called Peperoncino."

"Of course I remember! Some of the students took me out for dinner, Sarah. I must say I did not recall the name of wine, but I will never forget the special they had that day, *filleto di pesce* with tomatoes and olive oil, I think. Delicious."

"*Pomodorini e olive*," translated Willbe.

"That's it," exclaimed Professor Pfeiffer, "*pomodorini e olive*. Very good gastronomical memory you have, too, an absolutely divine dish. But please, come in and make yourselves comfortable."

In the living room, an elegantly dressed lady awaited the guests.

"This is my wife, Mathilde," he said to Willbe and Sarah, "and these are William Benjamin, who I met in Pisa last year and is now my new colleague at Columbia..."

The professor paused for a few seconds to kiss Sarah's hand and continued:

"And this is Sarah, his enchanting research companion."

They all greeted one another.

"Thus, end the formalities for the evening," announced Donald Pfeiffer.

Two hours later, with the discussion having moved through a broad range of topics, Sarah found herself fascinated by Professor Pfeiffer.

"Donald, do you mind if I make a somewhat odd comment?"

Willbe looked intrigued by Sarah's question.

"Of course not, Sarah, comment away. Knowledge is often built on odd thoughts," replied Professor Pfeiffer with a mischievous glance at Willbe.

"It's just that you are so knowledgeable and enthusiastic about the history of our country that I wonder why you chose mathematics as a career, and not history or political sciences, for example."

"That is a good question. I can tell you from the outset that deductive thinking, involving abstractions as it is normally done in mathematics, it's not entirely compatible with the fluidity of historical facts, and even less so with politics, where two plus two is often not equal to four. I think this contradiction attracts me, but I wouldn't mix the subjects at a professional level. I'm more suited to being a professional mathematician and armchair political theorist than the other way around."

"I'd say you are a bit more than an armchair political theorist," offered Willbe. "Your interpretation of the September 11 attacks, for example, is downright frightening, if proved correct."

"Has William told you about this, Sarah?"

"Only briefly."

Mathilde Pfeiffer got up and winked at Sarah:

"I'm going to make coffee and tea to bring out with the cake. I'll come back in about twenty minutes. That's about as much time as Donald needs to get started on this topic."

"Can I give you a hand?" asked Sarah more out of politeness than lack of interest in what Donald Pfeiffer had to say.

"Don't worry, my dear, I've got this. You stay and listen to Donald; I know where the conversation is going from here."

The professor shook his head and smiled tenderly at his wife's remarks.

"Don't believe everything Mathilde says, she also loves political gossip."

"Again, I'd not call your theories that. It sounds like you've given a lot more thought to them than if you were just gossiping," reasserted Willbe.

"True, that's the mathematician in me, I guess I can't help trying to be systematic."

Sarah seemed to agree with a nod.

"What about this looming economic crisis?" asked Willbe.

"Well that's exactly the topic of this op-ed I'm writing for the *Financial Times*. Economic crises are often described as unpredictable, but they do follow a certain pattern."

"You mean they can be detected by looking at stock price movements and indicators like that?"

"That's what economists and mathematicians tend to focus on when they talk about bubbles, to see if there's anything abnormal in the prices themselves, if they are not in line with what they call *fundamentals*. I have done work on this myself, as you know, Willbe."

"I certainly do, but I have a feeling you are about to tell me something different now."

"Yes, you see, focusing on prices, either of stocks, or houses, or whatever, is a bit too narrow. There are other variables one ought to be monitoring."

"Such as?" asked Sarah, making every effort to follow a conversation that she knew was important to Willbe.

"How much easy money is there in the system, for example? And I don't just mean the money that is provided by central banks, as one often reads in the financial press. I'm talking about money that is created by other agents."

"I'm confused now, Donald, I thought only the government could print money. Otherwise it would be counterfeit, no?"

"Ah, yes Sarah, I'm very glad you mention this, because it is one of the most fundamental misconceptions in all of economics," replied a radiant Professor Pfeiffer, who continued:

"Of course, only the government can print pieces of paper with the faces of dead presidents on them, but that's not the only type of money there is."

"It isn't?" now even Willbe was a bit perplexed.

"Absolutely not! When was the last time you actually used bills to pay for anything? I'm willing to bet that you used your debit card to pay for that bottle of wine you brought here tonight."

"Yes, I did. But I had the money in my bank account."

"Precisely, you had *money* in your bank account, not printed dollar bills. You see, the bank had a record of the size of your bank account before you bought the wine. When you used your debit card, all that it did was to decrease your account by the price of the wine and increase the account of the liquor store owner by the same amount."

"True," said Willbe, suddenly remembering how much the wine cost and trying not to think what the balance on his account was after purchasing it, "but I had to deposit my postdoc stipend from Columbia in my bank account to begin with. I still don't see how this was *created* by the bank".

"Very good! But do you think *everyone* first makes a deposit and then goes on spending? For example, when your parents bought their house back in Connecticut, did they wait year after year to deposit their salaries, saving a little bit each month, until they could pay for the house?"

"Well, no, they took a mortgage, like most people."

"Exactly! And where do you think the money for that mortgage came from? Sarah, want to guess here?" teased Professor Pfeiffer, trying to keep her interested in the exchange.

"Hmm, from the other clients of the bank, I suppose," she guessed.

"So you think his parents' bank had a pile of cash deposited by other clients and kept it stored away in a vault until people walked into the branch and asked for a mortgage? That sounds a bit inefficient, doesn't it?"

"It does... But how else would they find the money to lend to his parents?"

"Excellent point! And that's precisely what is so hard to understand about money. You see, people think it is something physical, like bicycles. Surely if you are going to lend bicycles you need to have the bicycles first, right?"

"Right," both Willbe and Sarah agreed.

"But that's not the case with money at all. Here's what happened when Willbe's parents asked for a mortgage to buy a house. The bank checked that they were creditworthy and decided to give them a loan. But they didn't use cash that was sitting in their vault or called their existing clients to see who would like to deposit some more money so they could lend it to this lovely couple."

"No?" risked Sarah.

"No, they simply increased the couple's bank account with an amount equal to the value of the loan, just like when Willbe bought the bottle of wine and the liquor store owner had his bank account increased."

"Now hold on a second," protested Sarah much to Willbe's surprise. "You said in the wine example that Willbe's account would decrease by the same amount," she continued, as Willbe tried to forget the amount that had been deducted a few hours earlier. "In this mortgage example, whose bank account goes down?"

"Nobody's does, and that's the magic."

"But that's cheating! The bank can't just increase the amount in one account without any consequence."

"You are absolutely right Sarah, but they didn't do that."

"But you just said that nobody's balance had to go down for his parents' balance to go up," contended Sarah, slighted exasperated.

"Yes, I did say that. But that doesn't mean there were no consequences. What happened was that the increase in his parents' bank account, which you should think as a liability for the bank, or in other words, an amount that the bank owes to his parents, is matched one-to-one by an increase in the assets of the bank. In other words, the loan that his parents now must repay the bank one day. It's a procedure called double-entry bookkeeping, and was actually perfected in Medieval Italy, as were most things related to modern banking."

The unexpected reference to a time and place that had been so fresh in their minds for the last few days shocked Willbe and Sarah.

Mathilde Pfeiffer returned to the dining room carrying a tray.

"Dessert, anyone?"

# 32

*August, 1367*
*Venice, Veneto Region - ITALY*

In the company of his youngest son Tommaso and a servant who was cleaning the office, Cristaldi tried to hide his anxiety by pretending to read some notes on the temporary measures he had put into place during Luigi's imprisonment, which had now lasted for three weeks.

The young Tommaso had been employed as an emergency solution, since Gianpaolo Fibonacci, as agreed, was to follow his father wherever he went. In his quest to win over the religious bureaucracy, in particular the Dominican friars in a position of power around the Veneto region, Giuseppe recruited the help of his older son, whose youth and physical strength could be put to use if the need arose.

Contrary to his partner, Cristaldi was still bound to the teachings of Christianity, not entirely because of actual faith, but by a cautious attitude that saw no harm in believing in a God that might not exist, whereas the alternative could lead to a lot more trouble. Even though a variety of earthly concerns occupy most of his daily life, the question of Hell still assailed him from time-to-time, and the thought of what was happening to Luigi compounded his agony.

The tempestuous entrance of Giuseppe and Gianpaolo into the office interrupted his thoughts:

"We need two thousand florins, Cristaldi. That's the price for Luigi's freedom, and we need to pay it now, before they take him to trial."

"Are you serious?"

"I have never been more serious in all my life. Stand up my friend, we need to collect payment on the bills of trade we discounted for some of the merchants here in Venice, see how much we can get back on short notice and, if needed, take some gold out of the vault to make up the full amount."

"And to whom are we paying this amount?"

"I offer you a bottle of the best wine in the Veneto if you can guess it..."

"Someone from the Holy Office?"

"Indirectly, yes..." Turning to the two young men, he continued:

"Gianpaolo, Tommaso, compute the interest the merchants will save on the promissory notes by paying them back early, and don't forget to record everything in the book. Do exactly like Luigi taught you, two entries for each transaction, in two separate columns, so they match and the book is still balanced."

"Does this indirect someone have a name?" insisted Cristaldi.

"It is best we don't speak of names, but I can tell you he is a cardinal."

"A cardinal?"

"Why the surprise, Cristaldi? The Church knows very well how to take care of finances."

\*\*\*\*\*\*\*\*\*\*\*\*\*

Giuseppe had laughed when he was informed of the place where he was to deliver the two thousand florins that would stop formal proceedings being initiated against Luigi: it was the tranquil meditation room of the monastery in Vicenza where hung the enormous wooden cross without a Christ figure.

Intramural and discreet. Due to the circumstances, the case now had to be treated with utmost secrecy. God and the Devil watching them in a bare monastery room. There, in the presence of the abbot of the monastery, the cardinal representing the Holy Office, and the young Gianpaolo as a witness, Luigi would profess his confession and repentance aloud. He would then be declared innocent and receive an absolution signed by Pope Urban V. With the ritual completed, Giuseppe would hand the Inquisitor the amount agreed upon for the *indulgence* received.

And that is how it was done.

After the authorities left the meditation room, a visibly weak Luigi, thin and disheveled, shuffled towards Giuseppe with open arms and tears rolling down his bony face. The embrace remained an intention only, for Luigi collapsed under the weight of physical and emotional exhaustion as he reached his friend.

Giuseppe and Gianpaolo helped the friar down onto the wooden bench, his eyes closed. Giuseppe rubbed his wrists while Gianpaolo went looking for a mug of fresh water. Luigi gradually returned to them and, for the first time in all the years he had known Giuseppe, saw two small tears forming in the eyes of his friend and partner.

"You were right, Giuseppe. Right here in this very same room, do you remember? With the purpose of opening a bank you tried to convince me of the power of money. Money was becoming a new god, you said..."

"Yes, I remember that evening very well."

"A god that just freed me from the claws of the Inquisition. I don't understand what is going on anymore, Giuseppe."

"Rest, Luigi. Let us not talk about this now. We are going to take you to my house and Marinella will take good care of you."

With the help of his son, Giuseppe made Luigi sit up on the bench and drink the water in the mug.

# 33

*September 16, 2008*
*Venice – ITALY*

M r. Bertolli was not overly enthusiastic about Piero de Lucca's invitation to join him for an early evening drink. Not because of the pleasantry per se, even though he did not think they were close enough to socialize outside of work. Piero's voice on the phone had a contrarian tone to it, which suggested to the *questore* that whatever his personal feelings on the matter, he had better see what the Inspector wanted.

The meeting place, Osteria Al Squero, was not very busy on a Tuesday, and Piero liked to unwind there at the end of the afternoon. He offered to take the *questore* there on his police speedboat and emphasized that the meeting would not take more than an hour, perhaps less.

On the way there, the inspector updated his superior on what he had been doing in the last 24 hours, deliberately leaving out the name of his Milanese friend who had helped him identify Hideo Akashiro. Mr. Bertolli's expression after listening to the brief report was far from reassuring.

The *osteria* was not very far from the Grand Canal, where the incident that motivated the second meeting between these two gentlemen in as many days had occurred. Piero had reserved two seats by the counter, as far from the front entrance as possible, with their backs to the large glass windows. He thought this would be enough to avoid drawing the attention of any curious customer, not so much to the conversation itself, which would be conducted in the appropriate tone and language, but to the documents he carried in his briefcase.

They could choose from several Venetian *cicchetti* - snacks freshly prepared for cocktail hour all around the city - and ordered a *baccala mantecato,* a creamy salt cod spread, accompanied by a selection of *panini, crostini,* and two Campari spritz.

The weather was still mild at the end of the summer, but the two men were dressed in the manner of officials of their rank, in suit and tie, with Piero carrying a black leather briefcase attached to his wrist by a small silver chain.

He opened the briefcase and discreetly took out papers and photographs one-by-one, sufficiently slowly that the *questore* could take a good look at each of them before he started his short speech on the need to clear the City of Venice of any responsibility for this incident.

The *questore* silently examined the documents one more time. After looking over the last one, which unequivocally identified the dead person as Hideo Akashiro, he took another sip of his Campari and asked Piero without any hint of emotion:

"What do you intend to do with this material?"

"That is the reason I asked to meet with you, *questore*. I have some ideas on what to do, but I wanted to consult with you first."

Giustino Bertolli did not know he was being recorded.

"As I mentioned to you before, our government's first priority is to avoid problems with Japan. The fact that he was a successful businessman in the naval industry, as it seems to be confirmed by these documents, corroborates to a certain extent the doubts you expressed the other day about his being in financial distress. Another possibility is perhaps some link with the Japanese security apparatus, which would make things even more difficult for us."

"But if that were the case, the Japanese ought to have informed us about his presence in Venice, no?"

"Certainly. And this seems to be an additional little mystery for us."

"You call this a little mystery? What if the Japanese media finds out that Hideo Akashiro was not in fact killed in a plane crash? That he was instead fatally wounded by a Japanese katana in Venice and given an indigent burial in an Italian cemetery? Would they also keep it a secret?"

"My dear Piero, at this point there is no way I can answer your questions. I tell you what though: give me 24 hours and we will talk again. This might be a bigger problem than you and I can imagine."

Mr. Bertolli drank the rest of his Campari without looking directly at Piero.

# 34

*August 23, 2008*
*New York City – USA*

"**S**o what did I miss? Any outlandish theories this evening?" asked Mathilde as she distributed generous portions of cake and ice cream around the table.

"Hardly, my darling Mathilde, I was simply introducing William and Sarah to some arcane concepts in accounting," joked the professor.

"I wouldn't call them arcane, more like mind-boggling, really. Makes you think that all of economics, or at least all of banking, is merely based on the debts owed to each other."

"You would not be too far from the truth there, Sarah. And bankers have always been acutely aware that trust is a big part of their business, from their Italian origins to the present."

Willbe felt instinctively defensive at the mention of Italian bankers and attempted to steer the conversation away from the topic:

"I'm still a bit confused about what all this money-creating business has to do with economic crises, which is how we began this conversation."

"That's the interesting part. As I was saying, one should look at more than stock prices to understand financial crises."

Mathilde knew that her husband was about to embark on one of his favourite topics and that she had a brief window of opportunity:

"Who's having tea and who's having coffee?"

Sarah and Donald picked coffee, Willbe and herself were having tea.

"The key variable is the supply of credit, which can be quite flexible, as we were just discussing."

"And why is that key?" asked Sarah, sensing that she was about to hear something to which the professor had given a great deal of thought.

"Because the supply of credit tends to increase in good times and contract in bad times. So when the economy is booming, people borrow more and faster than the pace at which the economy is increasing."

"Sounds reasonable, everyone feels optimistic, so they don't mind borrowing to buy new things," remarked Willbe.

"Exactly," continued the professor, "the problem is that the extra money cannot be used only to 'buy new things', as you just said."

"I'm lost again," sighed Sarah, turning her attention momentarily to her dessert. "Earlier I couldn't understand where the new money was coming from, and now I don't quite see where it is going."

"Well, these are two sides of the same problem. Yin and yang one might even say," replied Donald Pfeiffer with a wink to his wife.

"Ok then, so where does the extra money go?"

"Think a bit harder, Willbe, you almost gave the answer yourself. If the supply of credit expands faster than the economy, which already includes all of the 'new things' that people can buy, what can the extra credit be used for?"

"To purchase existing assets!" exclaimed Willbe suddenly getting the point the professor was trying to make.

"That's it! And examples of the 'existing assets' that Willbe just mentioned, Sarah, are things like stocks, real estate, artwork, etc. In other words, objects of speculation, whose prices keep going up fueled by more and more borrowers using extra credit to buy them from each other."

"Now that's quite the theory."

"Yes, but sadly for me, it is not my theory, Sarah, but that of a man called Hyman Minsky. Perhaps you've heard of the name, people have been calling what's happening in the world economy now a 'Minsky moment'."

"Yes, I have seen the term in the financial press. Is he quite well-known?"

"He was a force to be reckoned with. I attended some of his seminars towards the end of his career here at Bard College in New York and even got to have some conversations with him. I'm afraid mainstream economists mostly neglected his work, although I have a feeling this will soon change. What I just described to you is the first half of what he called the 'Financial Instability Hypothesis'. Between us, I think he called it that to poke fun at the 'Efficient Market Hypothesis'."

"What's the second half?"

"It's more or less the time reversal of what I just said, Willbe, what happens on the way down, so to speak."

"You mean when credit contracts and the bubbles burst?" asked Willbe.

"Exactly. Eventually something triggers a decline, a loss of confidence that prices will keep rising. And what you must keep in mind is that, in the same way that prices rise at breakneck speed in the euphoric phase of credit expansion, when they start dropping there's a veritable stampede, with all those borrowers trying to sell the speculative asset at the same time. The mania is replaced by a panic, leading to the inexorable crash."

"So it could be anything that triggers a collapse?" asked Sarah.

"Ah," Mathilde interjected ironically.

"My beloved wife knows me too well. Unlike some others who have investigated this question, I don't think the triggers are quite as unpredictable or random as they sometimes appear to be. Are you familiar with the Dutch Tulip mania of the 17th century?"

"Not specifically," answered Sarah, "apart from the fact that some people apparently paid more for a single flower than the price of an entire house, isn't that right?"

"Not exactly. You see, what the speculators were buying and selling were actually future contracts on tulip bulbs, not the flowers themselves. The most euphoric phases of the bubble took place in the winter of 1636-37, when the bulbs in question were firmly underground."

"I see."

"But that's a minor detail. The important bit is that the episode fits the Minsky model like a glove, especially the fact that most of the trade took place in Amsterdam taverns, or what they called 'colleges', with speculators using credit provided by the owners of the taverns to bid on the tulip contracts. In other words, drinking credit played the role of bank credit!"

"I didn't know that, it's quite funny."

"But that's not all. Nobody can know for sure what triggered the collapse in price of tulip futures, but one hypothesis is that proper tulip merchants, you know, as opposed to the drunken speculators, started handing out satirical pamphlets outside the taverns, warning people of the dangers of speculative investment."

"You are joking!"

"Not at all, they *wanted* to push the price down and end the party."

"Why?"

"Because it was bad for the legitimate tulip business to have all this amateur speculation going on."

"I suppose."

"And a similar pattern can be seen in other more recent episodes. The point is that in every major bubble in history, the trigger event looks very suspicious."

"Here we go," smiled Mathilde.

"It's almost," continued Professor Pfeiffer, "as if in each case the people in charge, you know, the captains of the economy, *wanted* the bubble to burst at a specific moment."

"The people in charge?" asked an incredulous Willbe.

"You believe a group of people are in charge of the world economy?" complemented Sarah timidly.

"You don't? When I question the links between the Bush family, for example, and the Saudi oil oligarchies people say that I'm a conspiracy theorist. But so what?"

"*Et voilà!*" exclaimed a satisfied Mathilde.

A small reflective silence descended upon the group after they stopped laughing at Mathilde's victorious exclamation. Willbe took advantage of it:

"Speaking of conspiracy theories, Professor, do you believe we are being monitored, that regular American citizens are being watched by the United States government? Say through wire-tapping, for example?"

"Without a doubt, my dear friend!"

Willbe, who up to that moment had not decided if he should tell Sarah about the phone call he received a few days earlier, felt his heart beat faster with the prospect of doing so now.

The episode, touching on a topic evidently dear to the host, could be subjected to his good-humoured yet, precise analysis. On the other hand, he would have to face a delicate situation with Sarah, who also seemed to be interested in the topic:

"Do you know of any specific instance of monitoring by the government? Are we really being watched by the national security apparatus in our daily lives?"

"I have no doubt about it, Sarah. I could talk for hours about the evidence confirming my convictions."

While she was intrigued by the change of focus, Sarah found Willbe's question slightly odd.

"Where does this suspicion come from, Willbe?"

"Well, here's the thing..."

Willbe adjusted himself on his chair, slightly insecure.

*************

Sarah was having trouble digesting the fruitcake and coffee she had just finished as she listened to Professor Pfeiffer talk about state surveillance conducted by the American government.

For her, hearing the surprising story told by Willbe about the anonymous phone call he had received was like being punched in the stomach.

"You never told me about this phone call, Willbe."

Feeling embarrassed and avoiding Sarah's direct gaze, Willbe tried to minimize the importance of the call, which in a way contradicted his keen interest in what Donald Pfeiffer had to say about national security. He knew, however, that Sarah was going to catch the inconsistency.

"It's just that I didn't think it was that important when it happened."

Professor Pfeiffer, sensitive to the faint atmosphere of discomfort that had entered the room, tried to diffuse it the best way he could:

"I would not think it was too important either, to be honest. Unless I'm mistaken, nobody connected to national security has ever threatened someone trying to read old books."

"And what about what happened at the Morgan Library, Willbe? You didn't think it could be connected to the threat? We were there looking for Desgranges' book after all."

"What happened at the Morgan Library?" asked Mathilde.

"Some lunatic driver trying to beat traffic almost ran us over on the sidewalk", answered Willbe in the most matter-of-fact manner he could muster.

"I thought that's what had happened, but hearing about this phone call changes everything."

Willbe knew she had a point, and he had not even mentioned the men he noticed watching them at the Bryant Park Café.

"It seems to me," started Donald Pfeiffer straightening himself up in his chair, "that the only way the phone call and the out-of-control car could be connected is if someone with a lot of resources is really watching your every move. But why?"

"That's what I'd like to know!" declared Sarah, looking less than amused.

Willbe regretted even more not having told Sarah about the call. He felt he was losing his grip on the situation, if he ever had had it:

"We need to be rational here. Unless we uncover more evidence, the most likely explanation is that the phone call and the incident at the library are indeed disconnected."

"Spoken like a true Bayesian, William Benjamin..." It had been clear throughout the evening that Donald Pfeiffer didn't like nicknames.

Sarah did not know who Bayes was, but she already disliked him.

"Tell us more about your time in Italy, Professor..." asked Willbe in a last-ditch attempt to move the conversation away from the unpleasant topic.

# 35

*August, 1367*
*Venice, Veneto Region - ITALY*

Friar Luigi, whose treatment at the hands of his tormenters in the Holy Office had not escalated to irreparable levels only because of the action taken by his friends during his incarceration, used the days he spent recovering at Giuseppe Fibonacci's house in Venice to reflect on his religious life, comparing what he had just experienced with the teachings of Christ, and considering the virtues of a simple life without sin.

*Why did I decide to become a clergyman?*

The question, raised many times before in his life, had always been answered with the firm conviction that serving had made him a more just and compassionate man.

Sitting comfortably against the cushions on a chair in the living room and absorbed in his thoughts, Friar Luigi did not notice when Marinella Fibonacci entered the room bringing the wild mint tea that he loved. He motioned to rise.

"Don't stand up Luigi, stay where you are. Just sit up straight so you can drink your tea. How are you feeling?"

"Thank you, Marinella, thank you so much. I don't know what would become of me without all that you and your husband are doing."

"Now, Luigi, don't exaggerate. And what you have done for us, do you forget that?"

"Allow me to say, Marinella, that you married an honourable man with a good heart. He was true to his word, and then some. I was even more impressed to see Gianpaolo by his side, helping him in anything he needed."

"You can't imagine how happy he is, Luigi, to be able to accompany his father and work alongside him. He can't hide his pleasure. His brothers are beginning to feel jealous."

"It is only natural; I'd be jealous too."

"They will help when it is their time. Giuseppe has plans for each of his children. You know him well; he would not have it any other way."

"It is I who have no plans any more, Marinella... After this experience with the Inquisition, I no longer know what to think."

"What are you trying to say, Luigi?"

"I'm not sure any longer, Marinella."

"I can see that your heart has more to say."

"Not that much more, but there is one thing in particular that is bothering me, torturing me in a way that not even the Inquisitors could accomplish."

"Then let it out, that's all you need to do. Otherwise, you will begin a long journey towards insanity."

"I'm not sure I'm ready to say it, or that you are ready to hear it."

"A woman is always ready to hear the worst, Luigi. Speak your heart."

Friar Luigi, still reluctant, finished his mint tea, returned the cup to the tray brought by his host, and leaned back against the cushions again:

"Marinella, I beg for your forgiveness for what I'm about to say."

He fell silent.

"Be brave Luigi, whatever it is, the world is not going to end because of it."

"I no longer believe in the Roman Catholic Church." Closing his eyes as if to gather the necessary courage, he completed his confession:

"I don't know whether I believe in God anymore."

# 36

*September 18, 2008*
*Ardennes Forest – BELGIUM*

M. Henry stared intently at the screen of his laptop, which displayed the results of the annual tests ordered by his personal doctor. Heart, lungs, kidneys, liver, blood, and lately prostate, everything examined in detail. He intended to live for as long as science, and wealth, permitted.

The bankruptcy declaration by Lehman Brothers on Monday had initiated a chain reaction of global panic exactly as M. Henry's peers had predicted at their weekend meeting in Brussels. The next two days saw unprecedented withdrawals from money market funds – a modern version of the runs that periodically plagued banks before governments started the practice of deposit insurance in the aftermath of the 1930s panic. Similarly sweeping action by the government was needed in the current crisis, and on Wednesday the Federal Reserve announced a record 85 billion-dollar loan to AIG to avoid bankruptcy. That, too, was part of the plan, and M. Henry could not help but chuckle at the sight of top government officials having to explain on television why AIG was different from Lehman.

Contrary to what people who did not know him well might think, he was not a greedy or ostentatious person. For example, having a private jet ready to take him anywhere in the world at short notice was not a luxury, but a necessity of his position. Part of his fortune was donated anonymously to universities, research institutes, hospitals, and schools in poor countries.

*It only makes sense to possess immense wealth if one can use it to create and enjoy the best the world can offer.*

Good health, for example, or trips to exotic places: to visit the tropics in winter and the polar regions in summer; to walk calmly down a cobbled street in Quebec City one weekend and through a park in St. Petersburg the next. Watching big game in Africa or a show of *fado* in the Bairro Alto in Lisbon. Or what gave him the most pleasure of all: spend a week in the high seas in the company of good music and books. Or again, simply have breakfast in the Belgian Ardennes, as he had just done. All of it without being recognized or bothered.

M. Henry missed his wife, who for forty years had helped him in countless ways both personal and professional, always full of energy and with her acute sense for detecting problems where no one else expected them. Above all, she understood his role and never made the slightest mistake in respect of their safety.

He was interrupted by a call from Rome. The same code as before, now with additional information about the investigation being conducted by a police officer in Venice. Disobeying orders from his superiors, this inspector had just found out that Hideo Akashiro had been killed in Venice and not in a plane crash in the Pacific.

M. Henry calmly resumed the reading of his medical results and tried to imagine what his wife would have said if she had been there to know about this little hiccup in Venice. The results of the tests for glucose and the various types of cholesterol were well within the acceptable ranges for a man of his age, as were blood pressure and PSA. The twelve pages of test results ended with a handwritten note signed by his doctor saying that he had the heart of a young man. He printed the report and stored it in a hanging folder in the right drawer under his desk. He then opened the left drawer and searched for a small silver key.

He rose and walked towards one of the bookshelves in his magnificent library, removed two books and pressed a small button revealed by the gap. A small section of the bookshelf rotated anticlockwise by ninety degrees, creating just enough space for one person to walk through.

He used the silver key to unlock the door that appeared in front of him. It was rare that he used this expedient – to isolate himself even deeper inside his already secure workspace – but sometimes the situation required it. He closed the door behind him, triggering the bookshelf to return to its normal position.

He needed to make a quick decision about the possibility that a police investigation in Italy could create an embarrassment for his business or a security breach, however small, for his organization.

The news of the airplane crash, with the planted information that the Japanese businessman was among the victims, had already disappeared from coverage.

*What, then, had gone wrong in the punishment of Hideo Akashiro? I need a full report of what happened.*

The room, a modest one hundred and fifty square feet in size, was sparsely furnished with only a desk and two chairs. Apart from the impeccable lighting and humidity control systems, the only unusual thing about it was the old-fashioned iron safe, painted in green, with a heavy handle and combination lock. A relic inherited from his maternal grandfather, evoking memories of his childhood.

After a few minutes of reflection, M. Henry opened the safe and took out his copy of the rare book by Jacques Desgranges, the object of recent interest by a relatively unknown mathematician at Columbia University.

*William Benjamin Fibonacci Hubbard.*

M. Henry had browsed the book innumerable times, identifying facts and historical coincidences, finding inspiration to solve various problems. The book documented in remarkable detail the evolution of thought and customs at the onset of the Renaissance, which was enough to put it in a league of its own for exceptional originality. More importantly, it was the only book that made explicit reference, in the chapter on banks, to a collection of notes that contained "recipes" for preserving an allegedly immense fortune.

Historically, it was quite natural that some of the pioneers in the banking business had tried to systematize the new ways of dealing with money, something that was happening on a previously inconceivable scale. It was the hint of secrecy and the suggestion that much more was hidden than was discussed in the book that made its reference to these files so cryptic and fascinating. All that it said was that a Society of the Guardians of the Venetian Files had been formed to protect them in perpetuity.

M. Henry possessed the third remaining copy of the book – all that was left from a limited-edition print run in 1570. His predecessor had given it to him during the ceremony appointing him Principal Guardian of the brotherhood. He returned it to its place on the top shelf of the safe and searched the lower part for a folio storing dozens of printed sheets, each containing the names of individuals to be contacted in special circumstances.

*I need detailed information on Inspector Piero de Lucca.*

This time around, his instinct was that the hurdle in Venice had to be managed without violence. He reasoned that if the police officer investigating the death of the unknown man in the Grand Canal were to be physically eliminated, the suspicions of the Italian police and Interpol would only increase, creating a fire that would be difficult to put out quickly, especially with everything else that would demand his attention in the days and weeks to come.

Later that same day Hank Paulson and Ben Bernanke would propose their emergency bailout to Congress, and M. Henry was deeply invested in it being approved.

*That was the whole point of letting Lehman fail, to scare legislators into action.*

He found the name he was looking for: the current manager of the Swiss Commercial Bank in Venice, whose office was located in the oldest bank branch in the city, near the port. He would receive instructions from another trusted bank director in Brussels.

One and a half million Euros - those were the instructions - were to be offered to the inspector leading the investigation in exchange for his silence. Or an even bigger sum, if necessary.

Having decided on that course of action, the resolution of another puzzle became a priority in his mind. For days he had been reluctant to evaluate the information he had received about the young math professor and his research associate. There was a reason for this, for if this William Hubbard turned out to be who M. Henry believed he was, the possibility of his eventually taking the reins of the brotherhood could be the realization of a dream - or Henry's worst nightmare.

# 37

*August 25, 2008*
*New York City – USA*

It was a Monday of heavy clouds and strong winds in New York. A day when nature reminded the residents of the city that they live in the Northern Hemisphere and that the warm days they had enjoyed in recent weeks would not continue for much more than another month.

After their dinner with Donald and Mathilde Pfeiffer on Saturday, Willbe and Sarah decided to spend Sunday apart visiting with their respective parents. The conversation about the anonymous phone call had left them tense with each other, and they had agreed that it would do them good to pause and seek the warmth of their families. Willbe felt guilty and promised to call Sarah on Monday, which he did as soon as he had finished breakfast.

Sarah woke up to the vibration of her cell phone on the glass top of her bedside table. She extended her arm reluctantly under the effect of a bad night's sleep. When she saw who was calling she hesitated before answering.

"Hello Willbe."

"*Sorry to wake you, Sarah, I just wanted to know how you are doing.*"

"Not great, Willbe, if you must know. I know it's a bit early in the morning to talk about these things, but I still don't understand why you didn't tell me about the phone call."

"*I just didn't want you to worry.*"

"I think there's something else going on, Willbe. I don't think you trust me to handle certain situations."

Willbe paused to think how to respond.

"*Even if that was the case, these are situations that are unrelated to our work or to what we feel about each other.*"

"How can you be so sure?"

"*I can't, but that's what I wish.*"

167

"I don't know, I need to let it sink in and think more about it."

*"Ok, but how about this? You think about it as we crisscross the North of Italy and visit Florence, Bologna and Venice."*

"You insist on this trip, don't you?"

*"I have my laptop in front of me ready to click ENTER and confirm the purchase of tickets to Italy. It's up to you..."*

"Right now? I'm not even properly awake yet."

*"Yup, right now. On a count of three: one... two..."*

"Alright, go ahead and click it," said Sarah, reticent, undecided, but touched.

Despite being entirely last-minute, Willbe's idea of a trip to Italy was indeed hard to turn down. She hung up the phone with her heart racing. Still a bit dazed, she wondered if she had done the right thing accepting the invitation. Now she had to start planning.

*Work will be the least of my problems. I have lots of accumulated vacation days and they are not as strict as I made out to Willbe.*

*************

The trip was booked for the first fortnight of September: departure on September 3, return on September 15. After that Willbe would begin teaching at Columbia.

He had two goals for the trip – apart from repairing his relationship with Sarah. The first was to visit the museum in Venice that had one of the three remaining copies of the book by Desgranges and, at last, be able to see with his own eyes something that made reference to the "Venetian Files".

The second, more personal and pleasurable, especially with Sarah by his side, was to visit his Uncle Emiliano in Pisa and reconnect with the rest of his Italian family. He also wanted to extract some more information from his uncle, for his intuition told him that for some reason the old man was holding back.

Bologna first, Venice last.

# 38

*August, 1367*
*Venice, Veneto Region - ITALY*

Marinella Fibonacci, her eyes fixed on Luigi, did not know how to react to the admission, at once spontaneous and painful, that came from her friend. She was not prepared to hear what she did, and lacked words to reply adequately.

"You should talk with Giuseppe and Francesco, Luigi, and tell them what you just told me. Let your partners know what is going through your head before life becomes more complicated."

"I thought about that, Marinella, and I indeed need to talk to them, especially Francesco, for I would not be surprised if I receive instant encouragement from Giuseppe to abandon my faith..."

"Francesco also has his doubts," added Marinella, "but, as far as I know, remains a true Christian."

Luigi fell silent for a while, looking at a woman from whom he had never heard any complaints. With some difficulty, he managed to stand up, supporting himself on one of the arms of the chair:

"And what does it mean, Marinella, to be a true Christian?"

Before she could answer, her son Gianpaolo entered the room and stopped to catch his breath:

"Hello, mother. Hello, Friar Luigi."

Marinella gave him a suspicious glance, noticing his agitation:

"What happened, my son? Is anything the matter?"

"No, nothing. Everything is fine, why do you ask?"

"You entered the room looking as if you had seen a ghost."

"Oh, nothing of the sort, mother. I just ran upstairs, and it looks like I am out of shape."

"I'm forced to agree with you," said Luigi with a smile.

"My father asked me to come and check on Friar Luigi, to see how you are doing."

"Thank you, Gianpaolo. You can let him know that I'm being very well treated by your mother and that I am even thinking of taking a stroll through the gardens, either in her company or with one of the servants."

"He will be very happy with the news, I'm sure. I also have a message for you, Friar Luigi..."

"*Va bene*, what do you have to say?"

"My father asks if you would like to be the head of our banking house in Florence?"

"What's that now?"

Luigi asked Marinella to help him walk across the living room, where he smiled at Gianpaolo:

"Could you repeat that, please?"

"He would like you to manage our bank in Florence."

"In my condition? I can barely stand..."

Marinella asked her son to help her and hold Luigi's other arm:

"What else did he say, son?"

"The message is exactly as I said. But I can tell you that I heard part of the conversation he was having with Cristaldi, when he mentioned the need to have someone in Florence who has their absolute trust, and that this way Friar Luigi could be away from Vicenza and Venice. Away from the wounds that had not had time to heal. And that..."

Luigi interrupted the young man with a hand gesture:

"Now, this is not altogether a bad idea."

This animated Gianpaolo:

"There's more. My father said that you would know how to put the books of the bank in Florence in order, and make note of any difficulties the business faced there, like you did in Venice."

"Even without admitting it, Marinella, it seems to me that your Giuseppe is a good Christian..."

Gianpaolo looked at both adults without fully understanding the meaning of Luigi's words.

# 39

*September 18, 2008*
*Venice – ITALY*

Piero de Lucca listened to the recording of his conversation with the *questore* Giustino Bertolli several times. He did not feel comfortable with having taped it, even if he had no intention of using it to blackmail his superior.

*No, that would be absurd, no need to resort to this kind of methods. For protection, maybe, if it got to that.*

The recording simply showed that he had had a frank exchange with his superior about the investigation. In all the years he had worked in Venice, he had never heard or seen anything that would call into question the integrity of the *questore*. He was just taking precautionary steps, perhaps unnecessarily, in the hope of bringing justice to a man who had *died twice* and was buried as an indigent, thousands of kilometers from his native land.

*Has the family believed the version in the newspapers?*

His beloved Venice was not a lawless place, and he was determined to ensure that it did not become one. The city founders were pacifists who wanted to escape the fighting between cities and the so-called barbarians who invaded Italy after the fall of the Roman Empire. Many took refuge in the small islands in the North East part of the Adriatic Sea seeking peace. Nature and the hand of man ensured that, with the passage of time, Venice became one of the most striking cities in Europe.

*Maybe it was time to take a few days off to relax.*

He decided to spend a weekend in Naples, where he had relatives and friends. At the very least a trip South would clear his mind and give him a chance to reassess his strategy for the investigation.

At this point he remembered the sales assistant at the formal wear store. He pulled his wallet out of his pocket, and from it the business card with her name.

*Claudia Celestini Sforza. Charming, provocative, intelligent…*

He looked for his cell phone, intent on following his desire. The call was answered by a male voice:

"*Signorina Sforza, per favore,*" announced Piero.

"*Qui parla?*"

"*De Lucca, Inspettore Piero de Lucca.*"

"*Un attimo, prego.*"

Piero did not really know what to say, but convinced himself that an invitation for dinner was appropriate.

"*Pronto*"

"*Claudia?*"

"*Si…*"

"*Sono io, Piero…*"

# PART 4

*What doesn't glitter could also be gold*

# 40

*September 18, 2008*
*Ardennes Forest – BELGIUM*

*Piero de Lucca… Inspector Piero de Lucca! So this was the name of the Italian police officer. Had they not tried to dissuade him from pursuing the investigation?*

As far as the brotherhood was concerned, the case of Mr. Akashiro was resolved. A member who put nationalism and the economy of his country above the interests of the brotherhood, rebelling against decisions made in meetings with his participation. The only lose end was this Italian inspector.

The manager of the Swiss Commercial Bank in Venice would receive the necessary instructions from headquarters in Brussels, where security around such matters was paramount. The president of the bank was a cousin of M. Henry and did not question his decisions. A man he trusted unreservedly, who apart from participation in the profits of the Commercial Bank was paid a generous seven-figure salary. He would know what to do.

*Nobody is indifferent to one and a half million Euros appearing out of nowhere. In this respect, human ethics has changed very little with the passage of time. Piero de Lucca was going to be no exception.*

Having decided how to deal with the issue in Venice, M. Henry felt compelled to return once more to the precious book stored in his safe. The book he had inherited from his predecessor in the brotherhood with the recommendation that he heed the wisdom therein whenever serious problems arose.

Attentive as M. Henry was to the book, it was unusual for him to refer to it twice in the course of a single day. And yet, today he felt the need.

*What may be the reason?* he asked himself.

Within its covers lay the centuries-old wisdom of the men who, for better or worse, made money the foundation of modern society.

Economists lie to tell a fairy tale story about money arising in early societies as a way to make barter easier. They imagine a time when people grew tired of exchanging the skin of an animal for grains and started using beads, then precious stones, and eventually gold to facilitate trade. An avid reader of history and anthropology, M. Henry knew that this was a myth. Even in remote times, before anyone could produce something in a scale large enough to make trade profitable, they had to borrow the means of production.

*Lend me the use of your carts and tools to cultivate my field and I'll give you part of the harvest as payment.*

Debt and credit relationships existed for more than five thousand years, with money appearing much later, mainly as a way to settle debt in situations of low trust. M. Henry knew that the early bankers in medieval Italy had no way of knowing this, but they understood very well that money, in the strict form of gold coins or other forms of specie, was still only a small part of the puzzle. The book by Desgranges touched on the extraordinary innovations created and perfected by these men, including double-entry bookkeeping – the foundation for the ability of banks to create money by extending credit to their clients.

*What were the young professor and his research companion looking for in the book? Why did they come all the way to Italy to read it?*

Apart from providing the historical background for the period when their secret society was created, the book was valued by the brotherhood for containing the only published reference to their founding documents. But it did not tell the entire story. The French author, under whatever pressures he faced in the 16th century, limited himself to pointing out the existence of some heavily guarded annotations about money, banking, and power. Without revealing the contents of these secret notes, Desgranges credited the knowledge in them as the source of the great wealth that had been accumulated by some Italian banking families in the two centuries preceding the publication of his book.

*Even if diligent Desgranges wanted to include more material about the files, it would have been impossible for him.*

M. Henry knew this because, according to a tradition that had been strictly observed since the late 1300s, only the three highest-ranking members of the brotherhood have access to the files, and Jacques Desgranges had not been one of them. They consisted of many handwritten sheets, securely stored in the impenetrable vault of the oldest bank branch in Venice, now under the brand of the Swiss Commercial Bank, that contained the first records of the business transactions between the great banking families of Fibonacci and Medici. Notes on the calculation of interest, diversification of investments, valuation of land and other business, and the type of precautions they had to take to minimize risks - *all kinds of risk.*

Like this note that M. Henry had translated from the Italian original, dated 1425 and carrying the invaluable signature of Giovanni de Medici:

> *"Accumulated wealth, be it in the form of gold coins or the promise to pay a debt, must be cultivated like the land where we plant potatoes, apples, and grapes. It is necessary to renew the soil and keep it fecund, or seek new ground, near or distant, increasing the value of the land and its fruits. With money, in any form, it is necessary to proceed in the same manner."*

Diversify the business. Discover new forms of investment. That was how the Medici built their fortune in Florence and the Fibonacci in Pisa and Venice. That and a firm grip on power.

Originally compiled by the legendary Friar Luigi di Vicenza, some passages in these files veered on mysticism, such as the belief that banking crises were the work of the devil or witchcraft. In other places the archives were remarkably practical; for instance, the advice it provided to early bankers on how to determine whether a crisis was about to spiral out of control or would die of its own accord. From a modern perspective, the advice was somewhat simplistic, but the importance of the notes was that they document how a group of powerful men attempted to get ahead of the crises by taking control of them. In some cases, that meant using their influence to trigger a crisis that would cause greater harm to their enemies. Naturally, this kind of power had to remain a secret. The real value in these Venetian Files was that they showed that such enigmatic brotherhoods existed.

The young couple had no way of inferring this simply from reading the book by Desgranges, unless someone else had helped them - someone who was no longer part of M. Henry's problems.

*Is the young William Benjamin the man I think he is? More precisely, is he the man I want him to be?*

Gathering the reports that he had received in the last two weeks from different Italian cities, M. Henry pulled out of his drawer copies of pages from the passport of the young professor, sent to him from Rome.

*He must find a secure way to finally meet William Benjamin Fibonacci Hubbard.*

# 41

*September 4-6, 2008*
*Bologna – ITALY*

The Alitalia Flight 611 landed at the Guglielmo Marconi International Airport in Bologna on a sunny Thursday morning after an uneventful crossing of the Atlantic Ocean. Willbe and Sarah planned to use the city as a base for short trips over the next few days to the neighbouring towns of Modena, Ravenna and Ferrara, where, according to Professor Pfeiffer, they would find the best preserved examples of Renaissance architecture in Italy. They were also eager to visit the University of Bologna, the oldest in Europe.

After Bologna they would travel to Pisa, the birthplace of the Fibonacci family, leaving Florence and Venice to the end.

From the airport they headed to the Hotel Maggiore on Via Emilia Ponente, their choice for the first few nights, with the understanding that they could change the following day if necessary, as they did not have time to research accommodations before they left New York. They were pleasantly surprised, however, by the cozy atmosphere and comfort of the hotel. Given the circumstances, they could not have made a better choice.

During check-in they were informed that the hotel had bicycles available for rental and that, if they wanted, they could make a reservation for that same afternoon.

"I wonder if they buy all the bicycles before renting them out," joked Willbe.

"What?"

"Remember? Professor Pfeiffer's example..."

Sarah rolled her eyes and told the hotel clerk they would prefer to walk around the city instead. They agreed that this would be the best way to explore the city with its narrow, cobbled streets.

After showering and changing into clean clothes, they left the hotel in search of their first Italian experience: breakfast *al fresco* in one the many charming little restaurants where food was served at outdoor tables by waiters merrily battling for space with the hundreds of tourists who walked the streets of Bologna.

On their way to Via Zamboni, Willbe had his camera ready and mentioned to Sarah that he wanted to take some pictures of the university to send to Mr. Carmona, as a reminder of the place where he had studied. It was a small gesture to thank the man who had charmed them so much and whose knowledge and professional expertise contributed to that trip in a most direct way.

"Incidentally," asked Willbe, "you never told me what you really think about all the legends surrounding this mysterious book."

"I had the same reaction as Mr. Carmona. I don't believe in those sorts of stories. Maybe they make sense to someone who has been initiated in a sect or secret society, but not to me."

"Are you sure about that, Sarah?"

"You don't believe me?"

"You seemed less certain when you heard about the anonymous phone call."

"I don't want to talk about this again, Willbe. I don't even think it is that important anymore."

"Ok, Sarah, I'm sorry."

They kept on walking through Bologna, making the most of their time. Willbe's heart already raced in anticipation of being in Pisa soon. *Anema e cuore...*

As they were about to enter the Hebrew Museum, out of nowhere Willbe had the impression of being followed. Nonchalantly, he asked Sarah to continue taking pictures of the buildings so that he could have a look around. He noticed another young couple, presumably tourists like him and Sarah, also standing nearby. The woman was wearing an egg-yellow blouse and the man looked remarkably like the younger of the two men he had noticed at the Park Bryant Café a few weeks earlier.

*************

It was time to leave Bologna behind.

At the end of the afternoon of the third day of their trip, Sarah and Willbe took a taxi towards Bologna Central railway station. The next two days would be spent in an environment familiar to Willbe and hopefully restful for Sarah, who had been tirelessly admiring the beauty of the places they visited.

Willbe was convinced that the trip had been his best idea to mend things with Sarah. He could see this in her eyes and attitude everywhere. Her happiness for being in Italy for the first time allowed her to take her mind off her work and the doubts that had made her irritable during their last days in New York. Willbe took great pleasure observing the spontaneous, almost puerile, cheerfulness in his girlfriend.

The train to Pisa passed through Florence, Lucca, and many other small towns. The beginning of September brought to the coaches a mixture of tourists, local workers, and students ready to start the new school year.

In the leg between Lucca and Pisa, Willbe thought he recognized the couple he had seen two or three times in Bologna. He felt slightly paranoid and tried to convince himself that it was a simple coincidence.

They arrived at Pisa Central Station early in the evening and were greeted by Willbe's Italian family: Uncle Emiliano, Cousin Carmela, who kept the excited family dog Pupo on a leash, and Cousin Aldo, who had offered to drive them back from the station to the family house in Ghezzano, a residential neighbourhood in Pisa popular with tourists looking for something other than the postcard views.

"Where is Aunt Antonella?"

"She is back at home preparing a *cacciucco*, the Tuscan fish stew that her darling nephew loves. You think she would not remember?"

Willbe smiled and said to Sarah:

"Aunt Antonella is a Neapolitan who fell in love with Pisa and Uncle Emiliano. I'm not sure in which order. She is a phenomenal cook, as you will soon discover. It will be hard not to put on weight around here."

Cousin Aldo's figure confirmed Willbe's joke.

Near the Strada Vicarese, after leaving Via G. Puccini, Aldo's Fiat took them around a small square with manicured flowers and shrubs and parked in front of a two-storey house where Aunt Antonella, wearing an apron and hair scarf, came to the front door to welcome them with open arms and rosy cheeks.

*"Carissimi, bienvenuti a casa nostra tutti quanti..."*

Sarah was quickly becoming familiar with the effusive way Italians greeted newcomers, with kisses on the cheek and tight hugs, Antonella was no different.

"You should get used to it," observed Willbe. "This is a very typical Italian family: loud, talkative, and very proud of their country."

"I hope they don't mind my shyness."

"Don't worry at all. My Cousin Carmela is also quiet and reserved. I'm guessing the two of you will get along very well."

Among greetings, hugs, kisses, and introductions, Sarah felt that the happiness they displayed was genuine, and the lack of pretense and formality made her feel at home. Locking arms with Antonella, Sarah admired the large house with a new understanding of Willbe's pride in his ancestry.

Uncle Emiliano grabbed Willbe by the arm in his jovial and expansive way and led him inside the house. Sarah stayed outside trying to converse with Aunt Antonella in a mixture of English and Tuscan dialect. Carmela, who spoke perfect English but was not talkative, tried to overcome her own shyness with a beautiful smile, delighted to see her cousin again and have the opportunity to meet his girlfriend. Behind them, Aldo and a neighbour were taking care of the luggage, under the supervision of Pupo wagging his tail.

Once they were all inside, Uncle Emiliano used the phone to let other family members know that the Americans had arrived and to confirm their presence at dinner.

Certain times in one's life are unforgettable and Sarah knew this was going to be one of them. In the last few days she had crossed the Atlantic, spent two nights in a hotel in Bologna, taken the train to Pisa and was now feeling the welcome embrace of *una famiglia toscana*. She realized they had work ahead of them in Florence and Venice, but for now all she wanted was to enjoy every minute of their trip.

The room the hosts had prepared for them demonstrated, among other things, how special Willbe was to his Italian relatives. Every detail displayed great care in creating an inviting and lovely space: the way the bed was made, the small table with pencil and papers to write on, and the special touch of fresh flowers next to a small bottle of Prosecco in an ice bucket with a small note that said *BENVENUTI*.

\*\*\*\*\*\*\*\*\*\*\*\*\*

## Ardennes Forest – BELGIUM

Anyone who consulted the rare book by Desgranges, either at the New York Public Library or at the Querini Stampalia Foundation in Venice, was immediately tagged and put under strict surveillance. The reports coming to M. Henry from New York this last few weeks were unequivocal: William Benjamin Hubbard, a recent hire of Columbia University's Mathematics

Department, had tried to gain access to the book and had not been deterred by the attempts to intimidate him.

*But for what reason?*

M. Henry could guess which part of the book interested the young professor. The book was classified as interdisciplinary, with content that could appeal to studies in mythology, anthropology, history, and economics. It covered many theological, philosophical, scientific and financial doctrines, many of which were used by different groups during the Late Middle Ages and early Renaissance, and each receiving a measure of praise or criticism from Desgranges. But the bulk of it was devoted to creeds, superstitions, and arcane customs in a few Italian cities in this period.

The medieval bankers, wise, cunning, and visionary as they were, found out very quickly in their daily practice what could be done with the money they had. In a nutshell, use it to gain power to be deployed to make more money. Then use that money to gain more power, and so on and so forth.

Everyone dreams of being able to make money, lots of money; but few succeed in preserving it. Why? Desgranges offers this:

*"Through all forms of money, from cowrie shells to coins made of gold, a mountain of silver or previous gems, or mere promises to repay debt, the Hellenic myth of King Midas has been the dream and the curse of men, whoever they are, in search of fortune and power."*

In all eras of history, this obsession has led man to great achievements and discoveries, as well as tragedies.

M. Henry was a living example. Born in July 1944 on European soil, one year before the end of World War II, he could not imagine then that on the other side of the Atlantic, in the small town of Bretton Woods, New Hampshire, destiny was working in his favour. The reconstruction of the world order after the War included the creation of the International Monetary Fund, the General Agreement on Tariffs and Trade and the International Bank for Reconstruction and Development, later the World Bank.

Had M. Henry, the son of an Italian who took up Belgian citizenship and became a banker after the War, not shown an aptitude for administering great sums of money, he would probably have ended up being an academic. As much as it amused him to think about this possibility, he never seriously longed for it. He had a natural talent for handling money, as well as the innate ability to spot those who chased money with the same eagerness as he did.

*And this young William Benjamin, an American with Italian roots from his mother's side of the family, was maybe one of them. What had brought him to Italy? Was it just intellectual curiosity?*

Each new piece of information he received from the people he assigned to follow the couple reinforced his suspicions.

# 42

*Circa 1375-80 AD*
*Florence, Tuscany Region – ITALY*

Luigi di Vicenza, now over sixty years old, would not live long enough to find out how profoundly history was about to change after the time he spent in Florence. In the next few centuries, the Renaissance and the Reformation would alter the course of humankind and of Christianity forever.

He had been very successful in the city ever since he took up his new responsibilities without the dragging fear of sin. Having accepted Giuseppe's challenge to manage the Fibonacci & Cristaldi Bank in Florence together with his friend's son Gianpaolo, Luigi at last found his true calling, and now struggled to forgive himself for wasting so many years in spiritual turmoil. He had not made money his new god, but he had come to regard the world as a place directed by humans, not by divine forces. Unknown to him, what he was experiencing were the incipient thoughts and change in attitude that were challenging the immense power of the Church over all medieval society.

When he was arrested by the Inquisition, Luigi realized once and for all that his vow of poverty, rectitude and simplicity, as taught by Saint Francis, had not been a personal choice guided by a kind God, as he had imagined. No, his choice had been guided by the need to survive in a world where material goods were beyond the reach of the vast majority of the population, who were subjected to the power of Kings and Popes.

The suffering that had been inflicted on him, in particular by his Dominican torturers, had severed his connection to God, and now it seemed more dignified to spend time working the land, for example, than isolating himself for long periods of praying for the souls of other sinners.

Setting aside his theological inhibition had allowed Luigi to become one of the most successful, and now publicly known, bankers in Florence. For this reason, the bank in which he was a partner was now considering association with a Tuscan family whose political power grew stronger every day: the Medici.

*Money was becoming a good like any other, and had to be cultivated before the harvest each year. With fertilizer and care of a different nature, for sure, but with much the same objective of increasing yield.*

He wrote down his reflections in his notebook.

Lost in his thoughts, Luigi did not notice Giuseppe Fibonacci and Francesco Cristaldi arriving in his office. They had come from Venice to spend three days in Florence. The friends and partners exchanged fraternal embraces.

"I think that you are working too much, Luigi. You should take some time off to rest," said Giuseppe.

"Have I not rested enough in my monastery days?"

"Luigi, you have proved yourself a thousand times over. I tell Gianpaolo all the time that your dedication to the bank here in Florence has surpassed all the expectations that Francesco and I had of you. You can relax without fear."

"This is true, Luigi," echoed Francesco. "It is a relief for us in Venice to know that you have the bank here in Florence under control."

"I would do even more if I could. You not only saved my life; you gave me a new one, and no amount of money can repay the debt I owe you both."

"With your help, Luigi, money is never going to be a problem for us, thank God."

Luigi could not help but laugh at Giuseppe's blatant hypocrisy.

"As you know," Giuseppe continued, "tomorrow Francesco and I will have lunch with Salvestro de Medici in his home. The same Salvestro we used to oppose, you recall."

"Yes, there have been significant changes in the politics of Florence."

"Exactly, and because of that, the first topic to be discussed will be the establishment of lasting peace between our families. We then want to acquaint ourselves with the younger members of the family. To that end, we are bringing Tommaso and Gianpaolo to meet Giovanni de Medici, Salvestro's younger cousin."

"The whole meeting is quite extraordinary. How did you arrange it?"

"Our wealth spoke for us, Luigi. Salvestro does not wield the power he once did. There have been troubles among some of the guilds and bad relations with some merchants, one of whom offered to broker this meeting with Salvestro."

"But can we trust these Medici?"

"I believe so. I had my reservations about Salvestro, but the real power in the family will soon be with Giovanni, who will come of age in three year's time."

"One of them was banned from Florence a few weeks ago," noted Francesco, who had been mostly quiet thus far.

"A bad apple in the bunch, among many healthy ones, Francesco. I don't think we need to worry."

# 43

*September 20, 2008*
*Venice – ITALY*

Deep down, Piero de Lucca was a clumsy romantic. He was thinking of taking Claudia Sforza to either the Club Del Doge or the Riviera. Both were posh and expensive, but he had a feeling that either could be the start of a memorable night. He worried that he had possibly mistaken Claudia's helpfulness for something else, but he decided that even if that were the case, a dinner in a comfortable restaurant would at the very least be relaxing. All that he needed at the moment was good wine, first-class food, and a beautiful and intelligent companion.

He chose the Club Del Doge, on the Dorsoduro by the Grand Canal, and opted for the sophisticated indoor dining-room. He arrived a few minutes before their 9pm reservation and enjoyed a glass of Prosecco at an outdoor table while waiting for Claudia to arrive.

"I hope I'm not late," said Claudia surprising Piero from behind.

As he rose and turned to greet her, Piero was taken aback by Claudia's extraordinary beauty, to which his memory had not done justice.

"You look absolutely stunning, *signorina* Sforza."

"And you are a charmer, *signor* de Lucca."

"Not always, not always... Shall we dispense with formalities this evening, Claudia?"

"Certainly, Piero. May I sit down?"

"We can actually move right inside if you want. Our table is ready."

With an old-fashioned, but entirely fitting attitude, the *maitre d'* ushered the inspector and his guest to their table.

The menu offered a choice of starters between steak *tartare*, garden salad, or *Vitello Tonnato* – cold sliced veal in a creamy sauce. For the *primo piatto*, cream of peas with mint, cod risotto, or one of the specialties of the place, the Hemingway risotto with fresh langoustines. The options for *secondo piatto* included lamb with mustard and carrot rice, Venetian-style calf liver, or the catch of the day with roasted vegetables. If they had any appetite left, dessert could be tiramisu, white chocolate cream with hot orange sauce or a selection of cheeses. As Claudia examined the menu, Piero perused the wine list and suggested a 2003 Barolo Vigna Rionda.

The vibration of his cell phone inside his jacket startled him. He apologized to Claudia and pulled it from the inner pocket, trying to identify the caller.

"Strange..."

"What is it?"

"A call to my work cell phone at this hour? Must be a mistake..."

He apologized again and answered the call, as his profession sometimes demanded:

"Hello... Yes, this is Inspector de Lucca. Who is this? Sorry, what's that? You are the manager of the Swiss Commercial Bank?"

Piero looked at Claudia with an expression that intimated he did not understand what was happening:

"And how did you get my unlisted number?"

*"Please don't be alarmed, Inspector,"* said the voice on the line. *"I tried to reach you this afternoon at your office to schedule a meeting with you, at the request of the CEO of our bank in Brussels. I told your assistant that I had to talk with you about an urgent matter and she gave me your number."*

Slightly irritated by what he had just heard, Piero excused himself and walked to the front of the restaurant.

"Very well, but I'm in the middle of a private dinner. Can we talk tomorrow?"

*"I won't take any of your time, Inspector. I just wanted to ask you to stop by our branch on Monday morning at 10am, if you please. Do you know the address?"*

"Yes I do, in the Dorsoduro, correct? But may I ask what this is about?"

*"Yes, number 2799 on the Dorsoduro. I prefer not to talk over the phone, but I have information regarding the investigation you are currently leading."*

"What did you say? How do you know which investigations I'm leading?"

*"As I said before, please don't be alarmed, Inspector. I am sure you understand that I cannot talk about this on the phone. I look forward to seeing you, and my apologies for interrupting your dinner."*

An even more irritated Piero returned to the table and apologized to Claudia once more.

"Don't worry about it. I bet it is not easy to be a police officer," she answered with a smile that made him melt inside and completely forget the call.

# 44

*September 7, 2008*
*Pisa – ITALY*

Willbe was the last to join his family and Sarah at the breakfast table, looking still half-asleep. Sarah made a discreet hand gesture for him to tidy his just-out-of-bed hair and then motioned to the multitude of breads, cheeses, cakes, and jams covering the table.

"What did I tell you, Sarah? Here you either eat or... you eat. There are no alternatives."

His Aunt Antonella smiled.

The house had a spare guest-bedroom, in addition to the master bedroom for Emiliano and Antonella, the bedroom used by their daughter Carmela, and a fourth one used by Cousin Aldo, whose parents lived in Milan but who was in Pisa to attend law school at the university where Willbe had also studied. Aldo's mother, one of Emiliano's younger sisters, had arranged for him to live with his relatives until graduation the following year.

The spare room hosted the many relatives who came to visit from out of town or abroad and was always meticulously prepared by Antonella.

"Are you ready to explore the best city in the world?"

"Emiliano," interrupted Antonella, "they have just wakened. Let them eat breakfast in peace. You'll have two entire days to buzz in their ears. I hope Willbe warned you about my husband, Sarah."

"Don't worry, Aunt Antonella. I can't speak for Sarah, but I slept like an angel. I'm ready for the tour."

"I also slept very well, Antonella, don't worry."Sitting beside Sarah, Emiliano told her in a low voice:

"Good, because we have lots to talk about" and continued in a slightly louder voice, "apart from showing the city to Sarah and taking her to our greatest monument. And, my dear children, please heed the advice of your old uncle: don't take those darn pictures pretending to be holding the tower up. I never understood how tourists could be so unimaginative."

"Sarah," whispered Antonella, "don't listen to him, he's always grumpy about tourists. He's right about the pictures, though."

Everyone laughed. After they all had enough to eat, Carmela rose, positioned herself behind Willbe and Sarah, and asked Aldo to take a picture of the three of them so she could frame it. Uncle Emiliano got up next:

"Alright then, enough chit-chat. Shall we go? Carmela, if you don't mind driving, Sarah can sit in front with you. Later in the afternoon we can switch. For now, I'll sit in the back with Willbe."

"And don't be late for lunch," stressed Antonella.

"*Va bene*, Antonella, we are going to be back here at 2pm sharp, don't worry."

"Willbe, you know how your uncle is when he starts talking with you... I'm making a *ragù alla napoletana* and it can't be re-heated."

"Don't worry, *mama*," interjected Carmela, "Sarah and I will take care of these two."

*************

Uncle Emiliano, who had a solid grasp of humanistic values, had prepared an itinerary full of historical and cultural significance for Willbe and Sarah, through both Pisa and Florence, where he had owned a souvenir store for several years. The two cities came first and second in his heart.

In the car, as Sarah and Carmela were getting to know each other, Willbe briefly told his uncle that they had shown the document he received at his graduation dinner to a specialist in New York who had confirmed its authenticity.

"And did you have any doubts, Willbe?"

"What are you two whispering about back there?" asked Carmela looking at them through the mirror.

"Willbe was just informing me that the present I gave him on his graduation dinner is authentic. Do you remember, Carmela?"

"Of course I remember. You have no idea, Sarah. More than half of the family came to celebrate, all proud that the American cousin had become a *dottore*."

"Yes, so Willbe tells me that the document was examined by an expert in New York, who concluded it was authentic."

"Did you have any doubts, Willbe?" asked Carmela echoing her father.

Sarah thought she should jump into the conversation with an explanation:

"To be honest, this was my idea. I wanted to show your nephew that he wasn't teaming up with a researcher who would just flip through books and agree with everything that was presented to me."

"And you did very well. Women are normally more suspicious than men, and that's a good thing."

Sarah and Carmela smiled.

"We are approaching our first attraction," announced Carmela.

Willbe and Sarah had no idea what was in store for them for the rest of the tour, but the first place they would visit was well expected. Partly to satisfy Sarah's curiosity, partly so that they would be done with it right away, their first stop was at the Cathedral Square, where they could inspect the famous *Torre pendente*, one of the most curious works of engineering in the world.

Sarah was speechless and Willbe encouraged her to climb to the top with him. Uncle Emiliano and Carmela agreed to wait for them at the entrance of the Baptistery. They marvelled at the seven bells on the way up, one for each note of the musical scale and with names like *L'Assunta* and *La Pasquereccia*. Having promised not to take any silly pictures, they ended up taking just three: one at the entrance, one by a bell, and one at the very top.

Looking at the city of Pisa from above, Willbe remarked that he felt more tired than the first time he had climbed the tower a few years earlier. Sarah, on the other hand, was feeling more energized each day, and Willbe could tell that the trip had brought back the thrill of the first days of their relationship.

"Your uncle is quite funny, Willbe."

"Wait until he starts telling you stories. I can't wait to see how he reacts when you start questioning their authenticity."

Their second stop was at the University of Pisa, so Willbe could show Sarah where he had studied and where Uncle Emiliano had promised to show them a family relic that Willbe had not seen yet.

It was the start of the academic year and Willbe felt nostalgic seeing a few students going in and out of the different buildings on a Sunday morning. Sarah asked one of them to take a picture of the four of them. As the student was searching for the best angle, Uncle Emiliano made a suggestion:

"I want you to take a picture of a small plaque in one of the inner gardens of the university, Sarah."

"Here we go," winked Carmela.

"I have a surprise for you all."

"You are not going to start telling us another family legend, are you *babbo*?"

They all laughed while the student, not understanding what was going on, ended up capturing an extraordinary photograph, as they would see later on Willbe's computer.

After wandering through the main building, where Willbe showed Sarah the classroom where he had attended the first lecture in his PhD studies, Uncle Emiliano suggested they used a side door to exit into one of the gardens. Guided by him, they walked along the small paths covered in stones of different sizes and shapes that divided the grass and flower beds until they reached a metal plaque sitting atop an oval stone on which one could read: IN SUPREMAE DIGNITATIS*- 1343

Under the engraving, almost erased by the action of time, three letters in gothic style could still be recognized:

*VGF*

Sarah and Willbe leaned forward to take a closer look.

"What do these letters mean, Uncle Emiliano?"

"I can't believe you don't recognize them, Willbe. Just now in the car you mentioned the document you received as a family present..."

"Vitorio Giuseppe Fibonacci!" exclaimed Sarah with enthusiasm.

"*Bravo ragazza!*" returned Uncle Emiliano with the same enthusiasm. "This is a plaque honouring one of the key supporters of the University of Pisa."

"Your medieval ancestor to whom our mystery book is dedicated," Sarah observed, looking at Willbe.

She had a twinkle in her eyes and seemed to have regained the professional eagerness towards their research that had faded in the weeks before they left New York. Willbe asked to borrow her camera and took detailed pictures of the historical relic.

"Well then, I see that you already know about the book stored in the Querini Stampalia in Venice. I was going to save that surprise for after lunch..."

"Do you know about the book, Emiliano?"

---

* with supreme dignity

"Not only do I know about it, Sarah, but I have another old document that I'm sure will surprise both of you."

Carmela broke her customary silence:

"We are tired of hearing about it at home."

"Only because you don't care about our family history! If you had the slightest interest, you might feel more pride and perhaps even help to try and find out what happened to the great fortune that our most famous ancestor managed to acquire."

Surprised, Sarah looked at Willbe, who took the cue:

"That's what I wonder, too. I can't understand how there is no record of what happened to one of the greatest fortunes in Tuscany. What I would like to find out is if it was connected to an economic crisis of some sort. That, incidentally, is the topic of the course I'm going to give at Columbia."

"Are you going to talk about the Fibonacci fortune in the Middle Ages?" asked an incredulous Carmela.

"No, I phrased that poorly. I'll be talking about economic crises connected to speculative bubbles."

"You ought to give some lectures to that *pazzo* Berlusconi. Have you looked at house prices in Italy recently? If that's not a bubble then I don't know what is."

They all burst out laughing at Uncle Emiliano's very Italian invective.

*************

After seeing the plaque in honour of Giuseppe Fibonacci in the gardens of the University of Pisa and walking around its majestic buildings, the group visited the Botanic Gardens and the Palazzo Boileau. It was then time to head back to the lunch being prepared by Aunt Antonella, who had made it clear she expected punctuality. On the way back Willbe offered to buy wine and bread for lunch. He loved everyday Italian bread – a *filone di pane* as they said. He bought a *sciapo*, without salt, and a *panini all'olio*, with a touch of olive oil in the dough.

The lunch table had been carefully set by a house helper under the guidance of Antonella and showed the important role played by food in Tuscan life. The table could seat up to ten people, but was set for the six present for lunch: Antonella, Emiliano, Carmela, Aldo, Sarah, and Willbe.

The main course was a specialty from Antonella's home: Neapolitan ragù – beef cubes, garlic, onion, olive oil, two glasses of red wine, and an abundance of tomato sauce, cooked for about three hours. Sarah and Willbe did not know what to say. It was impossible not to be touched by the thoughtfulness of the meal. Antonella watched her foreign guests closely, in anticipation of their comments, which did not take long.

Willbe raised his wine glass and stood to propose a toast to the wonderful lunch they were having. Sarah responded by trying out her Italian timidly: *grazie tante*. She then hugged her host and murmured another *thank you* in her ears. Uncle Emiliano watched everything with a satisfied expression, knowing that he was about to make the day even more memorable, especially for Willbe. He was sure of that.

*************

After lunch, Uncle Emiliano invited Willbe and Sarah to "an open and frank conversation" in the living room over almond *biscotti* accompanied by coffee and amaretto.

*What could this be about?* Sarah wondered, feeling the effect of the wine she had drunk with lunch.

Willbe could not hide his anxiety. Uncle Emiliano sat and took a sip of coffee, readying himself to end the mystery he had created at the University before lunch. He had prepared a small speech for this moment:

"My dear nephew, William. Even though my own family here and in other parts of Italy never understood my interest in the history of our family, I carried on doing research on my own, in my spare time, and to a certain degree hiding my 'obsession' with it, especially after I heard it suggested that one day I could end up in an institution..."

Antonella and her daughter exchanged glances at one another as they observed Willbe and Sarah.

"Your presence here in the past few years and the interest you showed in our conversations inspired me to continue, as I could see that I was not alone in my quest."

Willbe smiled with some embarrassment at the realization of how much he meant to his uncle.

"That was the reason I gave you a document, which as you told me earlier today was verified as authentic, and which if I'm not mistaken is one of the reasons for your return to Pisa."

Willbe agreed with a nod.

"Only this time accompanied by someone who has already captivated us with her grace and commitment to assisting you in your own search. A very special person, if I may say so."

It was Sarah's turn to show her embarrassment by blushing beyond the effect of the wine and almond liqueur.

"Having observed this dedication and knowing the reasons for your endeavor, I want to present you, my nephew, with another precious document, a relic I would say, that will without a doubt help you achieve your goals."

All eyes and ears were fixed on the old man, who relished their undivided attention with a well-timed pause.

"I obtained this document through one of the chance encounters that life puts in our paths, which I can explain on another occasion. I confess that I waited for this moment with great anxiety, so without wasting any more time I ask you to open this cylinder with all the care you can."

Emiliano passed the cardboard tube to Willbe, who decided to say a few words of his own before opening it:

"I must say, Uncle Emiliano, that ever since leaving Pisa for New York I had the impression that somewhere in this city, perhaps in your possession or with someone else of your knowledge, there was something that would justify our common interest in our ancestors. I'm truly thankful for this honour."

In turn, with Sarah's help, Willbe removed the metal lid from the cylinder and from inside it, with extreme care, an old manuscript, partially damaged and enclosed in protective sheets of tracing paper that allowed them to read an excerpt with the following words:

*società scritti per... il lavoro comune... banca di Medici e banca Fibonacci and Cristaldi... anno 1379... Giovanni di Medici, Tommaso Cristaldi e Gianpaolo Fibonacci... files di Venezia...*

Willbe and Sarah exchanged glances.

"Do you remember what your friend Sam Oliver said?"

"Yes, the fashion in late 15th century Italy for having old documents reprinted."

"Is this what I think it is, Uncle Emiliano?"

"Yes, Willbe. You are holding the proof that our illustrious ancestor Giuseppe Fibonacci became a partner of the great Giovanni de Medici in 1379, and that the whole deal was recorded in the Venetian Files!"

*************

---

* written partnership for... common work ... Medici Bank and Fibonacci and Cristaldi Bank... year of 1379... Giovanni de Medici, Tommaso Cristaldi and Gianpaolo Fibonacci... Venetian files...

Willbe and Sarah spent the afternoon visiting the other Pisa attractions suggested by Uncle Emiliano, who had decided to stay at home to rest. The enormous lunch and his momentous offering of the old document to Willbe had left him exhausted. When they got back to the house later, they were relieved to discover that dinner would be a much lighter fare – just some Italian charcuterie, cheeses, and breads. The next day they would travel to Florence, the third part of their trip, and they needed some rest, too.

The evening was, nevertheless, quite animated, with much of the conversations centering on Sarah, who found herself bombarded with questions about her country, family, work, and her relationship with Willbe. As the hours passed, though, tiredness began to take hold, first of Antonella, who excused herself and went to bed after a busy day. Next was Sarah, who in addition to being tired from walking all over Pisa was feeling the effect of the wine they had drunk at lunch and dinner – rather more than she was used to. Carmela took the opportunity and followed Sarah. Next was Aldo, who apologized for not staying up longer on account of classes to attend the next morning. Willbe and Emiliano remained in the comfortable dining room, as they had done on many nights during Willbe's studies in Pisa.

Willbe poured two more glasses of amaretto and asked if his uncle could stay for ten more minutes before going to bed.

"It is always a pleasure to talk with you, William. Nobody else pays attention to what I say around here."

"Uncle Emiliano, I have two questions I'd like to ask you."

"Please, go ahead."

"The first is how did you obtain the document you just gave me?"

"I'd be curious, too, if I were you. But if you don't mind, I'd ask you to be patient and wait a little bit longer. Until you arrive in Venice..."

Knowing that he would be in Venice in a few days, Willbe acquiesced.

"What is the second question?"

"Can you tell me again about your brother who left Italy right at the end of the War and lost contact with the family? He, his wife, and an infant son, if I recall correctly?"

"He wasn't my brother; he was my father's brother. What really happens remains a mystery, though. You know that we are a very close family, *una famiglia italiana, è vero*. They tried to look for him but gave up when they could not find any information. It shook everyone in the family to their core. My grandmother became depressed and never recovered until her death. I can tell you what I know, which is not much. Let's move to those chairs in the living room."

## 45

*Circa 1375-80 AD*
*Florence, Tuscany Region – ITALY*

The luncheon at Salvestro de Medici's house could not have been more fruitful and auspicious. The meeting between Salvestro and Giuseppe Fibonacci brought not only an end to the animosity between the families, but also the possibility of an equal partnership to create a new bank, combining their fortunes. Their intention, in many respects overly ambitious, was that the partnership control the bulk of financial operations in the regions of Tuscany, Veneto, and Umbria, and establish a branch in Rome with the goal of securing the patronage of the Papal States, one of the most lucrative clients a bank could have. This alone would guarantee an incalculable addition to the already sizeable wealth of the two families.

Despite Giuseppe's best efforts, the merger would take another five years to complete, when Giovanni de Medici reached the age of majority in the year 1379. In the end, the partnership was not quite equal, with the Medici controlling 55% of the new bank owing to the larger pool of capital held by the Florentine family, though this was substantially less than Salvestro had thought his family would control. Examination of both sides' books revealed that the Fibonacci & Cristaldi Bank had been more successful than its competitors had realized. Once the agreement was finalized, the papers were signed by the current owners of each bank and the eldest son in each of the three families.

Luigi, by then even more distant from the religious world where he had lived for so long, followed every step of the merger, making notes about the new risks and business opportunities arising from the union of such great fortunes. It was necessary to avoid misunderstandings, both large and small, that could lead to preventable losses. He also examined and learned a great deal from the Medici books and the family's methods of accounting, about which he also made detailed notes.

In the contract to be signed between the families, Luigi made sure to include three safeguards, inspired in part by his observation of business practices, but also by his suffering at the hands of the Inquisition. In essence:

*(1)  That each party would give the other parties the right of first refusal to join any new business external to the original partnership. In the event of refusal by any party, the party or parties entering a new business would disclose them to other parties, on an ongoing basis, any information relevant to the business of the original partnership;*

*(2)  That, as a result of new business not entered by all parties, each party would have the right to inject more capital and increase its share in the partnership;*

*(3)  That, under no circumstance whatsoever a partner would take any action or use any method that could lead to harm, either physical or material, to any member of the Medici, Fibonacci, or Cristaldi families.*

\*\*\*\*\*\*\*\*\*\*\*\*\*

A few weeks after the Easter celebrations in 1378, while still working on the merger in Venice, Luigi began to feel a pain in his chest of the same sort he had experienced years before on a trip back to Vicenza, though it was stronger this time around. When he mentioned the chest pains to Giuseppe and Marinella, he was told in no uncertain terms to take some time off and go to his house in Florence to rest. Business at the bank in Venice was good and could manage a few days without Luigi.

Privately, Giuseppe worried about Luigi's health and his absence from the bank in these final months of negotiations with the Medici. The day that Luigi left for Florence, Giuseppe and Francesco discussed the matter in Luigi's office at the Venice branch of the bank.

"Even a few days of Luigi not participating in dealings with the Medici makes me nervous," Giuseppe said. "Either of us could be there in his place, but I feel a lot better when Luigi is watching everything."

"I feel the same, Giuseppe; and I hope Luigi recovers soon. But perhaps the time has come for us to think about readying our own sons to take over from Luigi."

"You are right, Francesco. It's also time that for me to engage my youngest son with the bank here in Venice. Marinella keeps asking me to do so – Filippo Luigi is her favourite son."

"As the youngest often is for mothers..."

Giuseppe looked at Luigi's empty desk with the feeling that he would never see him there again. Tears came to his eyes, but he hid them from Francesco. He got up and walked towards the door to disguise his feelings. Francesco could read his mind though:

"Soon he will be back, he is a strong man."

Hearing no reply, he kept a respectful silence.

# 46

*September 22, 2008*
*Venice – ITALY*

Piero arrived at the Venice branch of the Swiss Commercial Bank on Monday morning punctually at 10am. He was accompanied by another officer of the Border Police, whom he asked to remain waiting for him outside ready to take a phone call from him. He was sure that he had nothing to fear inside such a respectable bank, but he was also suspicious of the way the manager had found him and liked to be prepared for the unforeseen.

He identified himself at the reception desk and was led to a small meeting room where a circumspect gentleman with grey hair rose from a chair to greet him and offered him coffee. Piero concluded that he was in the presence of the man who had called him on Saturday night. He did not look like someone who willingly involved himself in the affairs of other people, and this suggested that he was following orders.

Piero shook his hand, still uncertain as to why he was there. Replaying the phone call in his head made him think of the romantic dinner it had interrupted and the night he had spent afterwards with Claudia, a woman who exuded sensuality from every pore.

The gentleman with grey hair interrupted his train of thought:

"Inspector de Lucca, please take a seat. First of all, let me apologize again for having interrupted your dinner on Saturday. I was merely following orders from our Managing Director in Rome, who received instructions from Brussels to locate you as quickly as possible."

*Ok, there's something big here.*

"As I explained, I pressed the point when I called the Border Police and managed to obtain your number."

Piero indicated with a wave of his hand that he had already forgotten the inconvenience of the phone call.

In front of the grey-haired man lay a briefcase from which, after these introductory remarks, he pulled an envelope, which he then pushed deftly towards Piero. The gesture suggested professional experience with delicate negotiations.

Piero knew that he was meant to open the envelope, but instead he hesitated, his gaze alternating between the envelope and the man before him. Eventually, Piero spoke:

"Sir, with all due respect, because of my position as a police officer, I will not touch this envelope without first establishing the reasons for this meeting, which at this point are completely unclear to me."

"This situation is as uncomfortable for you as it is for me, Inspector. I know nothing of the content of this envelope or the reasons for this meeting, except that I am to give this envelope to you and ask that you open it only once you have left the branch."

"Why all this mystery? Couldn't it simply have been mailed to me?"

"It appears that you will find the answers inside," answered the man, displaying a small hint of impatience.

"Then why can't I open it now?"

"These are my instructions, Inspector. As a police officer, I'm sure you should understand the importance of following orders without question."

Piero began to think that he had walked into a trap.

*Should I take the envelope or leave it on the table?* It looked like he only had a few seconds to decide.

"May I use the bathroom, please?"

The bank manager was not expecting this request, but acquiesced with a nod, barely disguising his irritation.

Piero rose without touching the envelope and left in search of the washroom. Once inside it he called his subordinate.

"Marco, call me within exactly one minute, it's very important. Ask meaningless questions and don't worry about my answers. When I say *'grazie'* do not hang up. Stay on the line and keep listening."

"*Yes, sir.*"

Piero washed his hands and returned to the meeting room. As soon as he sat down again, he heard his cell phone ring and apologized for having to take the call.

The manager's face showed that he wanted to put an end to the meeting as quickly as possible. Piero, who was beginning to enjoy the situation, prepared to drop the cue to his colleague on the phone:

"No, I shouldn't be long here. Is it urgent? Alright then, *grazie.*"

He pretended to switch off the phone and left it facing down on the table next to the envelope.

"As I was saying, sir, please accept my apologies, but my position obliges me to ask you one last time if you know the content of this envelope?"

"And I can tell you again that I do not," answered the bank manager.

The inspector fixed his eyes on the man opposite him. Finally, he picked up the envelope and felt it around with his fingers. It seemed to contain one or two sheets of paper, at most.

*Perhaps a cheque? But why would the bank be offering me money?*

Piero rose and said goodbye with a polite handshake across the table.

"I trust that we won't need to meet again in more official circumstances," he said as he walked out, leaving the door open behind him.

The manager stared after him with just a little distaste on his otherwise implacable face.

*************

With the envelope tucked inside his jacket, Piero took a deep breath as he reached the sidewalk in front of the two-storey bank branch, ready to relieve his subordinate from the task he had assigned:

"We're done here, Marco, so you can drop me near my place now."

"If you need anything else let me know, Inspector."

"Thank you, Marco. After you drop me you can take the speedboat back to the station and go have some lunch."

"It's not even 11am yet, Inspector."

Piero checked his watch.

"I feel as though I spent hours in that room ... *Va bene*, go back to the station then and see if there's anything happening there. But only call me if there's something important."

"Alright, sir."

"And Marco..."

"Yes, sir?"

"Not a word about this meeting."

"Don't worry, Inspector."

Piero was fond of his subordinate, whom he had been grooming in the art of conducting a police investigation. If he continued to work as hard as he had done thus far, he would become an excellent officer.

As the speedboat began to move, Piero almost instinctively touched his jacket pocket. He remained silent during the short journey, torn between curiosity about the content of the envelope and concern at being confronted with an unthinkable situation.

\*\*\*\*\*\*\*\*\*\*\*\*\*

Ten minutes later, he climbed the steps leading to his apartment with a siightly faster-than-normal heartbeat. His building did not resemble the Hotel Danieli, evidently, but it was comfortable and well-kept. He hung his jacket on the back of a chair in the dining room and moved to the kitchen to prepare a stovetop espresso.

He drank the coffee working up the courage to take the envelope out of his jacket pocket. He had already concluded that this was going to be a turning point in his life, for there was no other plausible hypothesis other than that he was being offered money to drop the investigations on the death of Hideo Akashiro. All that was left to do was to confirm his hypothesis, and in that case, find out the amount and the conditions.

At last, Piero sat down and opened the envelope.

The fact that a bank slip with a numbered account fell onto the table did not overly surprise him; the balance printed on it, however, shocked him. His instinct, even before he read the letter that accompanied the slip, was that this was a matter of life and death. Nobody raised the stakes like that without being certain they would win. He worked up the courage to read the letter:

*Inspector Piero de Lucca*
*Chief of Security for the City of Venice*
*Border Police*

*We are aware of your reputation as a consummate professional. However, we urge you not to attempt to trace the origin of this letter. You will not succeed.*

*You now have forty-eight hours to accept our offer by accessing the numbered bank account provided and close the investigation into the death of Hideo Akashiro.*

*If you accept, we hope you will enjoy the benefits of our generous contribution to your retirement package.*

*If not, rest assured that you will soon join Mr. Akashiro in the San Michele cemetery.*

*VF*

Piero felt a shiver descend the entire length of his spine. Not because of the content of what the letter said, but because of the sudden recollection of the initials VF cut into the skin of Akashiro's bicep. Part of the case had just been solved.

He examined the bank slip again, still not quite believing the amount, and had just one thought:

*These are powerful people. What to do next?*

He walked to the small bar that he had installed in the living-room and poured a double dose of whisky with some ice. He then opened a box of Cuban cigars he kept for important guests and picked one up.

*Every dog has its day...*

# 47

*September 8-9, 2008*
*Florence – ITALY*

Willbe and Sarah stepped off the train on to the platform of the Santa Maria Novella Station in Florence, followed by the sprightly figure of Uncle Emiliano, who had insisted to accompanying them to the historical home of the Medici.

As they looked around, Willbe saw again the couple he had first noted in Bologna, and then again on the way to Pisa. They were dressed differently each time, but made no attempt to conceal themselves. He considered approaching the couple, but thought it would not be prudent. Unsure if he was simply being paranoid, Willbe, nevertheless, decided that this time around he would share his concern with Sarah, once they were alone.

Outside the station, the trio took a taxi to the Hotel Golf, a charming boutique *albergo* out of the year-round busy city centre.

After checking in, they agreed to meet again in the lobby at 7pm for a walk around the city and dinner at one of Emiliano's favourite local restaurants

*************

Sarah was impatient to see the city, but Willbe was adamant that he needed to share his concerns with her. He opened his laptop and called her over to the desk where he sat:

"Sarah, I want to show you something. These are the pictures we took in Pisa. There's one I want you to have another look at because of one detail that caught my attention."

Willbe scrolled through the photos and stopped at one taken in front of the University of Pisa.

"This is the first of a sequence by that student, remember?"

"Oh yes, your cousin asked the student, so we could all be in the picture."

"Exactly. Then you noticed that there could be a better angle."

"Yes, I remember."

"And what comes to your attention in this picture, which is in fact badly framed?"

Sarah examined the photograph on the screen for a few seconds.

"The hideous yellow shirt on this tourist," she answered, laughing.

"Exactly! Now, do you recall seeing her and the young man beside her in some of the other places we visited in Pisa?"

"No, I don't. Why, should I?"

"I have the impression that they've been with us since Bologna."

The smile disappeared from Sarah's face.

"With us? You mean following us? Why would someone be following us, Willbe?"

"I have no idea, but I think I saw them in Bologna, and I noticed them in most of the places we visited in Pisa, and today I'm certain that I just saw them at the train station here in Florence. I don't want to alarm you, but I also don't want to keep anything from you..." Willbe trailed off, sure that his meaning was clear to Sarah.

"There's something else..."

"Go on," said Sarah a bit more tersely than she intended.

"I think I have seen the man in New York before," Willbe continued intent on telling her all there was to know. "You remember the day we met at the Park Bryant Café, when I was showing you the electronic version of the first manuscript Uncle Emiliano gave me?"

"Yes, I remember that day very well."

"Well, that day I noticed two men, dressed like security agents or something, sitting not far from us at the café trying to look inconspicuous."

"Ok..."

"The thing is, I think they were watching us. That was the first thought that came to my mind when I listened to that threatening message."

"What made you think they were watching us?"

"I don't know, I had a hunch. But I didn't want to tell you precisely because I had nothing concrete to back it up."

"You shouldn't wait until you are absolutely certain to tell me these things, I think you should know this by now."

"Yes I know, that's why I'm telling you about this couple here in Italy."

Sarah stared at him pensively.

"Ok, the next time you see this couple, let me know discreetly and I'll try to snap another picture of them without them noticing."

"What will you do with the picture?"

"I don't know... just in case..."

*************

Uncle Emiliano resumed his role as tour guide in Florence and did everything he could to give Willbe and Sarah the best impression of the city he knew like the back of his hand.

He took them to the *Cattedrale di Santa Maria del Fiore* first thing the following day, where they saw the Brunelleschi Dome, and to the Leonardo da Vinci Museum next, where they spent the rest of the morning. At Emiliano's suggestion, they reserved the Basilica Santa Croce for the next morning, and so Sarah and Willbe used the afternoon to visit the *Giardino di Boboli* while Emiliano rested at the hotel.

As they were coming down the steps towards the *Fontana di Neptuno*, Willbe momentarily alarmed Sarah by kneeling in front of her with his back to the statue. With one arm extended as in a declaration of love and the other retracted towards his chest, he winked at Sarah and used his hidden hand to signal to her to photograph the couple that was coming up from behind him, pretending that she was taking a picture of him in the absurd pose.

"They sure look like tourists," said Sarah after they moved a few steps away.

"I agree. She looks German, or Dutch. I don't know. He looks American."

Surprised by Sarah's lack of interest in the possibility of their being followed, Willbe teased:

"So I see you believe in coincidences now?"

"This young couple following us through Tuscany? They're too obvious to be spies," she answered, exaggerating the last word. "You are becoming paranoid, Willbe."

Sarah descended the last flight of steps and leaned over the iron fence to snap a picture of Neptune in the best-known work of 16th century Tuscan sculptor Stodo Lorenzi.

*Go figure*, thought Willbe, relieved at Sarah's nonchalant reaction, but still not entirely convinced that she was correct.

*************

"The *Basilica di Santa Croce* is the most impressive Franciscan church in the world, and I could not let you come to Florence without showing it to you."

207

Construction of the Basilica Santa Croce began at the end of the 13th century and was concluded about 150 years later, when Pope Eugene IV consecrated the church in 1442. Among its most distinct features are the sixteen chapels built inside it, as well as the tombs and cenotaphs used for the burial of notable Florentines and other distinguished Italians.

"As you can see, the style is austere, despite how imposing the building is. This was a deliberate move to show the smallness of man before God. The effect must have been felt among the thousands of medieval and Renaissance worshippers who included the church in their pilgrimage, as it continues to impress us today."

They entered the basilica through the main entrance, flanked by the massive carved wooden doors. Emiliano directed them to the nave and pointed to the open timber roof. As they walked towards the altar he identified the tombs and funerary monuments of some of the most famous inhabitants of Florence: Michelangelo, Machiavelli, Galileo and Dante Alighieri, whose body was buried in Ferrara but in whose honour a cenotaph had been built in the basilica in 1829.

At the altar, Emiliano pointed to the Giotto fresco depicting Saint Francis, which showed the first signs of the humanism that began to manifest itself in the art of the period, announcing the arrival of the Italian Renaissance.

Knowing that Willbe and Sarah would travel to Venice that afternoon, Emiliano asked them to follow him towards one of the cloisters. On the way there, he told them about someone they had never heard of before: Friar Filippo Luigi Minardi, who lived in Veneto and Tuscany in the 14th century.

"How do you know so much about this Friar?" asked Sarah.

"I've always been an amateur historian, researching here and there, going to museums, libraries, visiting ruins and monuments, mostly here in Tuscany. I gathered from Willbe's emails from New York and from our conversations in the last few days that you two have just started your own historical research. It can become addictive once you start digging."

"True," agreed Sarah, smiling at Willbe.

"Luigi was the only religious man to become a partner of a bank in medieval Italy. It is quite remarkable that he did so, given that usury was a ground for execution during the Inquisition."

"Are there records of this?"

"It's all there in the book that you have been wanting to see."

"You never told us that you have read the Desgranges book, Uncle..."

"I haven't, but I know someone who has. Someone connected with the Querini Stampalia Foundation, who told me about the portion of the book that refers to the Venetian Files, where this friar is mentioned a couple of times."

"Wait, you know someone at the Querini Stampalia who has access to *Secrets of Italian Cities?*" asked Sarah, glancing between Willbe and Emiliano.

"Yes, a man who shared these stories with me because I'm a Fibonacci."

Willbe's face lit up:

"We're scheduled to visit the Querini Stampalia. Perhaps this contact of yours can help us gain access to the book, too. Do you think you can put us in touch with this man?"

"I have already arranged a meeting, Willbe, but you must wait until you arrive in Venice to know the details," replied Emiliano, patting his nephew on the shoulder.

************

The train trip to Venice was dominated by the expectation of finally being able to read the elusive book by Jacques Desgranges and make progress in their research. After a two-hour journey, the Trenitalia train slowly glided into one of the platforms of Stazione di Venezia Santa Lucia. Willbe and Sarah were waiting by the door with their luggage at hand and left the train as soon as it stopped, walking out of the station as daylight was slowly disappearing.

Sarah was tired and trailing suitcases through the streets surrounding the station was not the way she had imagined she would greet the city immortalized by Shakespeare and Thomas Mann. She was also not impressed by the *pensione* Willbe had booked, especially its yellow curtains and bedspread, her least favourite colour.

Willbe noticed her disappointment and decided to distract her while they settled in by telling her about the conversation he had had with Emiliano in Pisa.

"Do you remember when I told you the story about the couple who escaped from Pisa with an infant near the end of World War II?"

"Yes, who were they again?"

"I thought the man was Uncle Emiliano's brother, but of course it wasn't, as he is not that old. Turns out he was my grandfather's brother instead."

"Ok, carry on."

"Well, Uncle Emiliano also researched them and found out some of the circumstances of their escape. As it happened, the couple was fearful about their future in Italy, so they left with two suitcases filled with cash, some of it belonging to them, but some being the savings of other family members deposited in banks in Florence..."

"You mean to say that..." Sarah paused.

"That's right, say what you think, I won't be offended. They stole the rest of the family's savings."

Sarah could see the sadness in his eyes.

"It was a long time ago, Willbe, more than sixty years. You shouldn't attach too much significance to it."

"They had help, Sarah."

"Help? You mean to withdraw the money?"

"Probably, but that's not the worst of it. They had help leaving Italy quickly. Given the circumstances, they must have been helped by Italian and even German officials at the time. I was in two minds about telling you this..."

"Why?"

"You must have relatives who died in the war, I didn't want to upset you by bringing it up."

"That's kind of you, but I can handle it."

"Well, according to Uncle Emiliano, this granduncle of mine worked for the Mussolini government and was an admirer of the Führer. Most of my relatives avoid talking about him."

"Understandably."

"So that's part of what we talked about in Pisa. The other part is that we are going to have another surprise here in Venice, but you sort of already know that from the way he talked about arranging for us to have access to the book – at least I think that's what he was talking about when we spoke in Pisa."

# 48

*October 1378*
*Florence, Tuscany Region – ITALY*

It was an unusually cold October in Tuscany in the year 1378. Winter was coming early. On this particular Sunday, the streets in Florence were quieter than normal: most residents were either tucked away at home or enjoying some wine in one of the taverns, warming their hands and feet by the fire. Not a few others sought comfort, spiritual and otherwise, inside one of the many churches, celebrating the joys of a wedding or baptism, or mourning the death of a loved one.

In one them, Santa Maria Novella, inaugurated fifteen years before but still unfinished, the simple funeral ceremony gave little indication that the few people present were commending the soul of Filippo Luigi Scoppi Minardi.

Giuseppe Fibonacci, who had contributed towards the construction of the church, insisted that the prayers and services for the funeral of his partner must be conducted there by a Dominican priest. It was his private sense ·of revenge towards the Church to have the exequies celebrated by someone from the order that had inflicted so much suffering on his friend. After the funeral, obeying the wish expressed by Luigi himself, a procession led by four black rider-less horses led the small cortège to the cemetery of the Basilica di Santa Croce where he would be laid to rest among the Franciscans with whom he had lived for most of his monastic life.

Santa Croce, which would remain unfinished until mid-way through the next decade, had nevertheless, acquired great importance in its roughly eighty years of existence, not only for its location, but also by way of example in providing care of the most afflicted. In a similar spirit, the Basilica's priest had agreed to receive the body of Friar Luigi as proof that it did not abandon its brothers, regardless of whether they belonged to the official hierarchy.

Of course, the Franciscans were also aware of Giuseppe Fibonacci's wealth and influence, particularly since rumors of a partnership with the Medici began to spread. Families such as these were accustomed to special dispensations from the authorities.

Luigi's tomb was located in one of Santa Croce's cloisters, and the ceremony was short and simple. The Franciscan officiant reminded those present that all are equal before God, even those who had gone astray in life for inscrutable reasons. Psalm 23 gave the tone of the prayer: *The Lord is my shepherd, I lack nothing.*

It was one of the saddest days in the lives of Giuseppe Fibonacci and his remaining partner Francesco Cristaldi. It was also a unique event in the economic and religious history of the Middle Ages: the burial of an ex-friar turned banker.

After the ceremony, Giuseppe asked to be left alone. With no one around, he took a small golden coin with the image of King Edward III out of his pocket and placed it on Luigi's cold hands, in a final acknowledgement of his friend's prestige and wealth.

*May you remember our most fortunate days, wherever you are now.*

# 49

*September 30, 2008*
*New York City – USA*

Inspector de Lucca walked to the living-room of suite 710 at the Ritz-Carlton, next to Central Park, and drew back opened the curtains with a flourish. The view was magnificent. The top of the trees with their blazing autumnal colours resembled the palette of an impressionist painter. Piero stretched languidly, calling into action all the muscles of his body for a day to be spent walking around New York.

He had visited the city a few times before in a professional capacity, one of them as part of the security detail of a former Italian prime minister attending a UN meeting. This time, work was the last thing on his mind, and the purpose of the trip was to relax and enjoy his newfound wealth. One and a half million Euros in a Swiss bank account had made him feel like a new man. Imagining a trip like this had become a recurrent thought in the last few days in Venice as he reflected on the decision he had to make.

*I would not be the first or the last man to fail to resist the temptation of money. Besides, I am getting too old for problems of conscience.*

"Piero, where are you?"

The female voice brought him back to a very pleasant reality in which he now found himself and made his blood flow in his veins with more energy.

"I'm here, *amore*, admiring the Big Apple," he called out in response, affecting a bad New York accent for the last part of his reply.

"Come back to bed, it's early and I miss you already."

She did not have to say it twice. Piero returned to the bedroom and stopped by the door to observe the woman lying naked in bed. He could not contain himself:

"Claudia Celestini Sforza, you are indeed a wonderful woman."

\*\*\*\*\*\*\*\*\*\*\*\*\*

## Ardennes Forest – BELGIUM

M. Henry awoke in good spirits and completed his breakfast ritual with the appetite of a much younger man. Methodic as he was, he began each day reviewing his most recent decisions. He considered himself an expert chess player, but one who played with pieces of flesh and bone.

*As the Sage of Baltimore used to say, 'there is always a well-known solution to every human problem — neat, plausible, and wrong'. Every effort should be made to find the best, not the simplest, solution to a problem.*

The information received from Venice indicated that Inspector Piero de Lucca had accessed the numbered account at the Swiss Commercial Bank branch in the city where it all began for the empire that M. Henry managed. The police officer was a competent Italian civil servant who could have caused serious problems for the brotherhood if he had not been persuaded to abandon the investigation into Akashiro's death in Venice.

*It would have been simpler to send him to the same cemetery where Akashiro ended up, but this would not be the most adequate solution.*

M. Henry kept a copy of the message he had ordered to be delivered to the Italian policeman. The original sealed envelope had been sent to Venice with strict instructions that it reached the hands of Piero de Lucca. He had wished from the bottom of his heart that the inspector made the right decision.

The Akashiro/de Lucca issue was dealt with, but the unfolding economic crisis still demanded his attention. The day before, the U.S. House of Representatives defeated the 700 billion-dollar bailout bill proposed by Treasury Secretary Hank Paulson, despite Ben Bernanke telling legislators the week before that if they did not approve it, they might not have an economy the next Monday. It looked like legislators needed more than Chairman Bernanke's dire warning to spring to action, and M. Henry did not have to work too hard to provoke a massive sellout of shares in stock exchanges around the world, most dramatically in the United States, where the Dow Jones had its largest single-day point drop in history.

That seemed to have done the trick, as all reports indicated that the bill was on route to be approved in the Senate the next day, meaning that it would almost certainly be approved on a second House vote the following week. Politicians, as it turned out, also needed frequent reminders of who was in charge.

M. Henry now turned his attention to the next problem facing him at the moment: William Benjamin Fibonacci Hubbard.

*How to proceed? Under what pretenses?*

The night before, in the midst of examining the background reports on his various potential replacements, he had opened the safe where he kept some of his most valuable documents and removed his original birth certificate, registered in Pisa in 1944, as well as an old photograph of his mother holding him on her lap. He did not open that envelope often, as every time he did he was overcome with emotion, as he was again the previous night, his eyes watering.

*************

The arrival of the Allied Forces in Italy in 1943 resulted in thousands of casualties on both sides of the conflict, including many civilian deaths. Rumors that the Allied commanders intended to turn Mussolini's country into scorched earth spread throughout Italy. Despair took hold of the country when American troops invaded Sicily, and over the next two years many families fled North hoping to escape death by reaching the French or Swiss borders.

One of these families – a couple and their one-year old son named Domenico – managed to leave Pisa and reach Genoa and then Turin in the Spring of 1945, as news broke of an armistice between the Allies and the Germans. In Turin the young family used some of the money they carried in a suitcase to forge new identification and travel documents, and then travelled onwards to Milan.

There, they found themselves among a sea of people moving in all directions with a mix of happiness, anxiety, and grief for lost family members, dead or incarcerated in unknown locations. Inside his wallet, the father carried the address of a government official who was supposed to help them.

Enormous lines and huge confusion were the norm as people looked for news about the end of the war, information about friends and relatives, and a way to resume their lives in a minimally organized, albeit uncertain, fashion.

After waiting for three days, young Domenico and his parents were granted visas to enter Switzerland.

# 50

*September 10-11, 2008*
*Venice – ITALY*

The next morning, properly rested and confident about their purpose in Venice, Willbe and Sarah plotted their itinerary, having decided that they would spend the first part of the day exploring the city. After the disappointment of the *pensione*, Willbe suggested they began with a gondola ride.

*It's only money,* he thought to himself.

They picked a route that would drop them near the museum they wanted to visit with enough time for lunch nearby. From the list of restaurants marked on the map, they chose one whose name caught their attention: Osteria Ruga di Jaffa.

Two hours later, delighted after gliding through Venice's canals, they arrived at the restaurant, which luckily had a table for them, even though they did not have reservations. They decided to celebrate by ordering two glasses of prosecco and *prosciutto con mozzarella di bufala* as an appetizer. Since they still had work to do that afternoon, they agreed to have only a *primo piatto* for lunch. Sarah chose the *spaghetti alle vongole veraci* and Willbe went for the *gnocchetti al gorgonzola*, paired with a small *caraffa* of house red wine. For dessert, two *tartufi bianco e nero* and two *ristretti*.

At 2pm, after walking a few blocks from the restaurant, Sarah and Willbe finally found themselves standing outside of the Fondazione Querini Stampalia, where they asked a young man with an Australian accent to take a picture of the two of them in front of the arched doorway where a plaque identified the four-storey building.

There were many areas to explore inside the museum, where the mixture of styles was surprisingly beautiful. Each direction one looked in suggested a journey through a different period, from medieval to Renaissance, from classical to contemporary. It would be impossible to absorb all the complexity of the rooms, gardens, corridors, walls, and ceilings in just a few hours, and Willbe and Sarah agreed to head directly to the room where *Secrets of Italian Cities* was on display: the magnificent library housing more than three hundred and fifty thousand ancient and modern books.

The book was in a glass case similar to the one used at the Morgan Library and Museum.

"At last we meet again, old friend," joked Willbe.

"I wonder if we'll ever be able to read it again," said Sarah in a more somber tone.

"Perhaps I can help you with that," said a male voice in English with a light Japanese accent.

\*\*\*\*\*\*\*\*\*\*\*\*\*

Back in Pisa, Antonella noticed a change in her husband after his return from Florence. He seemed somehow relieved, she thought.

She knew him well. For many years Emiliano had kept a family secret so well that at times his own relatives worried that there was something seriously wrong with him. He knew that some of them only kept in contact because of the financial help that he provided to any relative in need. But now he had taken the first steps towards lifting the enormous weight that had sat atop his shoulders for so many years.

The groundwork had been laid years before, when Emiliano suggested to his sister in America that Willbe might consider continuing his studies at the University of Pisa. He had wanted to meet his nephew, of course, but there was a deeper motive: reconnecting the name Fibonacci to the history of the University and giving the young William Benjamin the opportunity to enter a world hitherto unimaginable to him.

*It was natural for Willbe to want to know where the ancient documents came from.*

Emiliano had come across the documents some years earlier when he was working in Florence in his souvenir shop for tourists. Out of nowhere, a man had approached him in the store and handed him an envelope from an unidentified sender. The envelope contained a letter with instructions to be destroyed, a bearer cheque for several thousand Euros, and the letter that Giuseppe Fibonacci wrote to his sons in 1380. He was not, after all, the *pazzo* that many considered him to be, simply for bringing up the topic of the family fortune lost many centuries ago.

In the next few years, money continued to come in a similar fashion, delivered in unmarked envelopes. His family suspected something was up when Emiliano's generosity reached new levels, but in the Italian way, they asked few questions.

*William Benjamin had no idea about what awaited him...*

\*\*\*\*\*\*\*\*\*\*\*\*\*

The Japanese gentleman introduced himself as Hideo Akashiro, a benefactor of the museum and an acquaintance of Uncle Emiliano. In a direct and businesslike manner, he invited Willbe and Sarah to attend a reception at the museum the next day, September 11, when they would have an opportunity to read the coveted book. They were told to rent formal wear for the party at a store on Calle degli Avvocati and meet him for drinks at the nearby Hotel Danieli before the reception. With a polite bow, he left as quietly and discreetly as he had come, before Sarah and Willbe could ask any of the many questions that came into their heads.

The following afternoon, suit and gown rented and hanging in their room at the *pensione*, Willbe and Sarah decided to take their minds off what lay ahead of them by visiting the Piazza San Marco and its extraordinary golden basilica. Inside the church, Sarah found herself peculiarly drawn to a 14th century mosaic that depicted a curious scene in which Salome held a tray with the head of John the Baptist and danced in a seductive red dress, presumably for Herod.

As they left the basilica, Sarah noted that Willbe kept looking over his shoulders:

"Still worried that we're being followed?"

"With this crowd, it's impossible to know, but I've had this sensation that someone is watching us ever since we left the museum yesterday."

"Well, Mr. Akashiro did seem to know exactly when we were going to be there."

"That's true, but I think my uncle had something to do with that, since he also knew when we were going to the museum and kept saying we would have a surprise in Venice. I have the feeling that this is something else."

\*\*\*\*\*\*\*\*\*\*\*\*\*

Willbe and Sarah arrived at the Hotel Danieli at 6pm, just as Hideo Akashiro had instructed them. He was not at the bar yet, so they assumed that he was staying at the hotel and asked to call his room at the front desk. Their assumption was correct, but Mr. Akashiro was not in his room. They went back to the bar and decided to have a coffee while they waited.

Another thirty minutes went by with no sign of Mr. Akashiro.

"Do you think he's still coming, or should we head for the party?" asked an anxious Willbe.

"I don't know, Willbe, he told us to come here first. On the other hand, he didn't look like the type that would be late..."

"No, but he did seem very busy, and he is a benefactor of the museum, so maybe he had to go there directly and didn't have time to stop at his hotel."

"Perhaps, but couldn't he leave a message for us at the front desk?"

"Maybe he's trying to be discreet. I say we head there and he will find us."

"Ok, no point in coming this close and not going, I guess," agreed Sarah.

The Querini Stampalia was less than a ten-minute walk away, but they would not make it there for a second visit. Shortly after they turned into the narrow Calle de le Rasse on the left side of the Danieli, Hideo Akashiro emerged from the entrance of one of the numerous shops and fell into step beside them.

"Walk with me, don't look alarmed."

It was easier said than done. Mr. Akashiro, impeccably dressed in his tuxedo, looked like he had seen a ghost himself, and the expressions on Willbe and Sarah's faces showed nothing but alarm. A few seconds later, they were walking through an even narrower passageway, and after making sure there was nobody else around Mr. Akashiro began to talk:

"I'm sorry I didn't meet you at the hotel, but there has been a change of plans. My position has been compromised and it is not safe for you to be seen with me."

Willbe and Sarah had only heard that kind of talk in movies, and had absolutely no idea how to respond, so they just kept walking.

"You must have many questions, and it had been my intention to have a much longer conversation with you, but I'm afraid that is not going to be possible."

He stopped talking when they reached a busier street and kept silent until they turned into another deserted passageway again - a pattern of broken conversation that continued for the next several blocks.

"The book you have been wanting to read, *Secrets of Italian Cities*, is at the head of a much longer story," Hideo informed them.

Willbe found the courage to speak for the first time since they had left the Danieli:

"Are you still going to help us read the book?"

"Yes. I have with me an encrypted flash drive with the entire contents of the book in digitized form. This is never going to be part of what the Querini Stampalia Foundation will make available to researchers, but being one of the biggest donors to the museum has its perks."

It was time for Sarah to regain her bravery:

"Why is there so much secrecy around this one book?"

"Because it contains the only published reference to a collection of archives that extremely powerful people want to keep secret."

"The Venetian Files?" they both asked in unison.

Hideo Akashiro made a crisp gesture with his hand for them to lower their voice and they all kept quiet for the next few blocks until they reached another empty stretch of street.

"Yes, the Venetian Files. They are not mentioned in any other printed book ever written, and very few people know of their existence. The only reason you have heard of them, Mr. Hubbard, is because your uncle Mr. Fibonacci mentioned them to you."

"And he only knew about them because you read the book and told him, is that right?" asked Willbe, remembering what Uncle Emiliano had told them about his contact at the Querini Stampalia.

A few more strides in silence.

"That is only partially correct. I did tell your uncle about the Venetian Files, but not because I read about them in a book."

Their zigzagging had led them to Rio de S. Zanirovo, one of the most charming of the smaller canals in the city, and they now walked with water to their right and buildings with closed doors and windows to their left.

"I have seen the files themselves," revealed Mr. Akashiro as they turned left into the minuscule Calle Rimedio, barely wide enough for two people to walk side by side.

"I am a member of a secret organization that has existed for centuries, the Guardians of the Venetian Files," he continued in a barely audible whisper. "In fact, I'm one of three people who have access to the files at any given point in time."

"What is the content of the files?" asked Sarah, putting her incredulity aside.

"The content is irrelevant, except as a historical curiosity. A collection of observations, annotations, contracts, rules, and procedures written down by early Italian bankers towards the end of the 14th century."

Another silence as they reached the Rio de Palazzo de Canonica and had to make room for some tourists crossing the bridge in the opposite direction before continuing on Calle Rimedio on the other side of the canal.

"What is important is that these bankers decided to form a secret society around the time that Cosimo de Medici was in exile in Venice in the 1430s. Cosimo was able to thrive in exile only because of the connections that his father, Giovanni di Bicci, had established many years earlier with some powerful families there, including the Fibonacci."

They took a right turn, crossed another bridge, this time over Rio San Zulan, and continued on Calle dell'Angelo for more zigzagging through narrow alleyways. Sarah and Willbe were devouring every one of Mr. Akashiro's words and had no intention of interrupting him.

"Cosimo and his friends learned the lesson that overt participation in politics can have dire consequences and decided that operating in secrecy was both safer and more profitable."

They made room for a group of tourists to walk by, and Willbe used the brief pause to ask a question:

"And did they succeed?"

"To an unimaginable degree. Cosimo was allowed to return to Florence where he led a long and exemplary life, while the secret society learned how to influence the world of finance away from the spotlight. They, or should I say we, have been involved in every major economic episode ever since, and we have made incalculable profits in the process."

The claim sounded improbable to both Willbe and Sarah, although it reminded them of Professor Pfeiffer's theories about financial crises and their less-than-accidental nature. When he thought it was safe to talk again, Willbe asked the obvious follow up question:

"Why are you telling us all of this now?"

"This is not a chance encounter, as I'm sure you understood by now, Mr. Hubbard. I have waited a long time for this. You might say that I put you on this quest. The suggestion your uncle made to your mother for you to study in Pisa, the arousal of your interest in your family history, the document you received as a gift from your uncle, the suggestion of the exact period in medieval history you had to search to find this obscure book..."

Mr. Akashiro broke off as they crossed another canal, Rio de la Fava, and Sarah noticed that a street sign with the word "Rialto" pointed in the direction they were going. Mr. Akashiro continued:

"... I followed your trajectory closely, making sure that the discoveries you made along the way would bring you here. After the setback at the New York Public Library, I was able to use my good friend Mr. Carmona, who I met through my association with the Querini Stampalia Foundation – and who has no appetite whatsoever for legends about cults and secret societies, but nevertheless, remains a loyal friend – to suggest that you come here."

At that, Willbe stopped on his tracks, suddenly realizing that everything Mr. Akashiro had just said meant that a large part of his life in the past few years – what he had up to that point thought was his private life – had been orchestrated by this man. With a knot in his stomach he looked sternly at Mr. Akashiro:

"I'm not taking another step until you tell us exactly what it is that you want from us."

"You have every right to be upset, Mr. Hubbard. As I said, it was my intention to have a much longer conversation with you today, in much more amiable circumstances. Rest assured, however, that I do not intend to harm you in any way. I earned the trust of your uncle, for example, who loves you like a son. But if we don't keep moving, I cannot guarantee your safety. Please come with me."

The mention of his uncle seemed to convince Willbe of Mr. Akashiro's intentions, and the trio continued walking.

"You still owe me an explanation."

"You are absolutely right."

After making sure that their brief stop had not alerted anyone to their presence, Mr. Akashiro continued:

"I have fallen from grace with the brotherhood. For years I have not been able to execute my duties as instructed."

"And why is that?" asked Sarah, feeling that she also had the right to ask a few questions of the mysterious Japanese man.

"There are other sinister organizations operating in Japan, Ms. Mayer, and unfortunately my family got involved with one of them – my son, to be exact."

Sarah was startled, but not entirely surprised, that he knew her last name.

"Suffice it to say that if I had carried out what the Guardians of the Venetian Files wanted me to do, my son, and perhaps the rest of my family, would have been punished by those other organizations as a consequence. I have avoided taking action for as long as I could, using all the trust I have built over decades in the brotherhood. But I could not delay things forever. My only remaining course of action was to try to expose the secret society before it was too late."

They could now see the top of *Ponte di Rialto* at the end of Calle del Fontego. Something in the way Mr. Akashiro spoke gave the impression that time was running short.

"But why me?" was the question burning in Willbe's tongue more or less since the beginning of their conversation.

"Because you are a Fibonacci, Mr. Hubbard, and therefore enjoy special protection within the traditions of the brotherhood."

They continued along Pescaria San Bortolomio as the red rays of evening light reflected themselves in the wavelets of the Grand Canal. The busy promenade did not allow them to continue talking, but somehow Willbe thought that Mr. Akashiro had said all that he wanted to say.

They walked for another fifty metres or so until they reached the Rialto stop for Route 2 of the Venice Water Bus. In full view of all the tourists, perhaps feeling protected by the presence of the crowd, Mr. Akashiro reached for his jacket pocket, pulled a flash drive from it, and handed it to Willbe:

"The password for the encryption will be sent to you when you are back in New York. Take the waterbus back to Santa Lucia Station now and you will be close to your hotel. Don't talk to anyone else in Venice - anyone!"

With a bow, Hideo Akashiro left them and continued walking along Riva del Carbon towards the small bridge that crosses Rio de S. Salvador. Willbe and Sarah bought tickets and were able to jump on the waterbus just as it was leaving.

From inside the boat they heard a splash, followed a few moments later by a woman's scream. As they looked towards the small bridge, they could see a man, soaked but elegantly dressed in tailcoat and black bowtie, lifting himself onto a gondola without apparent effort and disappearing in silence through a narrow corridor of green water.

*************

## September 15, 2008
## Venice – ITALY

Willbe and Sarah spent their last few days in Venice bunkered in their room, terrified of meeting the same fate as Hideo Akashiro. After seeing the person who they presumed was his attacker escape, they had followed the victim's parting advice and returned to their *pensione* on Thursday evening without talking to anyone else. They ordered food in their room and spent the rest of the night frantically discussing everything that he had told them.

In its own terrifying way, his story seemed to explain so many of the strange events of the last month.

The next morning, Willbe and Sarah searched for any mention of Mr. Akashiro in local newspapers, possibly in connection to an attack near the Rialto Bridge. They were shocked to find instead multiple reports that the Japanese businessman was among the victims of a plane crash in Malaysia. The stock photograph accompanying some of the articles left no doubt that it was the same man they had met the day before, which meant that the news was either a colossal mistake or a fabrication.

Mr. Akashiro's comments about his position being "compromised" had obviously been a significant understatement. Was there more to his warning that it was unsafe for Willbe and Sarah to be seen with him? Were they also in danger? The threatening phone call, the incident with the black Mercedes, the couple following them in Italy – it all made much more sense and suggested they had reason to be afraid.

They tried to change their flight booking to leave for New York as soon as possible, but the late summer period made it impossible. They yearned to be able to read the book stored on the flash drive given to them by Mr. Akashiro, but in the absence of the password this was also impossible. Instead, they sat glued to their screens, searching for whatever information they could find about Hideo Akashiro and the organization that it seemed had ordered his death.

They noticed, as anyone reading the news that weekend did, that the financial crisis that had been brewing for some weeks appeared to have reached a tipping point. Was Mr. Akashiro's organization involved? It seemed plausible, given what he had said about its participation in every major episode in world finance.

To their relief, the weekend passed without incident and Monday morning saw them boarding an Alitalia flight back to New York. Willbe grabbed a copy of the international edition of the Financial Times offered by the flight attendant as they settled in their seats and his eyes immediately focused on the headline: ***Wall Street crisis hits stocks***. He quickly scanned the article and stopped at a paragraph that made his heart sink:

*"The sudden turn of events came at the end of a weekend which saw top Wall Street executives locked in increasingly desperate talks over the future of Lehman and the state of the financial sector with Hank Paulson, US Treasury secretary, and Tim Geithner, president of the New York Federal Reserve."*

"Sarah, you must read this!" he said as he folded the newspaper and passed it to her. She understood from the expression on his face that something serious was going on. What she read defied belief: Lehman Brothers had filed for bankruptcy protection, Bank of America had taken over Merrill Lynch, financial stocks were in free fall.

"Do you think this has anything to do with what Mr. Akashiro told us?" she asked when she finished reading.

"I don't know, but this stuff is pretty unbelievable. They're saying here that the US government simply let Lehman fail. That alone defies all conventional wisdom about trying to control a financial crisis."

They stared at each other with worried expressions, realizing as the plane took off that they had stumbled onto something much larger than the fate of Willbe's family's lost fortune.

# 51

*January 1379*
*Florence, Tuscany Region – ITALY*

One month had gone by since the death of Luigi Minardi. Giuseppe Fibonacci and Francesco Cristaldi missed their friend greatly, and often found wondering, in response to new circumstances, "what would Luigi do?"

Luigi's influence lived on in the daily operation of the bank, particularly his discovery of the bank's ability to "create money", something that sounded a bit like alchemy to them at first. Giuseppe recalled Luigi's enthusiasm when explaining to him and Francesco that, although they always needed to have a healthy amount of gold in their vault to satisfy the needs of the occasional merchant who came to redeem part of his deposits, they could lend far in excess of the coins brought to them, as long as their clients kept paying each other with bills of exchange issued by the bank itself. Provided their bills kept moving in an unbroken circuit of trades, their bank was, in effect, creating money. It was better than alchemy, as no other metal had to be turned into gold for them to profit.

As Giuseppe and Francesco readied themselves to meet Salvestro de Medici one last time before signing the documents authorizing the opening of a new bank in Rome, they once again invoked their departed colleague.

"What would Luigi say about Salvestro de Medici?" asked Francesco.

"Nothing too complimentary, I suspect," joked Giuseppe with a loud laugh.

The young Giovanni di Bicci de Medici had, at last, reach the age of majority. The signing of the contract formalizing the partnership between the two most notable banking houses in Italy was marked by a simple ceremony and little public fanfare; while these bankers were intent on challenging the power of Kings and Popes, they understood that privacy and discretion were necessary to achieve their aims

The notary, who worked in a small office close to the house where Dante Alighieri had lived, welcomed Giuseppe and Gianpaolo Fibonacci, Francesco and Tommaso Cristaldi, and Salvestro and Giovanni de Medici in his modest chambers. The contract was printed in duplicate, one for each original banking house, stamped with red wax bearing the crest of each family, and signed by all present.

It was the beginning of the creation of the largest bank in Italy: the Medici Bank, so called owing to the Florentine's superior stake in the partnership. Only a few years later, the Bank would secure the Papal States as its largest client, ensuring its dominant position in the rapidly growing world of high finance. The extraordinary wealth and power it brought, though, would also be the seed of division between the partner families.

# 52

*October 5, 2008*
*Venice – ITALY*

Back in Venice after his sojourn in New York, Piero resumed his duties at the Border Police. He had resolved not to weigh himself down in moral quandaries, but he was, nevertheless, somewhat uncomfortable as he walked into the office.

*What would my colleagues, who always respected me for my conduct, say if they knew?*

He was especially concerned to ensure that his young assistant, Marco, would not find out anything. Piero would have to be discreet with the money.

*The trip to New York was just a small luxury, filled with pleasure and sensuality, after a stressful time. From now on, discretion, above all.*

He unlocked the drawer under his desk with a key he kept in his wallet and took out a folder containing the letter he had received a few weeks earlier. Re-reading the ending, his determination to solve the case - and keep the money - was renewed.

*The "enemy" is powerful, but everyone makes mistakes.*

The final threat in the letter had angered him. It was true that he had a price, like almost everyone, but it was much more than one and a half million Euros.

From the same folder he also removed the ticket for the Querino Stampalia that he had found in room 131 of the Hotel Danieli.

*How to continue with the investigation without attracting any attention?*

As he pondered this question, he found himself wondering, as he had done intermittently over the past ten days, why Claudia had not once mentioned the Japanese businessman since she and Piero had first met.

*Curious,* he thought to himself.

*************

228

## *New York City – USA*

Willbe found the sealed cardboard envelope in his apartment's mailbox. It did not include the name of the sender or a return address.

Since returning from Italy, he and Sarah had waited anxiously for the password that Akashiro had promised would arrive. Nothing had come through, and Willbe's friends in the Computer Science department at Columbia had been unable to open the heavily protected drive. Without access to the Desgranges book or any clue as to where they should look, Willbe and Sarah were beginning to wonder whether they would ever find out the truth about the secret organization and its Venetian Files.

Meanwhile, the financial news evolved at a pace that was impossible to follow even for experts like Willbe. They felt frustrated and confused, but also slightly relieved that no other strange event involved them personally in the past two weeks. Was the mysterious envelope about to change that?

*Maybe it's the password,* Willbe thought, as he impatiently waited for the elevator.

As soon as he was safely inside his apartment, he ripped open the envelope. Inside he found a letter, a few forms, a return envelope, and another smaller sealed envelope.

*Brussels, September 30, 2008.*

*Dear Dr. Hubbard,*

*The SWISS COMMERCIAL BANK, one of the most solid financial institutions in the world, has a tradition of recruiting talent from the best universities in Europe and North America.*

*Upon the recommendation of several of your peers, we would like to invite you for an interview for the position of Director of International Operations at our headquarters in Brussels between December 26 and 30, 2008. We hope that this period is convenient for you. Naturally, all your travel expenses will be met by the bank.*

*In the interest of both parties, we ask you to keep any information pertaining to this job opportunity strictly confidential, before and after the interview.*

*Attached you will find two copies of a Confidentiality Agreement signed by our Director of Human Resources. Please confirm your acceptance of this invitation by countersigning one copy and returning it to us in the envelope provided.*

*Sincerely,*
*M. Henry – Chair of the Board of Directors*

Willbe stared at the letter, perplexed. He knew of colleagues who had been recruited to work at major banks by headhunting agencies, but this seemed to be coming from within the bank - and from someone fairly senior at that. Should he take it seriously? Would he drop his academic career to become a banker?

His heart missed a beat and he felt immediately nauseous when he opened the other envelope: it contained a copy of the second document his uncle had given him a few weeks before in Pisa; the original was now safely stored in his apartment.

# EPILOGUE

*November 5, 2008*
*Ardennes Forest – BELGIUM*

M. Henry sat in his study watching the victory speech of president-elect Barack Obama. His expression was pensive as he tried to parse the meaning behind what he was hearing.

*"If there is anyone out there who still doubts that America is a place where all things are possible, who still wonders if the dream of our founders is alive in our time, who still questions the power of our democracy, tonight is your answer."*

*An impressive opening* thought M. Henry.

Obama, the first African-American to be elected President of the United States, was addressing an ecstatic crowd in his home city of Chicago.

*"It's the answer that led those who've been told for so long by so many to be cynical and fearful and doubtful about what we can achieve to put their hands on the arc of history and bend it once more towards the hope of a better day."*

M. Henry did not consider himself a cynic, so...

This had been an historical election, there was no doubt about that. But even though the expectations from voters were higher than ever, Mr. Obama seemed to know that the problems he would have to face were not small.

*"There will be setbacks and false starts. There are many who won't agree with every decision or policy I make as president. And we know the government can't solve every problem."*

*Indeed,* M. Henry said to himself as he poured another inch of whisky into his tumbler.

*"This victory alone is not the change we seek. It is only the chance for us to make that change. And that cannot happen if we go back to the way things were. It can't happen without you, without a new spirit of service, a new spirit of sacrifice. So, let us summon a new spirit of patriotism, of responsibility, where each of us resolves to pitch in and work harder and look after not only ourselves but each other. Let us remember that, if this*

*financial crisis taught us anything, it's that we cannot have a thriving Wall Street while Main Street suffers."*

At this point M. Henry switched off the television, after saluting the orator with a raised glass and an amused expression.

*So that's what the president-elect imagines the financial crisis taught us.*

He knew, more than anyone, that power could only be exercised in two ways: through force or through money. The two generally went hand-in-hand, as M. Henry himself had shown not two months earlier. However, his own power and that of his organization depended on how much they could influence people like the president-elect. It had been like that for centuries.

*What would Obama do about the banks that survived the crisis?*

Modern banks, to a degree that would be impossible for medieval pioneers to even imagine, had become the most powerful sector in the world economy. People, companies, and governments were beholden to them. But the survival of their privileged position relied upon skillful obfuscation and purposeful confusion about their inner works.

M. Henry placed his glass on the table and closed his eyes to plunge into his inner peace as he vaguely remembered a sentence from Ben Bernanke about the sophistication reached by banks in measuring and managing their risks.

*Barack Obama would still need them... he had no idea how much.*

M. Henry fell asleep within a few seconds.